WE PLAY GAMES

PREVIOUSLY PUBLISHED AS AN AUDIBLE ORIGINAL

SARAH A. DENZIL

Previously published as an Audible Original Jan 2024

PART 1

PROLOGUE

I can't live like this anymore. When I walk down the street, I look over my shoulder. The hairs raise on the back of my neck whenever someone comes too close to me. Fear is a shadow always following me and I don't feel like I'll ever be free.

There's no way to turn back time and stop myself becoming a victim. But at least I can be the last victim. No matter what happens now, I want this to stop. I want this story to have an ending.

I feel like my life is hanging by a thread because I know who is out there, coming for me. I used to have a bright future. But now life is dark, and I want to find the sun again. I know things between us are complicated but please, if you ever had any real feelings for me, help me. Help me put an end to this sick game once and for all.

CHAPTER ONE

EFFIE

I'm growing tired of letting my husband win. But there are times in a marriage when it's best to follow your gut and mine told me to give him this one. That doesn't mean I'm not fucking resentful about it, though. I'd rather be on a beach right now, sauntering across the warm sands of the French Riviera. Instead, we're at Ivy Oaks and the grey clouds are threatening to burst with spring rain.

The men from the removal company carefully place wine glasses in our display cabinet. I grab one, twisting it right out of his fingers, and fetch a bottle of Merlot.

"It's five o'clock somewhere," I say, using my husky voice, the one that makes young men blush and old men touch my arm. He laughs and continues unpacking. It's just gone midday.

All this noise is giving me a headache, so I make my way through to the front garden. The back garden would be more peaceful, of course, but I wouldn't be able to people-watch there, and I love people-watching. Somewhere from inside the house, I hear Ben's voice, a touch louder than usual. My lips thin. The thing about my husband is that he can charm the birds out of the trees but only if you play by his rules.

Don't get me wrong, I give as good as I get in our relationship, and I enjoy the games we play just as much as he does. But what happened last time has soured things a bit. I'd feel safer if I was in another country right now.

I move a deck chair closer to the drive, throw myself down and pour a glass of wine. The first sip tastes delicious—a full-bodied red. I'm drinking on an empty stomach, which means I'll get drunk quicker. Moving house is stressful, even when you barely need to lift a finger.

The sky is in between sun and rain. We're in "warm but overcast" territory. I slip on a pair of sunglasses, tinting the grey world sepia, and then I light a cigarette and wait. Surely someone in this community will be bold enough to come and speak to me. Someone will allow curiosity to beat their social anxieties. I look at the houses, one by one, wondering which door will open first.

Well, hello, house number five. The curtain twitches. Then the door swings open. I adjust my gaze to see the tiny woman exit the house. Her purple-tinted hair is cropped fashionably short and she wears big, thick-rimmed glasses, reminding me of the old-school fashion designers who aged ungracefully after the swinging sixties. She makes a beeline straight for our house. Lazily, I pull myself onto my feet and stroll down to the front wall, leaning my arms against the stones.

"You're brave sitting out here," she says. "Looks like rain."

I smile. "I needed a break from all the commotion." I tap the side of my head. "It's giving me a migraine."

"You poor thing," she continues. I notice how made-up she is for an older woman. Red lipstick bleeds into the wrinkles around her mouth. If I had to guess, I'd assume she's in her early eighties. Maybe late seventies, though the hint of frailty in her walk suggests otherwise. She glances at the removal men. "There's nothing more stressful than moving house, is there?"

I shake my head, allowing my blonde curls to shiver, then I remove the sunglasses. Her eyes are drawn to my hair, mouth, eyes. She'll see what everyone else sees: I'm beautiful and yet not beautiful. An ex-model who had many casting agents tell me there's nothing classically symmetrical about my face. I don't have those movie-star features, but everything taken together is striking enough to trick people into thinking I'm a natural beauty. I watch the hint of confusion on everyone's faces when I smile at them, and something about it gives me a small surge of power. I feel confidence flood through my veins.

"I'm Effie by the way."

"Beryl," she says. Her eyes narrow. "Are you Isabella Dupont's daughter?"

Before I answer that question, I take a long glug of wine to hide my annoyance. It grows tiring being constantly compared to your supermodel mother. "I am. Are you a fan?"

She hesitates for a fraction of a second. "Oh yes." Her smile stretches.

"Have you lived here long, Beryl?"

"Oh yes, longer than anyone," she says. "I know all about this place. Its history and everyone who lives here."

I lean closer to her. "Tell me *everything*. I'm nosey."

Beryl's eyes sparkle and she leans towards me, eager to gossip and give me what I want. Let the games begin.

CHAPTER TWO

BEN

I disconnect the call and stare out of the window, watching Effie as she works her magic on the neighbours already. She'll have this old crone eating out of the palm of her hand within minutes. As I gaze at my wife, not for the first time I wonder if I'm actually attracted to her. Attracted to the way she looks, talks, walks and thinks, the way other people are drawn to her. Or is it all convenience? After all, no one else enjoys the *extracurricular activities* we both do.

As I glance at the mobile phone in my hand, I think about our games and the rules we set long ago. *No lies. No ties.* Simple. Effie and I can't have any secrets between us. We're supposed to tell each other everything, no matter how dark the secret is. And God knows I've told her some horror stories. In return she's shared hers. The worst thing she's ever done to another human—which, to be fair, has haunted her a lot more than anything I've ever done has haunted me. The way she cut her family out of her life with zero regrets. The fact that she rarely felt more than a mild appreciation for anyone except me. I smile at that.

She's a fraud. Scratch the surface and what lies below runs deep. I have to be careful with her, manage her. If she knew everything, she'd leave, and that can't happen.

I place the phone back into the pocket of my slacks and hurry down the stairs, nodding at the removal men.

"Wine glasses, gentlemen?" I ask.

A young lad of about twenty points to the display cabinet and I nod him my thanks. Seeing as Effie already opened the Merlot, it would be rude not to join her. I can't let Effie have all the fun. I flip the glass in my right hand, catching it by the stem as I stride out to join my wife.

"I see you've started without me." I grin. Effie turns around and her face lights up. She raises the bottle.

"Oh, but darling, you should've brought a glass for Beryl."

I direct my smile to the OAP by the wall. "I'm so rude. Wait there a moment."

"Thank you, but I don't drink red wine," Beryl says, smiling.

"Can I get you something else? A glass of white? Or a cup of tea?"

"Thank you kindly, Mr..."

"May," I reply. "But please call me Ben. Mr May was my father and believe me, no one would want to be mistaken for him." I add a laugh to stop the statement from becoming too dark.

"Well, thank you for being so kind, Ben." Her eyes twinkle. "You remind me of my third husband."

"Oh, really?" I ask.

She nods. "He was the most handsome of the bunch."

Effie pours me a hearty glass. "Beryl knows everything about Ivy Oaks."

"There's not much to tell, though," Beryl says. "The people here keep themselves to themselves mostly. I'm afraid you've moved into quite a sleepy area. I do feel sorry for the young people when they move here."

Effie swigs her wine and waves a hand as though to say, "Don't be silly."

"If Ivy Oaks needs a wake-up call then maybe we're the ones to do it." She giggles and I can tell she's already quite tipsy. "In fact"—she turns to me—"what do you think, darling? Why don't we have a barbecue at the weekend? Get to know everyone. We can cater. The weather is supposed to be good."

"Oh, how lovely," Beryl says.

"Absolutely," I add, taking a sip of my wine. "We've got a lovely big garden at the back here. It would be a shame to waste it."

"Then it's sorted. Beryl, you must spread the word."

"Don't worry, I'll just tell Deepika. She organises most of the socials around here. The book club is always at her house. It's number six."

I stand back and watch as Effie and Beryl exchange contact details. I notice Beryl's pretty good at using her iPhone, which also appears to be the latest model. Perhaps she has family who regularly come over and help her. I picture a brutish-looking grandson with a heart of gold.

"Am I a genius or what?" Effie says through her smiling teeth as Beryl walks away.

"That's not particularly humble of you."

She lifts a shoulder. "We both know humility isn't high on my list of attributes." She moves away from the wall and flicks ash from a cigarette. "No doubt we'll find a good mark at the barbecue."

"Sure," I say. "As long as everyone comes. You didn't give people much notice. These people have lives, you know."

A flicker of tension works its way up her jaw. "They'll come. Curiosity will get the best of them. We're the new arrivals." She softens and throws her arms around my neck, planting a deep kiss on my mouth.

Even though I know this is part of the game, that she knows the neighbours are watching us from their homes, and that seeing a public display of affection will get people talking, I still can't help but wonder if it's real. The problem is, Effie has no idea. Not about anything, really. She doesn't know the full extent of what I did. Most of all, she doesn't know I've broken the rules.

No lies.

I've lied to her more times than I can count.

No ties.

She can't know about the many ties I've failed to cut loose. She can't know I keep putting us both in danger.

CHAPTER THREE

EFFIE

After returning my kiss, Ben walks away without looking at me. I sip the wine, stare at his back and wonder what he's keeping from me. No lies. No ties. That was what we agreed when we started our games. When does a secret become a lie? When you're in a marriage with a person and withholding information from them? A lie by omission, that's the phrase, and I'm convinced that Ben is withholding something huge.

I lean against the garden wall, watching the movers carry boxes into the house. One of them catches my eye. Tall, lean, dark eyes and a sheen of sweat across his forehead. It's not just the wine coursing through my veins. There's the thrill of knowing I could have him if I wanted. Fidelity isn't particularly important to us, as long as we're upfront about our affairs. Though Ben usually has plans for me and who I seduce. The freedom comes with strings attached.

Maybe I'm growing tired of that arrangement. It could also be the dark cloud that has followed me since we left the Beaumont Hotel a few weeks ago. I shake the thought away before it makes me nauseous again. It's time to move on. If I don't, I'll crumble, and where will that leave me? I have to be strong.

You will recognise by now that our marriage is not conventional. We're not regular people and even though we live in the perfect house in the perfect neighbourhood, we're far from the wholesome family you picture in a place like Ivy Oaks. Perhaps that family doesn't even exist. In my experience, people are rarely as pleasant as outward appearances suggest. Everyone has a dark side.

I'm about to head back into the house to pour another glass of wine when I hear a man call, "Hello there."

I turn back to the street and watch the stranger approach. He's smiling broadly and his eyes crinkle at the corners. Green eyes, I note, complemented by a teal T-shirt stretched across muscular arms. Okay, random stranger. You have my attention.

"Hi." As he draws closer I stick out a hand over the wall, inviting him to touch me.

He comes to a halt by the garden perimeter and grasps my hand with a warm palm. He gives it a quick squeeze. "I just saw the van and the boxes."

I glance over my shoulder at the house. "Yup. We're moving in. Here to raise hell in Ivy Oaks." I laugh.

"Oh, don't worry, Ivy Oaks is already in hell." His grin stretches. "I'm David Holt. I live at number four."

"Nice to meet you, David. I'm Effie."

"Effie. What an unusual name."

I adjust my weight against the wall. "It's short for Euphemia. And, yes, my parents were terribly posh."

He laughs. "Then you moved to the right neighbourhood."

"So I see," I say, glancing around the perfect rows of houses. "But why is it in hell?"

"This is where all the trust fund babies bring their families to die, which means there's no life in this place. If I were you, I'd run. You can still save yourself. Get a penthouse in the city."

I wave a hand. "Been there, done that."

"I bet." He grins.

As I take in his smile my hand grips the wall and I'm leaning close to him over limestone, my abdomen pressed against the cool surface. When I remember my alcohol breath, I shift away slightly.

"Tell me about these trust fund babies," I say. "Is it one of those neighbourhoods where everyone is in each other's business? Or does no one talk to each other, like in London?"

"Ah, I see you haven't been to one of the infamous Ivy Oaks neighbourhood meetings. I swear one of these days an ITV drama will be made out of the hedge wars and noise complaints." He lifts an eyebrow.

I laugh. "Sounds right up my street. I love a good opportunity to set the cat amongst the pigeons."

"Trust me, there are several cats roaming wildly through a herd of pigeons here." He smiles. "So, tell me about yourself, Effie. Do you have a family?"

"A husband," I admit.

Do I detect a flash of disappointment in his eyes? "Ahh."

A silence hangs between us.

"I'm sure lovely old Beryl will inform you, but in case she doesn't, we're hosting a neighbourhood barbecue next Saturday. Come along. Bring cake. Better yet, bring wine. Or both."

The smile on my face appears naturally. I didn't have to think about it, and that isn't like me.

"I will. Thank you for the invitation. I look forward to meeting you both properly." He steps away from the wall, and I can't help but notice the new rigidity in his torso that wasn't there before I mentioned a husband. "It was nice to meet you, Effie."

"Likewise," I say.

There's a splash of rain on my nose. I look up and the grey clouds are stitched even closer together. Another raindrop lands on my eyelashes. My gaze travels over to my new house, up to the third floor. Ben stands by the window, watching. No phone in his hand this time. Perhaps it's the break in the weather, but a chill spreads over my body. I swear the sight of my husband never used to elicit such a response, but I suppose sometimes things happen that change the way you see a person. What happened at the Beaumont Hotel altered our relationship on a fundamental level. I'm trying hard to move forward but when I wake up every morning, dreaming of blood, I wonder if there's anywhere left to go.

Once the moving company leave, I ascend the stairs to find my husband. I want to know why he's hiding out at the top of the house. So he can make secret phone calls?

"Who was that?" Ben asks as I step into the room he's earmarked as his office. Right at the top of the house, the view stretches over the front garden and across the neighbourhood.

I drift over to the window before I answer, noticing that it offers an excellent vantage point into the other homes. Ben crosses the space between us, his arms slip over my waist, pulling my back into him, and he rests a chin on the top of my head. We stand there for a second or two, looking out at the people living their lives.

"You can see right into number two." Ben points to one of the pretty ivy-clad houses. Inside I see a man pouring water into a kettle. In the living room a woman, presumably the wife, is tapping her phone screen. "And six." My eyes drift again to an identical house. A couple sit on their sofa watching television.

I want to tell him that I don't care anymore, that I want to stop. But it isn't true. I like this. I enjoy this power, and he knows it. His hands drift down, touching the tops of my thighs, slipping between my legs. Even though I want to pull away, I don't, because it feels too good. And yet I hate it, because after everything, he still has this way to control me. No matter how often I convince myself that I'm the one in control.

"Who was he?" His hands withdraw. He steps back and leaves me cold.

"David. From number four. He's coming to the barbecue, so you can meet him for yourself."

"You like him," Ben says. There's no question. He knows me well enough to know when I'm not faking it.

"I can't deny that he's hot," I say, as nonchalantly as possible.

Ben hesitates before he replies. "It seems a little soon, Effie."

I turn to face him now. "Too soon? Are you serious? You're already spying on them. What have you plotted already?"

He shrugs. He can't pretend he doesn't care. I see the ripple of tension work its way across his square jaw. I know he's angry. But why? Is he jealous? Ben has never once been jealous of anything I've done.

"It's too soon," he says again, walking away.

I change tack. "Are you going to tell me who keeps calling you?" I ask. "Is it to do with what happened at the Beaumont?"

"No."

"That's it? No elaboration? Just 'no'? And I'm supposed to carry on, am I? Knowing... what I did..." My hand flies to my mouth.

Ben spins on his heel, strides twice and grasps my wrist. "Stop, Effie. Honestly, what is the point in even talking about it?"

I nod and he lets go. It was only for a moment, but my skin is sore where he touched me.

"Sorry," he says. "I just hate thinking about it. We need to let it go."

"You brought us here," I remind him. "You wanted to carry on as though everything was normal. I wanted to get out of the country. I wanted to stop doing this."

He takes my hand, softly this time, and leads me out of the room, saying nothing. I don't pull away.

"What are you doing?" I ask.

"You need to see something," he replies. "You need to be reminded who you are."

I want to laugh, but I don't. "I know who I am."

"Do you?" he says.

We stumble down the stairs together. My fingers brush the polished mahogany.

"I remember the girl I met," he says. "A broken girl who needed putting back together. I showed you another path, didn't I?"

I nod. My breath is caught in my throat. I don't want to speak.

Once we reach the entrance hall to the house, he pulls me towards the cellar stairs. Part of me resists, another goes willingly. I don't remember looking at the cellar when we came to see the house. Why is Ben leading me down there now? My feet are bare, and they slap against the cold stone. A light comes on above us and I see a room that's empty, but clad with smooth floorboards and painted walls, a far cry from the spider-infested wine cellar at my family's estate.

Ben urges me into the centre of the room and stops.

He saunters over to a stack of what look like boards and lifts the one on top. Then he places it against the wall. On it, he's written "house two". I assume he has one for each house.

"Are you ready?" he asks.

I wrap my arms around my torso. The cold penetrates my cashmere cardigan but I don't mind; I want to be here. I want to see all of those boards up on the wall. I want to take a photograph and pin it to the board. I want to write what I know about these people. I want to find out who deserves it the most and who would be the easiest to manipulate. The thought sends a shiver of electricity up and down my spine.

"We'll do it right this time," Ben says. "No mistakes. We vet them all properly and figure out the best mark. No slip-ups. Nothing messy."

Nothing messy. I could laugh. Things always get messy with Ben. He takes risks. Without the risks it's not worth it for him.

"Don't you want to rip this community to shreds? Don't you want to play with them? Remember how good it feels."

"I'm tired, Ben." My voice isn't convincing.

He's on me in a heartbeat. I gasp. He claims my face with his hands. "This is what makes you alive, Effie. I know you and I know your heart." He kisses me.

Yes, he knows my heart. He knows it's an empty abyss just like his. When he manoeuvres me over to the wall and lifts me, I wrap my legs around him. But then as we kiss, I close my eyes and I picture green eyes that crinkle at the corners.

MODELBOARDS.COM

2015

Effie Dupont Mega Thread

Marilyn: After hearing all the chat at London Fashion Week about her behaviour, I thought it might be a good idea to open a support group thread here. You can stay anonymous if you want, but it's a good opportunity for us to air all our grievances about her. I know a lot of us have been targeted by Effie over the years.

Mossie1990: Thanks, Marilyn. When I worked a Chanel show in New York last year she spread rumours about me having an affair with another model's BF. And I'm pretty sure she ordered pizzas backstage. It's like... I dunno, she knows there are models with eating disorders so bringing in unwelcome food isn't right. You know? It was just to cause trouble and make us all feel bad.

Lagerfeld10: Fast food showed up when I walked Max Mara with her!!! Then all the photographers get excited and make us pose with slices of greasy pizza. I hate it.

Marilyn: Yeah, she knows what she's doing. I've done New York Fashion Week and a couple of other shows with Effie and backstage is always chaos. She told one model the designer thought she was fat! Not cool! She knows how hard it is for us.

Justanothermodel: Effie only books shows because of her mother. She's hugely privileged. Her name is Euphemia Elizabeth Catherine Fitzalan-Dupont. Her mum's a legend and one of the original supermodels, but Effie can't even walk. And I'm sorry but her profile says 5'9" and there's no way. No way! I'm 5'10" and I tower over her. And to think she booked Vogue at sixteen!!!

Oh, and her father? He's like this awful barrister who defends terrible companies. I bet that's where Effie gets her morals from. I'm sure it's hard to grow up to be a good person when your dad represents literal evil. He was the barrister defending that company that owned all those terrible psychiatric hospitals in the eighties. Gross human being.

KatieKat: I was Effie's housemate in Covent Garden... Yeah, I know some stuff...

Marilyn: OMG, spill!

KatieKat: OK, but it's going to be a long one. Buckle in, ladies.

Effie could be a lot of fun. She was very charming. When you have a conversation with her, she maintains eye contact with you. It makes you feel like you're the only person in the room. It's embarrassing to admit this, but I had a crush on her, and I think that's why I didn't notice what she was doing to the other girls before it was too late. I was young and figuring out some things, which I guess made me a bit more vulnerable to her charms.

She had her rivals—her targets. She never liked competition and even though I knew she didn't love being a model, she still wanted to be the best at it. But Effie was never tall enough, thin enough or pretty enough to be the best in the industry. Neither was I. After a while, I know that got to her.

She was under a lot of pressure to fill her mother's shoes, and no one believed she could, especially not her mother.

You guys have mentioned the fast food and rumours of chaos backstage. It's true, she did stuff like that allll the time. But the worst thing she did was to our housemate; let's call her Lily. This is intense, so trigger warnings for EDs.

Lily was young. About seventeen. She signed with our agent, Maggie, and me and Effie were meant to look after her. I don't know why Maggie thought it was a good idea to move Lily in with us, but that's what happened.

The problem was, Lily had a super competitive attitude. And she'd earned it already. Lily was the next big thing. She'd attracted a lot of attention in the press because she was genuinely extremely beautiful. She booked every job, walked a ton of shows, appeared on covers and even in a couple of TV adverts. Meanwhile, Effie was twenty and couldn't stay at the weight most designers wanted her to be. The jealousy was palpable.

Arguments used to erupt and I spent a lot of time acting as a mediator, trying to make them get along. But night after night they bickered. And it was petty stuff like Lily kept using Effie's expensive skincare. Obviously, Effie grew up rich and always had lots of money while the rest of us were getting paid in clothes. Effie could share with us, but she never did.

The more Lily booked jobs, the more it bothered Effie and soon I noticed Lily was hiding something from us. She lost weight. Okay, usually, that's a good thing for us, but Lily was skeletal. The press complained about her being too thin. They said she made young girls anorexic and that she promoted heroin chic 2.0. I encouraged Lily to stop dieting and I asked Effie to do the same, but Effie wasn't even talking to Lily at this point.

Lily told me she ate all the time. I didn't believe her, but she insisted that she did. We were all busy back then but for a week I decided to shadow Lily and find out if she was telling me the truth. That was when Lily confessed to me that she'd been suffering with terrible IBS and that every time she ate, she had horrible stomach problems. During that week I saw that she was telling the truth. She *did* eat. And it was at that point I became concerned that Lily wasn't dieting, she was ill.

I encouraged her to go to the doctors. But Lily told me she couldn't, that they'd know. It was very vague, and I didn't understand what she meant. I begged her to tell me, but she just closed down and refused to say anything more.

I had to leave for a few days after that. My older brother had his first baby, and I went to visit my family and meet my new niece. The break was welcome, trust me. I needed to get away from the craziness of the fashion world. Oh, it was heaven. It reminded that people can be normal. That not everything is about calories and inches and sample sizes. I think that was the moment I decided to call it quits. It was time to move back home, back to the north so I could try university again. I didn't want to watch girls bicker over face cream anymore and I certainly didn't want designers wrapping a tape measure around my waist ever again.

After a blissful three days I returned to London to see my agent and to give Effie notice on the flat. Guilt turned my stomach the whole journey there. At this point, I was the only person looking out for Lily and she was obviously in some trouble. I didn't want to leave her in that flat alone with Effie, but at the same time I needed to do what was right for me. While watching the fields roll by on the train, I decided to drag Lily to a GP about her stomach problems. I'd damn well make sure she was okay before I left. But what I came back to destroyed all of that.

I found Effie at the tiny kitchen table drinking a cup of

tea. She had a strange expression on her face. It was like her skin had been pulled tighter. I asked her if she was okay.

"Fine," she said.

I nodded to her and asked about Lily. At that, Effie paled. That guilty feeling gnawed at me again. Effie simply nodded towards Lily's bedroom. Something about the way she moved her head told me something was wrong. My spine straightened. I didn't know what to expect. I forced my feet to carry me over to Lily's door and I knocked, wishing I was home with my newborn niece again.

The door snatched open. Lily stood there naked, covered in sweat. It was the middle of December and our flat did not have good central heating. Effie called it the cardigan month because we'd always be wearing our thickest woollens.

"Good. You're here," Lily said. "Come and look at this." She grabbed hold of my wrist and dragged me into her bedroom. Her nakedness didn't bother me. We'd all seen each other naked at shows before. Her room, however, shocked me down to my bones. "What do you make of this? Look. Four hundred. Five hundred." She pointed to marks on the walls. Scrawled numbers. Then she stood on a set of scales in the middle of the room. "It makes no sense."

"What makes no sense?" I avoided looking at the scales. I didn't need a number to know how painfully thin she'd become.

"The calories. That's how much I eat. This is how much I weigh." She stepped down.

I allowed my eyes to roam across the room, noting the white powder lined up on her bedside table. "Lily, I think it's time to call the doctor now."

She started to cry then. I'd never seen her cry before. Like I said, Lily was always confident. But in this moment, she'd been broken down. I saw the pieces of her all over that room, in the dirty clothes piled up on the bed, the cocaine residue, the cigarette butts put out on the carpet, the rotting food, the greasy hair hanging over her face.

"I just wanted to be better," she said. "I don't want to hurt anyone." I pulled her into my arms and stroked her dirty hair.

"I know," I cooed.

Later, Lily told me that a doctor had found traces of laxatives in her urine. She said she didn't remember taking them but wondered if she'd mixed up her medicines and vitamins. We're models, of course we keep laxatives in the flat. But I knew it wasn't a mistake. It suddenly all made sense. Effie had poisoned her. Anger burned within me, but I didn't know how to direct it, how to deliver justice. I felt as though it might be a kindness for Lily to assume she'd made a mistake and allow her to recover without knowing what Effie had done to her. Before I left London, I made sure Lily went home to her family to recover. Then I packed up my belongings and never spoke to Effie again. I never want to see her face again. She's dead to me.

Mossie1990: What the fuck??!! She slipped Lily laxatives??

KatieKat: I think so. She could easily have replaced Lily's vitamins with the laxatives, or dropped them in Lily's drinks. Lily kept smoothies in the fridge most days.

Marilyn: That's awful. She's evil.

Lagerfeld10: I wonder what's happened to Effie anyway. I haven't seen her in a show for like six months.

KatieKat: Good riddance. Wherever she is, I bet she's doing the same manipulative shit. Leopards never change their spots.

CHAPTER FOUR
BEN

The problem with Effie is that she thinks she's better than everyone else, while simultaneously believing she's scum. When I first met her, she'd just quit modelling. She was addicted to painkillers, which kept her in a constant state of drowsiness, and she felt guilty for what she'd done to that girl. She needed someone to come along and fix her. It was my job to make her see that the way she messed with other people was a talent to cultivate, not a flaw to torture herself with. I made her see that messing with the minds of inferiors can be fun. That's the world we live in. Kill or be killed.

Effie needed to be trained to turn off that pesky conscience of hers, and with a little encouragement, she did just that. I pride myself on turning my wife into the predatory being she is now. I sculpted her like Pygmalion and his infamous statue. She owes me everything.

After we fuck in the basement, we hang the boards on the wall, adding names and house numbers to each one. Then we install a lock on the cellar door, not that anyone would want to come down here, but caution is everything.

Effie is quiet and far too thoughtful for my liking. She ends up going to bed early, but I don't mind. I like my own company. However, I'm not fond of silence and the house is extremely still. Painfully so. After downing a quick whisky, I decide to go for a walk. I pull on a pair of trainers and lock the door behind me, stepping out into the chilly evening.

Beryl was right about Ivy Oaks being a sleepy neighbourhood. Almost every light is on inside the houses. No one is out. They're all stuck behind brick walls, staring at a screen or a page. Is that what life is? A series of evenings on a sofa? These are rich people who will spend a few weeks out of the year on holiday, but in general this appears to be it. This life is not for me.

My phone buzzes. I sigh. Yet another text from Phoebe, an old mark.

Miss you.

I roll my eyes. This bitch keeps hanging on no matter what. I had hoped she'd be bored by now and that she'd just fuck off.

Miss you too, I respond, hating myself. I could ignore her, but I think I might be able to squeeze more out of her. And I do need the money.

Another text pings through before I can put the phone away.

Did you get the transfer? I just want to make sure you're all right.

Another ping.

Did you find somewhere to stay?

I sigh. I've told her this fifty times already.

I got it, babe. Thank you so much. You've saved my life so many times. I'm at a hostel. It's just temporary while I get my shit together.

She replies again. *And they're leaving you alone?*

For now, yes, I respond.

Good. Sleep tight, she says.

I send back the usual asinine response and carry on walking. It's a simple scam. I wine, dine and... well, you know, some impressionable young thing. I make her believe I'm an international businessman and that I could give her the world if I wanted to. And then I tell her I'm in trouble. I'm being framed. The police think I'm guilty of fraud, gangsters from London or New York or Moscow—I change the location each time, tweaking the lie—are after me. I've been hurt. They beat me up. I have no money. I can't go home... can you just send me enough to get them off my back? Enough for a place to stay and a hot meal?

And so it goes...

It isn't about the money. At least, it didn't start out that way. It's about the rush.

"Hi."

I lift my head, slip the phone in my pocket. It's a reflex. Whenever Effie is around, I don't want her to see my messages. But it isn't Effie this time.

A petite redhead stands on the other side of the street. She's close to a streetlamp, the glow illuminating her silvery-blue eyes and picking out the soft peach glow of her hair.

"Hi," I reply, lifting a hand. "Nice night for a stroll."

She smiles. "I fancied some fresh air." She glances at the house to her back. "My husband is watching a documentary about golf and I can't take it anymore." Her eyes narrow slightly. "You must be our new neighbour."

I nod. "Yeah. I'm Ben."

"Sophie," she says.

There's a knack to sizing up a new person without coming across as creepy. It's all about seeing someone through the peripherals of your vision. As soon as you feel your eyeballs moving up and down, you've fucked up because the woman knows you've taken in her whole body. Maintain eye contact while paying attention to the details on the outskirts of your vision.

Sophie is a slip of a girl with elfin features. She's short and petite, but I think she might be curvier than her clothes suggest. Her face is attractive too. I notice the rose-red lips and faint blush of her cheeks. Her hair isn't quite ginger, but strawberry blonde, which is much more alluring.

"Nice to meet you. Has Beryl mentioned the barbecue we're having? We're inviting the whole neighbourhood."

Her eyed widen. "Yes. Word travels fast in Ivy Oaks. Lewis and I will be coming." She pauses. "Lewis is my husband."

"Great stuff," I say. It doesn't bother me that she has a husband. I decided within half a second that Sophie is going to be my next mark. Sometimes you can tell by the smile on someone's face that they're pure. Sophie is one of those people. "My wife Effie is always complaining that we don't make enough couple friends."

"Do you have kids?" she asks, somewhat out of the blue.

"No," I reply. "At least not yet." It's my stock answer, but of course Effie and I have no plans to ever procreate.

"Same," she says. "Not yet." She breaks eye contact and gazes up at the sky. I take a note of it because she comes across as nervous in that moment. Clearly, this is a subject that means a lot to her, that perhaps has already wounded her. And I do love a wounded animal. "We're hoping to one day. But it's hard, isn't it?"

"It is," I say. I let out a soft sigh. "Believe me, I know. We've been through two rounds of IVF, but it never took. It's harder for Effie, of course. She's the one who has to inject herself and take pregnancy tests."

"I'm so sorry," she breathes. Shining eyes catch the orange glow of the streetlight. "That must be horrible." She shakes her head. "We're about to begin our first round, but I also don't want to lose hope that it might happen naturally for us."

"I'm sure it will," I say, concerned that I went too far with my fake IVF story. I don't want to make her *too* sad. She can't associate me with sadness. "Back in London, Effie and I knew this couple who had three unsuccessful rounds of IVF. Then they went on holiday and..." I raise my eyebrows.

"Really?" she says. "Wow. That's amazing. I know it's stupid, but I keep hoping for a miracle like that."

"Never give up hope." I smile, my widest, most genuine smile. I know exactly how it looks because I've practised it in the mirror dozens of times. "Never. Ever."

I see the effect it has on her. The way her shoulders move an inch or so back, and her chin lifts. It's not very often I see hope working its way through a person. I admire it for a moment.

"Thanks," she says. "I needed that." She sighs. "Well, I suppose I should be heading home. It's getting chilly."

I glance up at the stars, allowing a wistful expression to fall across my features. "It's always like that this time of year. Beautiful, but the cold creeps in." I meet her gaze. "It was really great to meet you, Sophie. I hope I'll see you at the barbecue?"

"Yes," she replies. "Definitely."

I lift a hand and continue walking along the pavement. That went better than I could have hoped. The perfect mark, ready and waiting, and I made a good impression on her. Now I just need to get Effie to play along with the IVF lie. She doesn't like playing pretend about baby stuff but I'm sure I can convince her.

I glance at my watch, wondering if I can slip away from

the house and drive to Reading, where there are a few casinos to hit. That exchange with a new mark has me wanting more. But I really should be giving up that particular bad habit before Effie finds out.

My phone pings. I suppress a groan and remove it from my pocket. What now?

Time is running out. Tick tock.

Huh, not Phoebe this time. I delete it. They're bluffing and it's nothing I can't handle. I'm the king of getting myself out of tricky situations. Even getting away with murder isn't a problem for me.

CHAPTER FIVE

EFFIE

I took up jogging when Ben and I started working suburban cul-de-sacs. It's a great way to move around the neighbourhood and take a peek in through windows. It's very easy to have an innocent-seeming look inside a house without appearing obvious. You have to use your peripheral vision and when you want a better view, you stop to tie a shoelace or place your foot on a wall to stretch out a muscle. Phantom cramp has allowed me quite a few prolonged gazes into many a family home.

Winter is usually the best time to get a good view of someone's house. Night falls early, before most families want to close their curtains, and the bright yellow glow of interior lights illuminates every single thing people do inside. Personally, I like watching families hang their Christmas decorations. You can tell how tight a family unit is based on how happy or stressed people are as they untangle tree lights.

I rushed myself this morning. Usually, I'd scope out the best times to do a little snooping. Early evening, around dinner time, is good. There's hustle and bustle going on through those large windows. Teenagers fighting over the television remote. Plates balanced on laps.

If I'm honest with myself—which, to be blunt, can be boring—the real reason for my rush to leave the house so early was witnessing David from number four slip out of the house in shorts and trainers. I'd already put on my running tights and a sports bra, so I hurriedly stuffed my feet into a pair of running shoes and jogged down the drive, shoving my keys into the tiny pocket at the back of my leggings.

Ben thinks it's too soon for me to pick a mark, but that's complete crap. He took an instant dislike to David, which of course makes David infinitely more interesting to me. I'm obviously going to pursue the one man that makes my husband crazy. I do love to play games, after all. But so far, I know next to nothing about my mysterious neighbour. A second chat with Beryl revealed that his surname is Holt, but when I searched for him on social media, all of his profiles were set to private. I miss the early days of social media when people were less guarded.

Luckily for me, David's circuit is within the confines of Ivy Oaks. When I left the house, I worried I might need to chase him down somewhere farther afield. I may still be slim from my modelling days—my mother's calorie obsession is proving hard to shake—but the running gear is really just for show. I'm too lazy to get into proper shape.

I push myself past a few houses and am soon sweating. My right thigh feels tight after not warming up, and I actually will need to stop and deal with a cramp. This isn't the first impression I want to give to the man I'm scoping out. I'm contemplating turning back when he crosses the road and spots me. He grins, removing an air pod before lifting a hand in greeting.

"You're a runner." His words are more of a statement than a question.

I suck in a deep breath. "Nope. Trying to be. Failing."

He laughs. "You started too hard. Here, lean on my arm a moment. Catch your breath."

I feel his warm skin as I do as he suggests. The closer I lean into him, the more of his scent invades my space. It's pleasantly sweet, like cinnamon and citrus. When I lift my chin, our eyes meet. This is how I seduce a man, I bat my eyelashes and lay on the charm. The only thing is, he instigated the touch and he's the one coaxing a smile from me. It's like the seduction is going the other way.

I clear my throat and lean away. "I'm out of practice. Too much of the high life, you know."

"Caviar, champagne, parties... I know it well." His tone drips with sarcasm.

"You only live once," I say.

We start walking down the street, almost in unison.

"If it isn't plainly obvious," he says, "I don't know that lifestyle at all. I'm actually pretty boring."

I tilt my head. "I doubt that."

"No, I am." He lifts a palm. "Scout's honour."

"Well, you're the most interesting person I've met here so far. Granted, I have only met two people..."

"Well, wait until you hear about Beryl's latest trip to the optician, because you're sure to change your mind. It's riveting. She told me all about it in the leisure centre last week."

I laugh. "Maybe you should've left."

"Why wouldn't I want to know about the cataract in her left eye?"

"Maybe you're too nice. You have one of those faces that attracts older women and small children."

"Oh." He nods. "You mean unthreatening?"

His shoulders square slightly and I can tell I've bruised his ego.

"No," I say. "Though there's worse things to be than unthreatening."

"Nothing says excitement and danger like a man in running shorts." He lifts a leg and I laugh.

After living with Ben for so long, I've become a great judge of character, and I can tell that David will make an excellent mark. Which means I should start asking him personal questions. I need to figure out every aspect of his life, every complication—who are his family? What does he do? Why does he live here of all places?

But I don't want to. I just want to enjoy a pleasant conversation about everything and nothing. I can't deny that David gives off clues in his demeanour. His voice is soft, not clipped like the men I usually meet in my circles. There's a faint hint of a northern accent. Everything he wears is good quality but not flashy. He has money but he doesn't show off. That suggests modesty. I've met many businessmen who purposefully check their Rolex for the time or remove a platinum credit card from a Hermès embossed wallet. Granted, I haven't seen him dressed up for an event, but I don't get that impression from David. He hasn't asked me where I went to school or what my parents do.

He sighs, pulling me from my thoughts. "This is great running weather. I love this time of year, the cherry blossom is in full bloom." He gestures to a line of trees along the street.

"I hadn't noticed," I say.

"Beautiful, isn't it? I went to Japan last year and the blossom is incredible there. Do you travel much?"

I shake my head. "I'd like to though."

"It's a passion of mine. I go whenever I can."

As we follow the road around a corner, I notice him

glance towards me. His face is filled with curiosity, as though he wants to ask why I don't go abroad. The answer is simple—Ben doesn't like to scam in other countries. He loves risks but isn't so keen on language barriers and the unfamiliarity of the legal system. There was one attempt in Sicily that we abandoned after a couple of weeks.

"Do you want to run for a bit?" David asks. "We could intersperse the runs with a couple of walks, keep it nice and easy?"

"Sure," I say.

I cast a guilty glance in the direction of my marital home. This second meeting with David hasn't gone as planned at all. My orchestrated meet-cute-turned-scope-out is more like a first date. But it's not all my fault. He's flirting as much as me.

No lies. No ties.

How am I going to spin this to Ben without lying?

The answer is, I can't.

CHAPTER SIX

BEN

It's always a rare treat to host at a new location. Effie and I relocate quite a bit for obvious reasons. When you play the kind of games we play, it's best not to stick around for long afterwards.

While Effie organises the caterers, I grab boxes of beer from the car and haul them in. The caterers are more than capable of providing and serving drinks, but neighbours expect a personal touch. It's all about men drinking from the bottle, standing around a grill. And if we're going to run our usual scams, I need to ingratiate myself with the husbands. What is Sophie's husband's name? I can't remember.

I walk through the house with the box on my shoulder, whistling as I go. On my way out to the garden I find one of the servers and let her know where to place the cooler boxes for the drinks. Then I make my way upstairs to change. Effie walks past me, her face tight. A doorbell rings in the distance.

"I'd better get that," she says, barely looking in my direction.

I shake my head slightly. I wonder what has rattled her. It's not like we haven't done this before. Perhaps she's still angry about the fake IVF story, because when I told her she had a fit over it.

The thing is, I don't understand why it bothers her so much. If there's one person on this earth who should not be a mother, it's Effie. And if there's one person on this earth who should not be a father, it's me. Deep down, she knows that. That's the real reason she's mad at me.

I quickly change into jeans and a simple V-neck sweater. There's a cool breeze in the air, the kind that requires long sleeves. We're nowhere near summer yet. Still, at least it isn't raining. The outfit is of course carefully calculated. Smart casual. I don't want to stand out. I need to make them think I'm one of them.

Effie is carrying bottles of wine out to the garden when I come down the stairs. This time I get a better look at her outfit and realise she's dressed in some awful frumpy thing that swamps her figure.

"Is that what you're wearing?" I grab a bottle from her and add it to the cooler box.

"Of course it is," she snaps. "What's wrong with it? I chose this outfit specifically."

"I thought you'd want to look sexy."

She shakes her head. "No, that's completely the wrong direction. I need to look unassuming so that I can make friends with the women."

"Yeah, but what about the men?" I point out.

"Men would find me sexy if I wore a potato sack. And speaking of outfits, what are *you* wearing, my love?" She grins, showing teeth, anger flashing in her eyes.

I take a step away, noting her mood. Sometimes Effie needs to be managed and it looks like I'll be keeping an eye on her for the day. I gesture to my clothes. "It's what they wear around here. It's dad chic."

"Sure. Whatever." She gives me a smirk before sashaying back into the house. I hear the doorbell ring again and, judging the time, realise it's probably the first guest.

I pause, listening. There's a woman's voice, then a laugh. Effie sounds flustered but perhaps that's by design. The relatable housewife. I make my way over to the grill to check how the chef's coming along with the food when our first guests make their way into the garden. A family comprised of a tall woman with striking eyebrows, long dark hair and brown eyes, a slightly shorter man with closely cropped hair and full lips, and two teenagers, one girl in dungarees, staring at her phone, dark hair piled into a messy bun, and a boy in jeans and a rugby shirt.

I lift a hand. "Welcome to the party. I'm Ben."

"Deepika." The mum extends a hand. "This is Aaron, my husband, Kalinda, my—"

"Kally," the girl says without pulling her eyes from her phone.

I can tell Deepika didn't like that. Her lips tighten.

"—daughter. And Danny, my son."

The boy raises a hand.

"We're from number six," Deepika continues. "We didn't get a formal invite, but Beryl mentioned everyone was invited."

"Of course," I say. "It's so nice to meet you all. Did you meet Effie, my wife?"

"I did." Deepika smiles. "She's pouring the kids some lemonades."

I glance at Aaron. "And what about the adults. Beer? Wine?"

"I'll take a brewski," Aaron says, his eyes brightening.

I grab him a bottle and toss it over. A *brewski*. I wonder if this guy's best days were at university in the early 2000s, at a ski trip pounding jelly shots and Jägermeister.

"You moved in a few days ago, right?" Aaron asks. "How are you settling in?"

"Perfectly," I say. "It's a great neighbourhood. And luckily the house doesn't need much doing to it. I'm sure Effie will want to put her own stamp on things, but for now we're happy to live in it for a while, get used to the house and figure out what we want to change."

"Oh, it's always best to do that," she says. "The absolute worst thing you can do is make changes right away..."

She carries on speaking, but I can already feel my attention drifting. I begin to wonder where Effie is and why she's taking so long with the drinks. Why is she pouring them herself, anyway? That's what the catering staff are for. Then I notice Beryl walk out into the garden with a younger woman at her elbow. The woman—in a nurse's uniform—helps her with a step. She's attractive in a sturdy way. Tall and strong with a steely expression in her eyes. Definitely not a mark. You don't go after the people with a calculating gaze, that's for sure.

And then Effie comes out with the lemonades. There is a couple I don't recognise walking behind her. My wife says something to them, laughs loudly, and then nods to me.

"... but I can give you the number of our interior designer if you like," Deepika says.

"She worked wonders on Kally's bedroom," Aaron adds.

I nod, noticing that the teenagers have disappeared, obviously bored by their parents.

"That's so kind of you," I say. "Thank you."

Effie approaches with the lemonade. "So sorry for the wait. It's manic in the kitchen and then we had an influx of guests."

She slips her arms into mine once the glasses are passed over. "We'd best mingle, darling." Her attention turns to Deepika and Aaron. "The food is almost ready. Help yourself as soon as the chef calls us all over."

As we move away, Effie says quietly, "Did she keep going on about not being invited?"

"She did mention it," I say.

"Insufferable," Effie mutters.

CHAPTER SEVEN

EFFIE

The doorbell rings again and I make my way back into the house to greet the next guests, leaving Ben alone with the neighbours.

The woman I see standing on the doorstep looks so much like Ben's dead mother, Emily, that it catches me in my tracks. I hope she doesn't notice the way the blood runs from my face.

"Oh, hi," she says, her voice as sweet as the strawberry-blonde hair framing her face. "We're here for the barbecue? It is here, right? And today? I didn't get the wrong date?"

My gaze travels over to the man standing to her left. He contrasts her elfin features with his rather average build and face. Or perhaps he just looks average because he's standing next to her.

"Yes," I say. "Sorry. I've got a to-do list about three miles long running through my head right now. It's a wonder I can even remember my name. Which is Effie, by the way."

"Sophie," she says.

"Lewis." The man leans forward and shakes my hand.

"Come in, guys, grab a drink—"

"Sophie, you made it!"

I turn around slowly to watch Ben enter the kitchen. How does he know her already? I watch him carefully, noting the way his eyes are fixed on her. Of course they are, considering who she looks like. Although I wonder if he's even made the connection. He's grinning from ear to ear. Even as he shakes Lewis's hand, he keeps staring at her.

This isn't good, I think. Ben hasn't smiled at a woman like that since he met me.

"Come into the garden, guys. I have beers, burgers, all the good stuff." Ben slaps his hands together.

The way he's acting like *one of the guys* is grating on me, but I smile and follow them like the dutiful wife. As we walk through the kitchen, Beryl approaches me.

"Do I look tired?" she asks.

I open my mouth to answer but she carries on.

"I was up all night, Effie. Someone sent a pizza to my house. A pizza! How ridiculous! Well, I felt bad for the young man who delivered it, so I just accepted. Paid for it and everything. But then, of course, I had to eat it. And then I was up all night with terrible stomach ache." She lowers her voice. "The *constipation*."

"Oh, dear. How awful." I wince. "Can I get you anything? Some antacids?"

"A Rennie would be wonderful, dear. Now, I have to let you know that I can't eat much today. It's nothing personal."

"Of course not. We completely understand."

One of the servers hurries past and I click my fingers. "Could you get Mrs..." I pause. "Beryl, I don't know your last name!"

"Scott," she says.

"Could you get Mrs Scott a Rennie from the pantry. And then take her through to a comfortable seat in the garden."

"You're an angel," she says, and I do actually feel a little guilty.

Last night the nerves got to me and I pulled a juvenile prank I haven't done since my modelling days. I called a local takeaway and ordered pizza in Beryl's name. Only I never expected her to eat it and then hear about her constipation. That's karma for you, I guess.

During the next hour the only other guests to arrive are Sam and Alex from number seven and a sinfully boring middle-aged couple obsessed with where people went to school. In fact, school seems to be a favourite topic around here. For much of the day I end up chatting to Deepika about how she chose not to send Kally and Danny to one of the *top* private schools, even though they could most definitely afford to. They didn't want them to board, she likes having an actual relationship with her family.

I smile and nod and sympathise about the decision not to send a crotch-goblin to a fancy prep school, but inside I'm relieved when the doorbell chimes. My heart lifts. The only person who hasn't turned up yet is David. And seeing as Ben has been talking to Sophie and Lewis for the best part of an hour, it's time for me to have my fun too.

"Excuse me for a moment," I say, moving away. I quicken my pace, wanting to beat the servers to the door.

When I swing it open, David lifts a bottle of wine in his right hand and then a shop-bought cake in the other.

"You remembered!" I say, holding out my arms to take both from him. He follows me through to the kitchen, where I hand the goods over to the caterers.

"Ah, you have help," he says. "That's not a proper barbecue."

"We have a barbecue and we have meat. That's literally

the definition of a barbecue. We don't technically have to be the ones cooking it."

He leans his hip against the table. "Where I'm from, a barbecue is where family and friends gather to watch you burn sausages that'll eventually give everyone food poisoning."

"Where *are* you from, David?" I ask, suddenly interested.

Perhaps I imagine it, but for a moment I swear he grimaces. "I'm not from your world. Let's put it that way."

"Nothing wrong with that," I say. I want to embellish about *my world* and how it looks much nicer from the outside looking in. But I don't. That would be tacky.

We walk out into the garden and he grabs a beer from the ice cooler. Ben zones in quickly, I think sensing a shift in my demeanour. He even wraps a protective arm around my waist, which catches me off guard. I find myself picking Sophie out of the small crowd of people, hoping she sees it. Perhaps it's petty but I don't care.

"Afternoon," Ben says. "You must be David."

"Guilty." David smiles. "And you must be Ben."

My husband nods. They maintain eye contact for a second or two too long and that drawn-out moment soon turns awkward.

"I don't think you told me what you do," I say to David, hoping to get the conversation flowing again.

"I'm in insurance," he says. "Or at least I was. I made my money, got lucky with a few investments, and got out. Retired at forty-two. Can't complain." He sips his beer.

"And you retired to Ivy Oaks?" Ben says, almost rudely. "Why not the Caribbean or French Riviera?"

He laughs. "Well, firstly, because I didn't retire *that* rich. But also because I wanted to stay close to my daughter, Lori.

Her mother and I are separated but she goes to the same school as Aaron's kids, so Ivy Oaks is nice and close."

It's typical of Ben to forget that other people love their families. Regular people like David and Deepika want to spend time with their children. They want to be a family. The thought brings on a wave of shame and I swallow too much wine with my next sip.

I'm about to break the silence again when Ben's phone rings. He backs away from us, his arm falling from my waist, and goes inside the house to take the call. I stand there watching, desperate to get my hands on that phone. Who keeps calling him?

"You two make a handsome couple," David says.

"I suppose so," I reply.

"You used to be a model, didn't you?"

"A long time ago," I admit. "I wasn't very good at it." An image of my old flatmate Louisa scrawling numbers across the wall of her bedroom flashes into my mind. I drink more wine, blocking it out.

"I'm sure you were," he says. "You're very beautiful."

I wait for a joke or piece of banter to follow but nothing comes. He seems sincere.

I shift from one foot to the other and roll my eyes slightly, hinting at self-deprecation. "That's sweet, but it's all smoke and mirrors. I'm just an averagely pretty girl who knows her angles and how to apply make-up."

Before he can correct me, I notice Sophie and her husband approaching. I give them a little wave and call them over.

"Do you three know each other?" I ask.

David nods. "I know Sophie from book club."

"Oh. I love a book club." I widen my eyes. "When do you meet up?"

"Every other Thursday at eight," Sophie says. "You should come. It's me, David obviously, Deeps, Sam and Beryl."

"Sounds great. Count me in. Do you guys need any more drinks?"

Lewis shakes his head even though Sophie seems to be opening her mouth to answer. "This salad is delicious, by the way."

"Thank you," I say, as though I made it myself.

David wanders off to mingle and I end up making small talk with Sophie and Lewis. At first, I'm disappointed, but I also need to know more about my husband's next mark. Innocence is his weakness, and it comes off Sophie in waves. That's why he married me. I'm the least innocent person you can imagine, which means he can never break me. If Ben married the kind of woman he craved, he'd either drive her insane or... well, kill her. And as I nod my head and sip my wine, it occurs to me what a fucked-up thing that is to think about your own husband.

Sophie is a housewife and Lewis is a solicitor at a medium-sized firm in Oxford. She's the one with the softly upper-class accent, and the classic tell-tale signs of money. Her jewellery is quietly expensive and not at all fashionable. The gold bracelet could be an antique. She wears designer jeans and a striped cotton shirt, a Barbour gilet over the top. It's giving young Princess Anne. To me, it seems obvious that Sophie is the one with the money and Lewis isn't as well connected or rich. I wonder how that plays out at home. It's important to suss out the power dynamic right away.

"I'm so sorry about your struggles," Sophie says, almost out of the blue.

I smile thinly. "That's so sweet of you to say."

"If you ever want to talk, our door is always open."

Sophie reaches out and places a hand on my upper arm, stroking it lightly. "I hope you don't mind me saying. I bumped into your husband the other night. Somehow, we ended up talking about children and it came up that you've been through IVF. It's such a stressful thing to go through. I'm so sorry."

She's so sincere I can't take it. Sweat beads across my forehead and the wine sits sourly in the pit of my stomach.

"Thank you. I really appreciate it. Sorry, I just need to go and check on something. Would you excuse me for a moment?"

I back away, dump my wine glass on the closest trestle table and hurry into the house, nausea rising. What is the matter with me? Why am I so rattled? Bile rises in my throat and for an awful moment I think I might be sick. I walk up the stairs to the first floor and use our ensuite bathroom. After splashing some cold water on my face, I feel somewhat normal.

"Effie?"

I towel-dry and step out. Ben sits on the bed, the top of his phone poking out of his trouser pocket.

"I didn't see you there," I say.

"What's going on?" he asks.

"Nothing. The heat got to me." I shrug. "And the wine. One too many glasses, I think."

He stands, and his phone slides out of his pocket onto the bed. I force myself not to let my eyes linger on it because Ben hasn't noticed. He walks towards me, completely clueless of the gift he's left behind.

He leans over me, his right fist closed tightly. "Well, pull yourself together. Or you're going to make fools of us both." There's tension in his expression, as though he's holding something back.

I step around him and sit down on the bed. *On top of his phone.*

"I'll be down in a minute," I say. "I'm just going to retouch my make-up and sober up."

He nods. "Good idea."

I'm shaking as he leaves the room. He has no idea I'm sitting on gold. The one prized possession he never lets out of his sight. I know he's been lying to me. It's time to find the proof.

CHAPTER EIGHT

BEN

I glare at my wife, making it clear that she needs to sharpen her game. Then I take the stairs and head back to our garden full of guests. As I cross the threshold I look out for Sophie. It's a shame she's so conjoined with her dull-as-fuck husband. But chatting up the husband is part of the process and I've already agreed to give them both financial advice. Sure, I'll come out of retirement just this once. Anything for neighbours.

Instead of Sophie's bouncy red hair drawing my attention, I find David's green eyes looking at me. He reminds me of some corn-fed farm worker. Perhaps it's the grass colour of those eyes, or the sun damage along his cheek bones. He doesn't belong in our world. He doesn't have the right smell. No wonder Effie likes him. Deep down Effie longs to be far away from here, probably up north in Yorkshire or the Highlands. I could picture her nursing a baby at her breast, with crinkly-green-eyes over here farming the land.

But it'll never happen because Effie is mine. I know how to keep her in check when she's getting out of line and I'm the one who convinces her to play my games. Not that it takes much persuasion.

Anyway, I don't like the way this guy is looking at me. Could he take me? No. He might be stockier, but I fight dirty. I nod and flash him my best smile. He knows it's fake but who cares? To my horror, he walks over. I'm beginning to resent this whole barbecue nonsense. At first it seemed like a good idea to get to know the neighbours, sniff out the weakest of the pack. I didn't anticipate having to make polite conversation with the guy Effie wants to fuck.

"Need another beer?" I ask. The go-to of the modern man. Talk beer.

"Nah, I'm good." He raises his bottle. "I'll probably be heading back soon so I thought I'd come over and say thanks for this."

"You should probably thank Effie," I say. "She put in most of the work."

He nods. "I will."

His voice is clipped as he talks to me. It was soft when he spoke to Effie. This bloke does not like me one little bit.

"She's freshening up," I say. Then I grin and raise my shoulders into a shrug. "You know how it is."

"How what is?" He shakes his head slightly.

"When you can't keep your hands off each other. Even when there's a party going on downstairs."

His eyebrows raise. "I can't say me and my ex had that kind of relationship."

I smile more broadly. "Effie's a bit of an animal. She'll pounce on me wherever we are. You wouldn't believe the places we've fucked." I watch him become uncomfortable. I'm enjoying every moment of this.

"Sure," he says, turning away. "Well, thanks again for this. It's been great."

I watch him leave. His beer is so full that when he slams it down on a table, a dribble of foam splashes down the neck. It's a small victory, but I'll take it. He's the one lusting after another man's wife so it's on him.

I catch sight of Sophie in the distance, but before I can get to her, another dad rocks up, beer in hand. Aaron again. Mr Brewski himself. Behind him, I see his wife and kids talking to Beryl. Now I understand why he's making a beeline for me.

"Great party," Aaron says. "This is exactly what the street needs."

I nod my head. We stand side by side, like dads at a junior football match.

"Did I see David leave?" he asks.

"Yeah, he left quite abruptly. Which is a bit weird."

"That's the half of it." Aaron sips his beer. I turn to him, interested now. "The guy is something of an oddball if you ask me. His daughter goes to school with our kids, so we see him a lot. He's one of those dads always getting involved, you know? Like, mate, go play golf like the rest of us."

"What makes him an oddball?" I ask, irritated that Aaron's only scoop is the guy being a decent dad.

"Well, maybe 'oddball' is a bit strong, but he's not exactly chatty. He comes to every neighbourhood gathering but doesn't join in. He never dates anyone, not men or women. He's on social media but doesn't friend anyone. I dunno. Maybe he's just socially awkward or something, but he gives off the wrong vibes. You know?"

I'm not sure how much I trust Aaron's judgement, but I am intrigued as to why David is so private. It could be innocent. We live in a heavily monitored world and not everyone likes that.

"I don't trust single men," I say. "They're always the lone

gunman, right?" I smile. No harm sowing a bit of fear amongst neighbours.

Aaron nods. "Deepika won't let Kally go to a sleepover with David's daughter, Lori. She doesn't want Kall to stay over at his house."

Aaron and Deepika sound like the kind of parents that want to ban books from the curriculum, but I don't say that. I just nod my head. "Probably for the best."

After Aaron is waved over by his wife and ends up in a conversation with Beryl, I wonder how I can use that information against David. And then I remind myself that I've already chosen Sophie as a target. Sophie is the perfect mark. Trusting, innocent, already in pain: vulnerable. While watching her interactions at the barbecue, I've already noticed how she and her husband never hold hands, kiss or even touch. Trying for a baby puts a lot of strain on a relationship. Sex becomes a chore. I've never experienced it myself, but then I'd never bring a child into this world.

It's been a while since I got a text or phone call, so I slip a hand into my pocket to find my phone. The right pocket is empty. I try the left pocket, and then both back pockets. Fuck. Where did I leave it?

"Hey."

It's Sophie and she's alone. She's frowning, her eyes sad and downcast. Is she upset? Or is this her natural expression?

"Hi," I say. I open my mouth to tell her I need to go into the house, but she cuts me off.

"Um, Lewis left, so I'm going to go."

"He left? Without you?" This is interesting. Maybe I should stay and find out what happened between them. But if Effie has my phone...

"Yeah, we had a tiff. Nothing major. He didn't like me telling you about our problem conceiving so he's been in a mood all day. He's probably right. I did ramble at a stranger about personal things, so..." She trails off. Idly, she makes shapes with her hands, fingertips touching fingertips. It's oddly erotic.

"But you didn't do it to be malicious," I say. "Sometimes it's easier to confide in a stranger."

Her eyes brighten. "Right! That's what I said. But he took it personally." She glances towards the house. "I should follow him and make sure he's okay."

"Maybe he needs time to cool off," I point out. I should be searching for my phone, but this is too perfect. "Look, do you fancy a cup of tea? It's a bit chilly out here now."

She lifts her head to the sky. There are clouds overhead and it'll rain soon. That'll put an end to our barbecue.

"Sure," she says.

I lead her through to the house. This is my opportunity to plant seeds, to be the man whose shoulder she cries on. The missing phone is an issue but at least if Effie finds it, she won't be able to get in. I made sure of that when I chose my passcode. She'll never guess it.

CHAPTER NINE

EFFIE

Of course, there's a passcode. I try his birthday, my birthday, our anniversary, and then I put the phone down because I can't think of any more significant dates. Knowing Ben, he used a random code to make sure I couldn't figure it out. But what am I going to do now?

I use my own phone to search for ways to hack into a phone without the passcode or fingerprint. There's recovery mode but it'll erase what was on the phone. I can't do that. I just need to guess Ben's code.

Not a birthday.

Not an anniversary.

Ben is not a sentimental man. That has never bothered me, of course. I knew what I was getting into when I married him so any notion of me being naïve or taken advantage of is stupid. He's older and we met when I was quite young, but I was and always have been capable of the same manipulations he is. Ben just thinks he has control over me. It works in my favour to allow him to think that.

What other dates could he have used? A death? A shiver

runs down my spine. My mind casts back to the terrible night at the Beaumont. The body at the bottom of the stairs. How quickly we dealt with the aftermath. How close we came to losing it all.

I tap in the date.

The phone is still locked.

There's movement downstairs. I toss the phone on the bed, but it lights up. Ben has received a notification. I tap the screen and it shows me a bubble branded by his bank—one of his private accounts separate from our joint finances. Because of what we do, we spread our money into several accounts so that Ben can split up any large sums of cash into small deposits. It attracts less attention than several thousand pounds being deposited in one lump sum. Most of our accounts are offshore, where regulations are much lighter. I also have money in places Ben has no idea about. But that's another story. This notification is telling me that Ben is overdrawn.

Overdrawn?

But Ben is loaded. Isn't he? Not only were his parents rich, but he earned a lot during his time in the city, invested it well and profited. And that isn't counting the... how to put it... extracurricular money-making schemes he runs. Out of the two of us, Ben has always been the richest, though I can certainly support myself.

I put his phone back on the bed and open up the app for our joint bank account on my own phone. I pay attention to it when the bills come out, otherwise I don't check often. Ben is the finance guy. He works out where we'll get the best mortgage and does the sums for the month. Now, as I scroll through the withdrawals, several stand out to me. The money isn't going to a utility bill or council tax or any other dull expense, Ben is making the withdrawals himself, and there are quite a few of them.

None of them are large sums of money. £500 here, £350 there. They certainly add up though. Why is he taking all this money out of our joint account? What is he using it for? He clearly factors these payments into the monthly figure I transfer from my private account. So, he plans in advance that he'll need to withdraw this money. But why?

I pace the bedroom. Ben doesn't do anything for no reason. He's the most calculated man I know. He has also swindled thousands of pounds out of unsuspecting women. It's what he does best. It's never enough to engage in an affair with them and mess with their emotions, he needs the money to exert power over them too. And yet, he's overdrawn. So, how has he spent all of his money? *All of it.* I let that settle in. My very rich husband, a multi-millionaire, has spent all of his money and now he is draining mine.

No lies. No ties.

This is a whopping great lie. This is double life territory. I'm like one of those stupid women in a crime documentary talking about how they never saw the red flags. Then it hits me full force. I'm the idiot. *I'm the one being scammed.*

Ben has broken the golden rule. While we mess with other people, our games rely on a certain amount of trust. In order for our partnership to work, we have to trust each other. But if I'm really honest with myself, there is no trust. He doesn't treat me like his equal, he doesn't treat me like a wife. I'm not special. I'm not loved by him. I'm just another mark.

I sit down on the bed, unable to breathe. Perhaps I should be in tears, but I'm not. I'm filled with rage. And now I need to decide how to handle this. My first instinct is to stride out into the garden, find him, throw the phone in his face and get out of here. After all, I never wanted to come to Ivy Oaks in the first place. This saccharine, gated community has an oddly bloody history I wanted to avoid. No, I wanted us to go abroad, become anonymous, to never speak or think about what happened at the Beaumont again.

What happened has taken a huge toll on me and I work every day to put it behind me. It isn't easy. But I do it for him, because I can't imagine ever finding anyone else who would suit me as well. He's the only one who could ever understand who I am. I never deserved a good man, so I found a bad one instead. We are soulmates. Aren't we?

Which leads me to a decision. I know exactly how I'm going to handle this betrayal. I'm going to do what I do best. I'm going to play a game. I'm going to play *our* game.

ERIC LANSDOWN SURVIVORS GROUP

About

This is a private group for anyone who has been victimised by Eric Lansdown. We don't actually know his real name, but his image is in the profile picture. You may have known him as someone else.

Eric Lansdown is a liar and a fraud. He pretends to be rich, meets vulnerable women, and then scams them out of money.

This group is not about exposing Eric, it is for support only. No one should be pressured into going to the police. That's not what we're about. Obviously, if anyone wants to report him, that's completely up to you. But we know Eric is clever and doesn't leave any trace.

Group Rules

No doxing of group members.

No spam or advertising.

No screenshots shared outside this group.
No guilt or judgement.
Be kind.

Lucy Turner

Posted 467 days ago

This is my story with Eric.

We met in a bar one night and he gave me his business card and told me he'd like to go on a date with me. He wore this pristine, perfectly fitted suit that I can remember even now. I thought he was too handsome to be interested in me and I almost didn't call, but my friend told me I was being ridiculous.

To cut a long story short, Eric took me on the best date of my life. It started in a Michelin-star restaurant and ended at his amazing apartment overlooking the city. He'd been so kind to me all night, telling me I was beautiful and funny. We had a great time. But looking back, it was probably all a lie. He told me many lies that night.

He said he was the CEO of a new pharmaceutical company that was going to change the world of medicine and save lives. He literally told me that he was going to cure cancer. I was drawn in by every word at the time but when I look back, I feel so embarrassed. If someone told you they were going to cure cancer, would you believe them? But he was so confident, and he clearly had a lot of money. I was just impressed to see he was doing good with his money. So many of these guys don't care about others, they just care about profit. I thought I'd found a unicorn. I was so happy.

We had a whirlwind romance. He told me he loved me and that he'd never felt like this before. He took me to Paris one weekend. He bought me designer bags, a beautiful gold necklace. I've never been so swept up in another person before. And he was *fun*. He made me laugh, he took me to clubs, we drank a lot, sometimes we even popped pills. I was twenty-two at the time and I guess he was about thirty, but I don't know, he never told me. I remember thinking he was young to be a CEO but I guess there were those Silicon Valley millionaires at the time like Mark Zuckerberg who were all young too.

After about five weeks, everything changed. Eric changed. He cancelled dates and told me he was too busy to meet. There were problems at the company, a big investor had pulled out and then there were issues with a competitor. He sounded so stressed, but he still sent me messages telling me how much he loved me and how sorry he was. He sent me roses and apologised profusely whenever he was late or had to cancel. We'd meet at strange times. He'd send a car over to my flat to take me to his at midnight. Sometimes I'd get there, and he'd be arguing on the phone. I felt bad for him. I massaged his shoulders and made him food. There wasn't anyone else around to take care of him, so I thought it was my job. But not long after this, things became even stranger.

He told me that his company's medical technology was causing problems, that they'd uncovered something dangerous that the government couldn't know about. He said he was in danger. Look, I know it sounds bizarre and you probably think I'm an idiot, but by this point, he'd been working on me intensely for nearly two months. I was completely head over heels for him and I was scared for his life.

From then on, we communicated by text and phone call. And in every single one, he sounded panicked. He said the government had frozen his assets, that he'd been kicked out of his apartment and that he was being followed. He thought it might be government agents after him or something. The website for his company went down. I went to his apartment to find he'd moved out. He told me he was living in a hotel, but by the time I got to the hotel, he'd already left because someone was following him. He wasn't safe and needed to move all the time. I sent him money. So much money. In the end, it drained all my savings. Over two or three weeks I sent him around ten thousand pounds. All of which he promised to pay back. He never did. I never saw him again.

The moment I realised he was a con man was the lowest point of my life. I remember I'd turned up to a hotel lobby expecting to meet Eric. But he was gone. And this time he'd promised me that he was going to stay there until I arrived. I waited for three hours until a member of staff came and politely asked me if I as okay. Embarrassed, I left. I never heard from Eric again.

Why didn't I go to the police? I can't begin to explain how ashamed I felt. Can you imagine admitting to everything I just described? The thought made me feel sick. I kept picturing the police officers laughing at me behind my back. I couldn't bring myself to say a word. Which is cowardly, I know. If I had said something, he might have gone to prison and been stopped from doing all of this again to other women.

Rachel Berry

Posted 467 days ago

Welcome to the group, Lucy. I'm so sorry for what you

went through. All of that is painfully familiar to me. Only I knew him as Samuel Brown.

Lu Chen

Posted 466 days ago

I knew him as Eric Lansdown too. I hope our experiences didn't overlap. Somehow that would make it worse.

Francesca Sizemore

Posted 15 hours ago

I think I might have met the same man as you guys. But I knew him as Ben May. He didn't just con me, he conned my husband too. It was awful, we lost our house. We lost everything. Ben, Eric, Samuel, whatever his name is, deserves to pay for his crimes.

CHAPTER TEN

EFFIE

I met Ben when I was twenty-three. My attempt at a modelling career had failed spectacularly and I was not popular in the fashion world for obvious reasons. I lived alone in Covent Garden in an apartment owned by my mother. She wasn't talking to me because she was ashamed of my failure, but she hadn't asked for the keys back either.

Ben tried to scam me. He told me he was the CEO of a daring pharmaceutical company that would cure cancer. He completely underestimated me, as he still does to this day. I went along with his ruse until the morning after we had sex. I stole his watch, money from his wallet, and left his business card on the bedside table with the word "bullshit" scribbled on it. You could say it was the beginning of a beautiful love story, but I doubt our romance would be described in that way by anyone apart from us. Perhaps not even us.

He found me a week later in the same bar. Perhaps I continued to go there in the subconscious hope of seeing him again. Or maybe I'm just lazy. I'd already sold his watch by then but he never asked for it back. He told me his real name and we discovered that we had some mutual friends and may even have been at a Swiss ski resort at the same time. I wasn't surprised to hear that he came from money. I grew up with enough of those boys to understand how they tick. To understand their boredom.

We never dated. We didn't call each other and organise a time or place to meet. Whatever our relationship was at the beginning, we both fell into it. We became each other's emotional crutches, in a way. I told him about my housemate Louisa and what I'd done to her. He told me about his disciplinarian father. I told him about my mother's disappointment in me and my father's disinterest. He told me about being carted from one boarding school to the next.

Playing games was part and parcel of being with Ben. It felt familiar to me and in an odd way it became a sort of coping mechanism. I'd been drifting for so long, unwilling and unable to find a purpose. Ben told me that I was beautiful without being beautiful and I believed him. He drew me into his schemes, using me to strengthen his game. I fainted in hotel lobbies, flirted with lonely men and chatted to wives. Looking back, he was working me as much as the people we scammed. Only I didn't recognise it because of that first night when I'd seen through him. I was a little bit too pleased with myself. I thought I'd be able to see through him always.

This life crept up on me. Before I knew it, I was seducing his friend Paul to punish him for bad investment advice. Ben lost a lot of money thanks to Paul and as payback, I was sent in for sex and blackmail. I've been nothing but a cog in Ben's manipulation machine ever since.

But at least I'm doing something I'm good at. Would I be playing games with people on my own if I'd never met Ben? I can't deny that I did it before him. I never meant for it to go *quite* this far, and maybe I have been in over my head at times. I've done things—one thing in particular—that makes me hate myself but fundamentally I'm a bad person and always have been. How much responsibility truly falls on Ben's shoulders?

We drank champagne bought with the money Paul paid me to keep quiet. It tasted better knowing how we paid for it. A week later, we found two witnesses on the street, stepped into a registry office and got married. I made sure Ben used his own money to buy the ring, and I made sure it was a real diamond, too. I remember how willing he was to go through with that and it helped me trust his love was real.

I'm not sure how we fell into what we do now—choosing a neighbourhood to tear apart. After we were married Ben moved into my rent-free central London designer flat, of course, and life was thrilling for a while. But the same schemes and formulas started to wear thin and the noise and dirt of London got under my skin. Then one day I stepped out of the flat straight in someone's vomit on the pavement. I had to throw my favourite suede Valentino boots away. I'd had enough. For the first time ever, I dreamed of my parents' home. The meadows. Mother's horses. Dad's sports cars. I even took Ben to meet them, which went relatively well. Both parents approved of the match because Ben is from "good stock" as Dad said. They managed to make me feel like a brood mare of course, but anything is better than disappointment.

It was on the way back to London in Ben's Porsche that I told him I wanted to move out of the city. I needed to get away from the noise. I asked if he would be happy commuting from somewhere like Buckinghamshire or Essex. He shook his head. He said absolutely not. And yet, somehow, I eventually got what I wanted. That was five years ago, and we've moved half a dozen times already. I got what I wanted, only at a price. Perhaps that was Ben's plan all along, to punish me for wanting to change our lives.

I pull my thoughts back to the present, to the computer screen in front of me. I click "add to bag" and then I put in my debit card details for my private account. I'm on the old laptop that barely works with the fan that makes a whirring sound. It's the only laptop I trust Ben won't have installed keystroke tracking software on. I'm probably being overly cautious, but I'm not taking any chances.

My first task is to purchase a mailbox that accepts packages. One I can drive to and collect my post from rather than have it forwarded to me. Then I use incognito mode on the ancient laptop to buy tracking devices. I get a few, though I only actually need one for his car. The others I can hide in case I need them for something else.

As I check out, I consider the option of walking away from all of this. I have enough money to buy a small house somewhere up north and start over again. But then I remember what happened at the Beaumont. There's no way Ben would let me walk away. My stomach flips as I think about that time and how it changed everything. And what does Ben have from the hotel to hold over me? He has dirt on me, I know it. But I have something on him that I've kept up my sleeve for a long time, too. Something that could cause him serious damage.

I think of the life Ben has made for us and what he's taken away from me. There's still plenty he could take. I have a lot to lose, and not just money. I need to think smart. I need to play him at his own game. There's no fucking way I'm going to let him win.

First things first. Where is my money going? That's what I need to know.

Look, when it comes to other women, I understand the deal. And while it bothered me at first, I saw it as mutually beneficial in the end. After all, I get to be with other men too. It's never quite as glamorous as it sounds, considering there are certain marks to be seduced, but the power still turns me on. Most of the time.

But when it comes to my money... That is an entirely different matter. There is no such agreement between the two of us.

Which is why I don't feel any guilt for following him.

A few days after the trackers arrive, Ben tells me he's heading out for a bit without telling me where he's going. I kiss him on the cheek with an unsuspecting smile and wait until the front door closes. I watch him leave in the Range Rover and I power up the old laptop. Immediately, the tracker shows me that he's driving towards Reading. I watch it moving through the streets until it stops outside a casino.

My husband is at a casino on a weekday afternoon. Is that where my money is going? Ben always told me it was one way to clean dirty money. Buy chips at the casino. Spend a bit of time there, and then cash in the same chips, obtaining money from a legitimate source. But it's also not something he does often, and not on a weekday afternoon.

I consider jumping in a taxi and following him there, but I decide not to bother. It's not like I need to see him in action to know what's going on. Besides, he might see me in there. Instead, I sit on the sofa and watch the tracker. It's stationary for several hours. There's no way he'd be in there all this time if he wasn't gambling.

"Ben, you fucking idiot," I mutter.

Of course, it all fits. He needs risk. Every game we play is a gamble, and I've known for a long time he's addicted to our scams. Could he be addicted to wasting our money, too? I find myself pacing the living room, trying to figure out what I'm really mad about and what I want to do about it. And then it hits me. It doesn't matter to me why Ben stole my money. I've had enough of this life. I'm tired. It's time to get out.

CHAPTER ELEVEN

BEN

The thing that Effie doesn't understand is that when she forced me to move out of London, she sucked out my lifeblood. The city pumped me full of it. Bustle, noise, people, a million opportunities to scam, it all got my heart pounding. Out here, it's asphyxiating. And since she forced me to move, I've had to find another way to stir up some of that old excitement. The games are one thing, but I need more.

Gambling has always been a good way to launder money, but it's also something casinos keep an eye on. In the end, I got bored and ended up gambling for real. And the thing is, casinos and card games are only fun at high stakes. When you're rich, a lot of doors open. Effie and I have always had a certain arrangement. She knows I can't stay in the house watching television. And she knows not to ask questions when I leave. In the weeks between our games, I need a distraction. Finding high-stakes poker games is a great way to do that. The problem is, I lose more than I win.

When your income is obtained through blackmail, there's always cash inside the house. Stacks of it. Thousands. And I spent it all. Then I started borrowing to compensate. Without my old job, I don't have the income to replace the lost earnings, or to pay back the rather unpleasant men I borrowed the money from in the first place.

Luckily, I have several marks I can manipulate a few thousand out of, a couple of dodgy men I can blackmail every now and then. I considered calling in my favour from Dominic, a man I met at poker, who's involved in organised crime, but I'm saving that for a rainy day. And there's always Effie's money. She's both loaded and cautious with her money—a good combination. Not that it stopped her from spending my money when she felt like it. For example, the whopping diamond ring she insisted I buy her. But then I saw it as an investment, like a Rolex. Some people need a visual representation of wealth and diamonds are extremely visual. It was useful to our game to have that status symbol hanging off her hand.

If Effie knew about the money I'd taken from her, my life would not be worth living. The truth is, I've been careless. Once I realised she didn't notice the extra money coming out of our joint account, I took more. And I lost more. It was only supposed to be a couple of thousand. It ended up being much, much more. But at least I've managed to get the loan sharks off my back now. I can move on. Kick the gambling habit and focus on something far more fascinating—the next game.

I toss a few chips onto the felt table. Nothing high-stakes today, unfortunately. A little poker, maybe some blackjack later. I wheedled some money out of a woman who thinks I just escaped from a prison in Thailand. Every now and then I send her a photoshopped picture. Poor Miranda. She really is a sweet soul and she's probably sent me something like twenty thousand pounds over the last three years.

Miranda is chasing that high I gave her the first time we

met. Effie and I were living together at the time, so I had to rent a flat in London for a few weeks. Miranda met Eric Lansdown, of course. I remember I took her for a steak at a nice place. Just a really good steak, no Michelin-star chefs or anything like that, because Miranda didn't read like a woman who wanted luxury. She wanted to feel special, but not in an extravagant way.

What I do involves tailoring the method to the person. Hayley wanted jewellery. Fiona wanted to be hugged after sex. Diana wanted to be controlled. Lu wanted compliments. Rachel wanted a Chanel bag.

Effie wanted to be the smartest. My wife hates it when she's outwitted. If she isn't the smartest person in the room, a little part of her implodes. Don't get me wrong, she's an intelligent woman, and she genuinely did see through me the first time we met, but I've managed to play her for years now. That's been interesting for me because it has an element of danger about it. No one else in my life has the power to meet me at my level. But now she's stopped wanting to play games and I'm getting bored.

Since we left the Beaumont, Effie has changed. I suppose part of me expected it, but I was hoping she might be able to move past it all. There's nothing stopping her from forgetting about it and moving on. That's what I did. And it's why I went to great lengths to ensure she didn't know everything about what happened that night. It's for the best, after all.

Frankly, I'm disappointed. If Effie can't move past this, then, no matter how I feel about her, or the history we've had together, we can't go on. She fits so well into my lifestyle, but I can't help but wonder if she'll eventually outlive her usefulness. And if she does, who could replace her? I need someone smart, who looks the part and sounds the part, and who will keep up with my games. I sigh, collect the chips I've won and glance at my watch. I don't have the sort of marriage where my wife tracks my movements, but I also can't push it. Besides, I need to think about my next move with Sophie.

Sophie is everything Effie isn't. Innocent, open and sweet. But is she corruptible? Turning Effie into my life partner was one thing, but what if I did the same to a woman like Sophie? It would certainly be a challenge.

On my way out of the casino, my phone buzzes again.

Tick tock.

I pause. What is this? I thought the messages were coming from the loan shark, and I paid them off more than a week ago. *Fine. If you want to play*, I think.

I type back. *Tick tock until what?*

Until I tell your wife what you did.

A waitress smiles at me from the bar. She's pretty. Young, maybe twenty-one, with strawberry-blonde hair that reminds me of a certain neighbour. I smile back. I wonder when her shift ends.

Rather than leave, I take a seat at the bar. I drum my fingers against the polished surface, considering my next response to the texter.

Go ahead, I type. *I don't know who you are and what you think you know but my wife and I don't have any secrets.*

The response is quick. *Are you sure about that?*

CHAPTER TWELVE

EFFIE

Ben stands back, admiring his handiwork. I have a thumbnail jammed between my front teeth, biting back what I want to say. That I know what he's doing with my money. That for the last few days I've been pretending. From now on it will be nothing but pretense.

"It's starting now, Effie," he says. "I'm going to get into Sophie Morgan's house and set up the cameras. Then we'll take it from there. What are you doing?"

"I have the book club on Thursday," I say. "I can begin planting seeds."

He nods.

We're in the cellar again. Ben's cheeks are flushed and his voice is breathless. I haven't seen him this animated for a long time. It's Sophie who has him all riled up. I would be jealous but I'm frankly too angry for that. After he spent that time at the casino, I've fumed over it as the days pass on. Sometimes I barely manage to be civil. But I have to remind myself that I'm playing a long game.

"I can't wait to get into their house," he says. "I have a

good feeling about this neighbourhood. I think we can do some of our best work."

It strikes me then—as he calls this "work"—that we haven't had a real reason for our games in a very long time. The first time we picked apart a couple it was for revenge. Whenever I think about Paul, I remember his swollen fingers and the way his stomach touched mine when we had sex. Ben seduced the wife, and I seduced Paul. I tricked myself into thinking I enjoyed it.

I told Paul I was pregnant and needed to get an abortion at a private hospital. I asked him for money and threatened to tell his wife. He handed the money over quick as a flash. The guy was loaded so it wasn't much to him. It wasn't much to us, either, but it was the principle of it—according to Ben. No one screws over Ben May.

What Ben did to his wife, Olivia, was crueller. He took pictures of her and posted them onto a revenge porn site, cropping his face out of every dirty shot. Then he created an anonymous email address and sent them all to Paul. It makes me cringe thinking about it now: the kick I got from it, how we celebrated with champagne. What has changed since then? I'm older now, I suppose. Perhaps I'm finally growing up. Either that or the sheen of being Ben's wife is beginning to wear thin.

"I don't want to pretend about the IVF," I say.

Ben shrugs. "You have to. It's our in."

"You know I don't like faking baby stuff. You know that and yet you did it anyway."

He wraps an arm around my shoulders, placating me. I want to shove him away but I need to be smart. I can't stop thinking about the money. We've both done some horrible things, but we promised we'd never hurt each other. Ben clearly doesn't care about that anymore. I'm fair game to him, which means he's fair game to me. I pull him closer.

"We won't be here long," he says. "Six months at the most. I promise." He kisses my neck and I pretend to enjoy it. "This might be our last scheme. Let's just go with it. Make the most of it. Yeah?"

"Our last scheme?" I scoff. "You've said that before and you never mean it."

"I do this time." He strokes my cheek, so softly, as though he really does love me. No wonder I used to believe it. "I promise, Effie. You're going to get the life you want."

"What's that?" I ask. "What do I want?"

He pulls back to regard me. Every muscle in my body tenses in anticipation. What does Ben think I want?

"Well, to slow down. Maybe not completely, but enough so that we don't have to move around all the time. Perhaps... Yeah, maybe we could go abroad like you said. Somewhere warm. You in a bikini by the pool, wearing those heels I like. Sipping champagne. We could play a few minor games with people but nothing... legally complicated. Nothing that involves surveillance or breaking and entering." He grins.

"And you could live like that?" I ask.

He kisses my neck again. "As long as I'm with you."

Liar.

There's no way Ben would ever give up his way of life. He's addicted to taking risks. I even have proof now that he's a gambler. There's no way we could ever live in the manner he's proposing.

"Does that sound good, Effie?" He continues to nuzzle my neck. "One last scheme? Let's go out with a bang, shall we?"

He's not backing down, which means I have to. If I don't, he'll be suspicious.

"All right," I say. "But let's play it carefully. Don't lay it on thick. Okay?"

"Okay," he murmurs softly into my ear.

I don't want the thrill of excitement to shoot through me, but it does. I hate that his fingers running along my jaw heighten the bolt of electricity making its way through my body. There's nothing I can do to stop my body reacting to him, craving him. Despite everything I know, and all the rage twisted up inside me, I want this.

There's something wrong with me. With us. Deep down I know I can't keep living like this. I want—no, I need—to get out. And yet I do nothing to stop him. Pushing it all aside, I ride the burning wave crashing through my body until pleasure spreads across my hot skin like a flame.

CHAPTER THIRTEEN

BEN

It takes over a week to learn Sophie and Lewis's routines. He leaves at seven every morning to go to work. Her routine is more sporadic. She doesn't work. Her comings and goings vary from day to day. But I soon find out she has a few regular appointments that have her out of the house for at least two hours. Tuesday at 9am is her Pilates class. She then meets a friend for coffee at about half past ten. At least, that's what she does on the two Tuesdays I stalk her movements.

Effie is still asleep as I watch Sophie leave for Pilates as normal. It's always a pleasant surprise when a petite woman unveils her curves with tight sportswear, and I smile to myself as she puts her yoga mat in her car.

I have at least an hour and a half to get into their house. My bag is packed ready. I won't have long when I'm inside but I can do it. I've already been in their house to give them my financial advice, and while I was there, I slipped Lewis's key from the hook in the hallway. I watched them like a hawk all week to see if they called out a locksmith. They didn't. From our upstairs window, I saw them search the house and then I assume Lewis went to get a new key cut. All too often people assume their carelessness is the problem, when actually it's a nasty piece of shit like me.

Now, getting into their house may seem easy with a key. The hard part is making sure no one on the street sees me do it. But of course, I have a plan.

I tiptoe down the stairs, not wanting to wake Effie. At one time she would have been keen enough to come with me, but not anymore. I don't have the energy to deal with her moods. It's much easier to let her stew around in bed.

When I leave the house, I make a show of going for a walk. I move past Sophie's house towards the security gates, nodding to the security guard as I leave Ivy Oaks. Then I take a right turn that leads me to the perimeter fence. I have a backpack on. Whenever I carry one, I feel incapable of "fitting in". They look ridiculous on me. But I don't think the guard paid much attention and the street around the perimeter is quiet.

On a walk earlier this week, I marked where Sophie and Lewis's property met the fence, and then I surveyed the area for weaknesses. I checked for security cameras, ran my fingers across the wood, looking for any potentially loose slats. There were no cameras and no loose slats, which means I'll have to climb it.

I toss the bag over the fence, place my hands on the top rung, which is around six feet. I'm six feet one so it's only a slight reach. Then I press one boot against the fence and heave my weight over. I land with a thud and duck behind the hedge as I double-check the surroundings.

My one great worry is that they may have a security camera in the garden that I didn't catch during my observations. During my hour at their house, I excused myself to go to the bathroom, stuck my head out of their guest bedroom and checked the garden. I saw the light fixed to the wall, but no cameras. Still, I worry that there's one somewhere out of sight that catches my drop into their garden. I'm not sure how I could explain that, especially if they had the kind that sent a notification to the owner, like the doorbell at the front of the house.

When I stole Lewis's keys, I took them all. I have keys for both the front and back door, along with keys to his car. I hurry over to their patio door, work through the keys on the chain and unlock the door. There's no blaring alarm. Sliding the door behind me, I'm now in their house. I take off my boots, put on a pair of gloves, and slide a beanie hat over my head. I need to work fast.

The conservatory at the back of the house is filled with floral sofas and wicker tables. I hurry into the house, sliding open the bifold doors leading to the kitchen. This room is never the most interesting. I need to cover the living room and, of course, the bedroom.

I bought the smallest recording devices with the longest battery life that I could find. Some are shaped like a USB stick, others the size of a credit card. But the best I found was a hidden microphone inside a four-socket plug adapter. I've never known anyone who does not have one of those. And when I check around the back of the television, I find one.

It takes me just under ten minutes to swap the adapter. I keep one eye on the window, checking for anyone passing by. But I'm too low to be seen.

I don't bother with a video recorder in the living room, since I can see them from my house anyway. I move further into the house, hurry up the staircase and find their bedroom. When it comes to hidden cameras, there are several designs you can try. Cameras hidden inside casing that resembles an air freshener. Those that look like an alarm sensor. Cameras designed as a portable radio or a smoke alarm. You can buy them to look like a computer mouse, or a sound bar. It feels illegal to be able to buy so many sneaky ways to capture another human being, but they're all available online. It is, of course, illegal to break into someone's home and bug their house, but I'm not planning on getting caught.

Now, from my experience some people won't notice a new air freshener or smoke alarm pop up in their home. Renters may assume that they'd never noticed that smoke alarm above their bed. Some single men don't pay attention to décor once bought by their ex. But anything like that would stick out like a sore thumb in this house. The camera I bring is a plug adapter. This time for an electrical appliance.

When I see the headboard, I can't help but smile. They have a customised shelf built into it with phone charging stations and an alarm clock. A camera at the back of the headboard will give me a great view of the room. Quickly, I grab the alarm clock, unscrew the adapter and add my own. Then I plug it back into the socket and pocket the old adapter. I check the screen, make sure the clock is working properly and arrange everything so that the camera has the perfect view.

I'll need to watch out for Sophie or Lewis rearranging their items on this shelf. I could do with another angle just in case. I check my watch. I've been twenty minutes so far. I don't want to stay much longer if I can help it. But there's a lamp on the other side of the room and I have one more plug camera. I hurry over, unscrew the old adapter and screw in mine. I'm nearly finished when I hear something. It breaks through from downstairs, loud and startling. A creak, followed by a thud. The front door. Someone is home.

"Fuck." My heart in my throat, I swear under my breath. And then I remember my boots are still in the conservatory and the bifold door is open. There's no way I can get to the conservatory without bumping into whoever is downstairs. I hear a cough, it's Sophie. All I can do now is hide and hope she doesn't go through to the kitchen. I flatten myself against the carpet and shimmy beneath the bed. My heart thunders. And yet, I'm smiling. Adrenaline surges through my blood. I could be caught at any moment. She could call the police, or try to attack me or something else, and that is the thrill of it all.

It's all or nothing now. My fate is in luck's hands. All I can do is adapt, which is exactly how I like to live.

I hear soft feet on the stairs. She's coming.

CHAPTER FOURTEEN

EFFIE

Ben thinks I'm asleep when he sneaks out of the house in dark clothing and a backpack. I'm not. I've woken up now in every way.

By the time he's out of the door, I'm up and getting dressed. Ben thinks he's sneaky, but he's not the only one who knows that Sophie goes to Pilates on a Tuesday.

I pull on my yoga pants and a vest top, grab my dusty yoga mat and a water bottle and hurry out of the house. I jump into the car and wave at the security guard as I leave. Then I drive to the class, park up, and sprint around the corner to where Sophie is waiting for the doors to open.

"Effie, hi! I didn't know you took this class," she says brightly.

I lift a hand, but I make sure not to smile. Instead, I allow my eyes to dart around, and I keep my body taut like I'm stressed.

"Yeah, well, I usually come on a Thursday, but I have an... appointment this week."

"Right," she says, nodding.

Then I run my fingers through my hair and adjust my

weight back and forth, almost bouncing on my heels. "Actually, I really don't know if I want to go in." I let out a long sigh.

"What's wrong?" Sophie asks, concern brimming out of her.

I force tears into my eyes. "Oh, nothing."

She steps towards me. "There's definitely something wrong. Do you want to chat?"

"I took a pregnancy test this morning. It was negative," I blurt out, as if I can't help myself.

She nods grimly as though my words confirm her suspicion. "Come on. Let's skip Pilates and grab a coffee. I know a great place around the corner."

Sophie leads the way. We make our way to a tiny independent café and I hope the cappuccinos are good. As we settle into our chairs, she offers to buy me a drink and I protest at first, but she insists. A few minutes later she returns with two large coffees on a tray.

"I knew as soon as you walked over that something was wrong," she says. "I'm so sorry about the pregnancy test."

I stir my coffee. "You're so intuitive." I smile. "Thank you. I really should be used to it by now but every time it happens, it's like a stab to the stomach. You know?"

"I get it. I feel the exact same way."

"Sorry I ruined your morning."

She waves a hand. "Honestly, I'm relieved. I woke up with a headache this morning. And I usually go for a coffee after, but I'll just have my fix now."

Perfect, I think.

"Maybe you need a lie down." I touch her lightly on the arm. "You know, I think the stress of all this comes out in our bodies. For me it's stomach aches and neck tension."

"I think you're right."

"So, how are you and Lewis coping with it all?" I ask. I

may as well get some further information out of her. Though I need her to go home soon and catch Ben in the act.

"We're fine." She sips her coffee before shaking her head. "That's such a lie. We're far from fine. I'm beginning to feel like Lewis doesn't care about this as much as me. He's sick of making love when I'm ovulating. He says there's no romance and it makes sex a chore." She rolls her eyes. "He's not the one who takes the vitamins and keeps to a strict diet and has had to cut out alcohol. Yet somehow this is harder on him."

"All the men I've known find the mildest of inconveniences intolerable while women adapt to almost anything," I say with honesty, though Ben is one man who can put up with many inconveniences if it means him getting his own way further down the line.

Her eyebrows rise. "That is so true. My dad was like it with my mum, too. And my brothers. Mum coddled them of course." She scoffs. "The truth is I'm tired and, honestly, I'm beginning to feel like maybe it's not worth it. But then I think about holding a tiny baby in my arms and suddenly it feels like everything."

My chest tightens when she says that. There's a strange, dull pain in my abdomen. I blink, pulling myself back from those thoughts.

"I know what you mean," I say. "But I don't think it's ever going to happen for me."

"Oh, Effie, don't say that."

"It's true," I say.

She squeezes my hand and I clear my throat, turning to stare out of the café window. "I'm so sorry, Sophie. I think I need to head home. I'm exhausted."

"That's okay," she says. "I'm glad we talked."

"It really helped. Honestly." I pull on a light jacket over my top. "What are you doing now?"

She bites her lip, thoughtfully. "I think I'm going to head home as well. I'm like you, I feel worn out. It's the fertility stuff, isn't it? God, it's a lot to go through."

I place my hand on her shoulder before I leave. "If you ever need to talk, you know where I am."

"Likewise," she says, staring up at me.

I walk out of the café trying to suppress a smile. Ben thought he'd planned his morning to perfection. No doubt he found an ingenious way of getting inside their house. He timed his outing well, made sure he could get in and out without being noticed. But he underestimated his wife. Now Sophie is going to go home, and he'll still be inside her house. And I can't wait to return to Ivy Oaks and watch it all happen from my window.

CHAPTER FIFTEEN

BEN

Under the bed, I strain my ears to listen for my prey's next move. After the shock of Sophie's return home has settled, I seize the adrenaline coursing through my veins and use it to give me power as I've done many times before. Hearing her footsteps on the stairs is a good thing. It means she's not going into the kitchen. If she sees my boots, this is all over. There's a slim chance I could get out without her recognising me, if I kept my head down and ran, or knocked her unconscious perhaps, but that's messy and I run the risk of making things worse for myself if the police get involved. My plans tend to rely on the *don't get caught* principle.

When the door to the bedroom opens, I concentrate on keeping my breathing shallow. She's a quiet mover, making minimal sound as her feet move towards me. Then I see her yoga mat drop to the ground. A moment later, her bare heels face me as she sits on the bed. She lets out a noise of pleasure, probably stretching her muscles. Then her feet disappear and I know she's on top of the bed.

This is not good. How long is she going to stay up there? Is she taking a nap? I don't know how heavily this woman sleeps. And how would I know if she's even asleep? She's almost silent as it is. The only thing I can do is wait.

I close my eyes. Effie once tried to teach me how to meditate. I didn't enjoy it, not because I couldn't switch off my mind, but because I didn't see the point. I didn't take it seriously. Now I reluctantly employ those methods. I concentrate on my breathing. I flex my muscles and tighten them. The more I can focus on my breathing, the easier I'll find the silence. At least in theory. I could also fall asleep and start to snore.

Above me the bed creaks as Sophie finds a comfortable position. I hear her plumping the pillow. Every now and then she makes a *tsk* sounds with her tongue or lets out a soft laugh. She must be browsing her phone. I picture her scrolling through social media, laughing at memes, clucking at opinions she doesn't share. I wonder what her political leaning is. She comes across as a leftie, but you can be surprised by young women from a privileged background. Most like to come across as a bleeding heart but deep down they just don't want to be taxed. None of it bothers me but it's useful to know when trying to suss out a mark.

I'm not sure how long I'm there before her feet drop back onto the carpet. Every muscle in my body tenses. I breathe softly through my nose. But now she's making her own noise, humming quietly to herself as she walks across the bedroom. I hear another door open. The bedroom door? Then the sound of running water. A shower! She's in the ensuite. Thank God for that. But I have no idea how long she showers for. It could be two minutes like me or twenty-five like Effie.

I wait until I hear the muffled sound of the shower door close. Then I shimmy out from underneath the bed. The room is empty as I flee silently, making my way down the stairs. My blood is pumping. I'm sweating beneath the beanie hat. I haven't felt this alive in a long time and I have Sophie to thank for that; her unpredictability is alluring.

I'm positive that I'm making too much noise, but I can only hope she doesn't hear through the sound of gushing water. Finally, I make it to the conservatory and grab my boots. And then I freeze. The ensuite shower overlooks the back garden. I can't go out there. Quickly, ducked down behind one of the sofas, I pull on the boots and assess the situation. There's no way I can climb over the back wall. Running across the garden is too risky, and if she saw me and alerted security, they would catch me outside the perimeter. My best bet is to stay flat against the house and edge around the side. I'll have to avoid their doorbell camera and make it look like I've just come back from a walk. But that means the security guard won't see me return to Ivy Oaks. Is that something he'll remember? I don't have much of a choice. I slide the bifold door and hurry along, keeping my back against the wall.

About halfway along, I hesitate. I have a decision to make. Unless I climb over the wall at the front of the house, I'm going to be seen by the doorbell camera. There's just no way of doing it. But climbing over the wall might attract the attention of someone else in the neighbourhood. This is beginning to annoy me now. If Sophie hadn't come home early, everything would have moved along smoothly.

My eyes are drawn to movement across the street. Effie must be up and about inside the house. Can she help in some way? Create some sort of distraction? My fingers rest on the shape of my phone inside my trouser pocket. Things with Effie have been delicate but she's still part of this. She still enjoys the games. At least I think she does. I edge out slightly to check the street. Most people are either at work or school. I mentally make a list of those who might be home. Beryl, who gets a clear view of almost everything. David, who lives next door to Sophie and apparently doesn't have a job. Sam, the writer, who works from home. Beryl is the most dangerous because she's so nosey. But would she recognise me from here? I'd be some random intruder to her. I guess it'd shake things up on the street if they thought there was a burglar around.

And then I consider another option. I could hop the fence onto David's property, edge around the side of his house, and leave from the front. He doesn't have a doorbell camera, I've checked. He might see me if he's sitting in the living room at the front of the house or one of the upstairs bedrooms. But what are the chances? And what would my excuse be?

Before I can overthink it, I'm climbing the fence. A rose bush snags my trousers and I'm glad for the gloves as I make my way through. I keep the gloves and my beanie hat on until I'm near the front of the house. Then I shove them into my bag and have a better idea. Dusting myself down, I walk around the side of the house and straight up to the front door. I ring the doorbell.

Thirty seconds later, the door is snatched open.

"Hi," David says.

I wait a beat. He says nothing about me emerging from the side of the house so he can't have seen me.

"Sorry to bother you, mate. I wondered if I could borrow a Phillips head screwdriver? We're putting some furniture together and I've lost mine."

"Sure," he says.

He doesn't invite me in, but I don't care. When he goes back into the house to get the tool, I know I've got away with it. And I can't keep the smile off my face.

CHAPTER SIXTEEN

EFFIE

That lucky bastard. I wait by the window. I even get snacks—salted Kettle chips—and pour a glass of Merlot. I don't have binoculars because it would look too suspicious. Instead, I wait and wait for something to happen; police cars rushing through the gates, a piercing scream to break the perpetual quiet of Ivy Oaks.

Nothing happens. Not a thing. Sophie goes into the house and I expect her to find Ben there setting up his spy network but he doesn't emerge for at least fifteen minutes. I wonder where he hid, inside a wardrobe or under the bed? Behind the sofa?

When I see him pop up around the side of the house, I move myself to a different room to get a better view. At this point, I expect him to call. He's obviously stuck. For some reason he can't get out at the back and the Morgans have a camera on the front of the house. I watch my phone, but it never rings.

My fingers drum against my wine glass as I wait for him to do something. A moment later I see him climb the boundary wall to reach David's property. He removes his gloves and hat, tidies himself up and *rings the doorbell*. The man is so brazen. I'm floored by it. I'm impressed and furious all at once.

When I can see him heading to the house, I tip the wine down the kitchen sink, pour myself a glass of water and swill my mouth. The door opens and with a spring in his step, he strides in. He walks straight up to me and kisses me, palming a breast at the same time. He's buzzing.

"Where've you been?" I ask. "Have you been putting something together?"

"Oh, yes," he says. He grabs his phone from his pocket and opens an app. Then he turns the screen towards me.

Sophie Morgan is naked in her bedroom getting changed into fresh clothes. I find myself examining her body, the surprisingly full breasts and hips, the bruises on her stomach from where she must have to inject herself for the fertility treatments. She pulls on plain white knickers and a bralette. She values comfort over sexiness, I note.

Ben starts watching it and I turn away.

"You did well," I say. "We'll learn all their secrets now."

He nods, still staring at the screen.

I know my husband. I know he didn't do this to learn more about the people he wants to scam. We don't need cameras for that, Sophie is enough of a walking wound to manipulate as it is. We don't need to see her naked or having joyless sex with her husband. Honestly, the thought of watching that depresses me. But Ben likes it because it's a power trip. I glance at him. He's transfixed. It's funny, because he isn't a pervert. This doesn't turn him on, at least not exclusively. I genuinely think he is intrigued. I think he wants to know her. All of her.

And that's interesting. That's something I can work with.

For the next few days, Ben is glued to what he calls The Real Morgans of Ivy Oaks. I'm less interested. Instead, I focus on my own game plan.

I've been thinking of ways to get into his phone or laptop, but Ben watches both like a hawk. The laptop is the one I have the better chance with. He doesn't take it with him when he leaves the house, but at the same time, it's password protected and I can't crack the code. I've spent many hours scribbling out ideas on a pad, but none of them are clever enough to be used by him. I'm at a loss. Frankly, it's pissing me off. I'm a walking ball of simmering rage.

Then I see the screwdriver on the coffee table. Ben dumped it there after he came home from his escapades. It's time for me to have my own fun. I grab it and run out of the house. I'm not sure Ben even notices me leave to be honest. Not that I mind, because it gives me more freedom. Continue to underestimate me, darling, it will make victory all the sweeter.

David answers the door quickly after I ring the bell. He smiles when he sees me holding up the screwdriver.

"My husband is too lazy to bring this back," I say.

"Fancy a cup of tea?" he asks.

"Got anything stronger?"

He shrugs. "Whisky."

"Perfect."

When I'm inside the house, I place the screwdriver onto a narrow table in the hallway and follow him through to the kitchen. My eyes are drawn to pictures of his kid on the wall. There are none of his ex-wife, just David and his daughter, Lori, smiling for the camera. In one she's on a pony and he has his arm draped over the pony's neck. In another he's holding her as a tiny, red-faced baby.

"Your house is lovely," I say as we walk through.

"Thanks."

This short hallway is more of a home than any of the houses I've lived in with Ben. David likes music, I can tell from the miniature guitar on the wall, and the vintage Clash poster. We reach the kitchen and I smile at the brightness, coral-painted walls with cream cabinets. When he opens up the pantry to get the whisky, I notice how delightfully messy it is in there, tins of soup stacked on the shelves, opened bags of crisps. He walks back towards me, past the fridge, which is cluttered with colourful magnets.

I point to them. "From your travels?"

He nods. "Whenever my ex has Lori for the summer, I pick a place and go. I can't get enough."

I scan the places—Lisbon, Cairo, Seoul, Berlin.

He passes me a cut-crystal tumbler of whisky and clinks glasses. It runs down smooth, burning my throat in a good way.

"Do you have a good relationship with your ex?"

He perches himself on a stool next to the breakfast bar. "It's a fragile one. For a while there we were at odds. She didn't want to let me in and if I'm honest, I don't blame her. I wasn't a good husband to her, and I know it's clouded the way she feels about me as a dad too."

I want to ask more questions, but his body language is telling me not to go there. He folds in on himself when he talks about her. Rather than pry, I nod and stay quiet.

"How long have you been married?" he asks. Then adds, "If that isn't too personal a question."

"About five years."

"He's older than you," David says. "What are you, thirty?"

I nod. I tend to avoid telling anyone my exact age. The more precise the detail, the easier you are to find once you've moved on. Ben taught me that.

"And he's..."

"Forty-seven," I say.

I'm being honest for a change. Ben looks more like forty because he has a dermatologist, but for some strange reason I want David to know the truth. His eyebrows lift in surprise.

"How did you two meet?" he asks.

"On a dating app," I say. "Sorry it's boring."

He laughs. "Not at all. It's actually quite interesting."

I smile to myself. Everything I'm saying is making David dislike Ben even more. Ben scouting a dating app for younger women is not a good look. It's not true, obviously, we met in a bar, but the principle is the same. He still approached me knowing there was an age difference. He's one of those cliched men who doesn't find women his own age attractive.

We sip our drinks and a question burns in my throat. "What happened with your wife?" I blurt out.

David winces.

I cock my head to one side. "You did ask me a personal question. Aren't I allowed one in return?"

"You are. I suppose." He drains his glass and places it on the kitchen counter. "It's one of those stories you'll have heard many times. We married when she fell pregnant with Lori and we thought we could make it work. But I was an ass." He smiles, but it comes across as more of a grimace. "I felt like a failure. She nit-picked everything I did, and I couldn't handle it. Every time I got Lori's formula wrong or swaddled her the wrong way, I took it personally. I was young. And I grew up in a family where... well, let's just say the compliments weren't in abundance. So, I found a way to get compliments elsewhere. That's how insecure I was."

"Other women?" I ask.

He nods. "Lots of them." I'm impressed by his honesty.

"What changed?"

"Family court," he says. "I sat there and listened to all the times I was late, or didn't turn up to Lori's school play because I was out with another woman. I had to be reminded of the time I took her to the doctor's and couldn't remember her birthday or middle name. She was right about everything. What I saw as nagging was justified, it was because I didn't put the effort in. And then I fucked things up even worse by screwing around. I had no one to blame but myself."

I sip my whisky. "You don't seem insecure now."

"Therapy," he says with a laugh. "I guess that's one advantage of having money."

"I don't like therapy," I say. "I tried it for a while. It seemed like hokum."

He smiles. "Hokum."

"What's funny about that?"

"Nothing, you're just very posh."

I start to giggle. The whisky again, no doubt.

"Seriously, though. Why didn't therapy work for you?" he asks.

I suddenly feel the weight on my feet, and I walk over to David's small dining table, pull out a seat and sit down. Lifting one leg, I remove my high-heeled shoes and stretch out the arch of my foot. "Oh, I'm a lost cause. You see there's nothing actually wrong with me. I'm just a bitch."

He smiles, lifting the left side of his mouth. "You're not a bitch."

I chuckle then, shaking my head. It's not like me to let my guard slip. "I've had too much of that," I say, jabbing a finger towards the offending glass.

"It certainly loosens the old tongue," he says. "I haven't told anyone about my infidelity in a very long time."

"I tell everyone I'm a bitch," I deflect.

David lets out a roar of laughter. The sound makes a lightness bubble up from my belly. Sitting there in his kitchen, I start to feel like someone else. Someone better. But it's an illusion, isn't it? The good of someone else has rubbed off on me for a short time. Soon I'll have to get up, leave this house, and go back to the spider web where I belong.

CHAPTER SEVENTEEN

BEN

Sophie and Lewis are hanging on by a thread. It's not that they argue, it's that they don't do much of anything. I watch the camera footage with interest, noting how long Lewis keeps away from the house. Sophie doesn't have much of a social life, which means she's undoubtedly lonely. The one thing she enjoys doing is putting records on and dancing when Lewis isn't there. I hear the scratch of the player in their living room. She's into vinyl. It's actually kind of hot, even though I know nothing about records.

Their sex is robotic. It's embarrassing to watch. One night, I pulled Effie onto my knee while we both watched. Halfway through, Lewis lost his erection and Sophie began to cry. She told him they'd never make a baby like this. He screamed at her about the pressure. Effie got up from my knee and walked out of the room, which surprised me. When did she grow a conscience?

And what else is Effie up to? Her reluctance to play the game is becoming more and more noticeable with each day. She made little effort at the barbecue and she keeps complaining about the IVF story. I'm not sure if she'd go as far as to sabotage my plans, but something nags at the back of my mind—why did Sophie come home early that day? What if Effie had a hand in it? I can't know for sure. Effie doesn't seem to have had the energy for anything like that, but I'm not ruling it out either.

For three days, whenever Sophie leaves the house, I get in the car and drive to the nearest music store. Finally, on the third day, she walks in.

"Oh my God, Ben! I didn't know you liked vinyl."

I smile and kiss her politely on the cheek. "Honestly, I'm a beginner. Effie gave me a record player for Christmas and I've only bought a few albums so far. I don't really know what I'm doing."

"I can help if you like," she says enthusiastically.

"That would be amazing, thank you," I reply.

The thing about lying is that it has to be realistic. I could research vinyl, pretend I'm a collector and impress her with my knowledge, but there's always the chance I'd slip up. On the other hand, if I'm honest enough to admit I don't know what I'm doing, not only will she want to help—which means putting more effort into it—but now she knows I'm willing to admit my weaknesses. Wherever possible, show vulnerability. It's a green flag to women. Arrogance is the biggest and most noticeable red flag a man can put out into the world.

"Do you like jazz?" she asks.

"I like Nina Simone," I say.

"Great. Good choice."

She takes me around the stacks, pointing out good albums to buy, whispering that I can get cheaper online, and showing me modern alternatives to the jazz greats. Soon an hour has whizzed by and I'm paying for an armful of records. Of course, now I need to actually buy a record player to ensure I don't get caught out.

"Do you fancy a coffee?" I ask.

She hesitates for a moment but then nods her head.

That hesitation is important. It could be interpreted two ways. One is that she thinks it's inappropriate for a married woman to have coffee with a married man but seeing as we're neighbours, and we just spent an hour in a record shop, she doesn't see the harm. The other is that she's harbouring feelings for me and isn't sure whether to indulge them or shut them down before they flourish.

We go to the nearest café and I order an Americano. Sophie gets a latte. It's busy inside and out, with people enjoying the sunshine as they eat their toasties for lunch. I've always hated the smell of coffee shops. It's the aroma of cheap cheese melting out of those toasties that turns my stomach.

"Thank you for helping me," I say. "Effie's going to be thrilled when I actually start playing records."

"I'm so glad," she says. "And it was no problem at all."

I note that she seems relieved that I mentioned my wife's name. It reminds me to proceed at a snail's pace with her.

"I'm hoping it'll be a nice gesture. We've been arguing a lot recently and the record player came up. She thinks I've been ungrateful because I haven't used it." I sip my Americano. "I mean, she's not wrong about that."

"Oh, I'm sorry," she says. "It's hard, isn't it? The little things build up so quickly."

"Whoever said you have to work at a marriage wasn't lying," I agree, angling my head down as though I'm sad. "The truth is... Well, it's even worse than one argument. We're... sorry, you don't want to know about this."

"Of course I do," she insists. "If I can help, or at least listen, I'd love to."

"We've been on the rocks for a while. Especially with the fertility problems. It's like everything is coming to a head."

She nods. I wonder if she's thinking of her own marital issues. "Has something specific happened? Or is it just general problems?"

"A little of both," I say. "Effie doesn't want to do IVF anymore. She's given up. She says it's too hard. That's her choice and I respect it. But I want to look into other options, like adoption. She doesn't."

"Oh, that's tough," Sophie says.

"If we don't at least try to adopt a child, it means we'll never have the opportunity to be parents if we stay together." I lean back and run a hand through my hair. "What a decision to make. My wife. Or a child. And I'm forty-one. I'm not getting any younger."

Sophie reaches across the table and places a hand on my arm. "I'm so sorry. That's awful. But maybe she'll come around. Like you said, you've been through a really difficult patch. She might change her mind."

Her hand stays on my arm for a few moments and I make sure to maintain eye contact. Eventually she takes it away and clears her throat.

"Honestly, we could do with a distraction right now," I say. "What are you and Lewis doing tomorrow night? Do you fancy a double date? We could grab some food and go for cocktails."

She mulls it over for a moment. Does she want to say no? Finally, she answers, "That would be fun. I'll double-check with Lewis, but I think he'd welcome a night out. Things have been a bit—"

Before she can finish that sentence, an alarm blares out through the café. Sophie's body jolts in shock. I glance over at the tills to see if it's something routine, but the staff begin to shepherd everyone out. There's a sense of urgency. Sophie stands, and I notice smoke seeping out from under the toilet door.

"Blimey," Sophie says. "I wonder what's going on."

"Nothing to worry about," a barista calls. "Just a small fire in the bathroom and it's already been put out by staff." The young girl rolls her eyes. "Smokers."

As we head out onto the street Sophie turns to me. "I need to make a move anyway. Tomorrow night, then? For the double date?"

"Shall we call round at yours about seven?"

"Sounds great." She half turns, but then pulls me into a hug instead. "Everything is going to be all right. I know it will."

When she pulls away, I let my arms drop to my sides. I can still smell the scent of her shampoo as she walks away. Strawberry. My thoughts are dirty. They're full of selfish acts. All the things I want to do to her. But she's not someone who can be rushed. This is going to take time, and unfortunately, I'm going to need Effie's help whether she likes it or not. Whatever mood she's been in needs to change. We need to work together.

My phone chimes and I grab it from my pocket.

You can't escape me. I know what you did and if you don't respond I'm going to make sure your wife knows everything too.

I start moving, the bag of vinyl weighing down my arm. Whoever this is, they're starting to make me angry now. It's a short walk to the car and once inside I stare at my phone again, debating how to respond.

Don't fuck with me. You'll regret it, I fire off.

A reply comes back quickly. *I could say the same thing to you.*

And then two pictures come through. I wasn't expecting that. I'm screwed.

CHAPTER EIGHTEEN

EFFIE

I'm relieved to see Ben is finally off the sofa. He's been watching the camera feed for days now, sometimes forcing me to watch it with him. I don't want to see their depressing sex or listen to them deciding whether to watch *Gogglebox* or *Game of Thrones*.

This morning, rather than plonk himself in the same spot, he grabs his car keys and leaves without telling me where he's going. *Off to the casino again to lose my money, darling?* I watch him drive out of Ivy Oaks and open the tracking app. But he doesn't head towards the casino this time. It seems he has something other than gambling on his mind, and I intend to find out what it is.

I book an Uber, then I tie my hair back and pull on a brunette wig, just as Ben taught me. I don a pair of sunglasses that aren't my usual style and throw on a pair of dungarees and trainers. Ben never sees me in anything other than tight dresses, designer jeans and high heels. From a distance, I'm sure I could fool him but close up he'd know. But I'm not intending to get close.

The Uber drops me off at a car park in the centre of

Oxford and I spot his blue Mercedes immediately. But after that, it takes a while to figure out where he is. I try some of the nearby shops and cafés but he's nowhere to be seen. Finally, I see him, and Sophie walk out of a record shop. Sophie. Of course. It's always about her.

They head to a coffee shop, which makes me smile. I know how much Ben hates cafés, particularly cheap-looking ones, and that he'll have to suffer through it to get closer to his target. I sit on one of the outside tables for a few minutes, nursing an espresso and watching them chat. Sophie places a hand on his arm. I wonder what they're discussing. Me, probably. I'm always to blame for whatever shit Ben complains about to his marks. It's an easy way for him to gain sympathy with these women. God knows they love an inattentive wife to turn into a villain.

I've had enough. I have a powerful urge to rain on his parade. I head into the toilet and light a cigarette. For good measure, I set alight some of the tissue in the bin and add the cigarette to the small blaze. Then I hurry out, leaving the flames behind me. I walk right past their table, out the front door and hurry around the side of a chip shop. There I shed the dungarees and wig, emerging in a pair of black yoga pants and a tight black top. I pretend to be jogging for a few minutes —just in case—before booking an Uber home, smiling to myself.

It's a small victory, but interrupting his seduction brings me joy.

Later that evening, I attend my first Ivy Oaks book club. It's at Deepika's house and I'm not in the slightest bit surprised to see that it's spotless. We are all gathered in her lounge on pristine cream sofas, shoes off of course. On the far wall hangs a large canvas print of her family. I stare at it for a moment, taking in what this portrait represents. I see it as Deepika's heart and soul, the part of her that matters the most. And, yes, I'm sure she loves everyone in that portrait very much, but it isn't just about love, is it? It's about the people in this picture living up to her standards. This large picture tells me that everyone inside the portrait needs to step up and match her expectations. Kally has her hair long, plaited to the side, a blue sari pretty against her olive-rust skin. Danny sits up straight, hands on his lap, hair parted neatly to the side. Aaron smiles adoringly at Deepika, who is in a matching blue sari, her perfect teeth visible between glossy lips.

I can't help but wonder how much control Deepika has over everyone and everything in this house. And right on cue, she comes out from the kitchen carrying a large tray of snacks. Warm samosas, a bowl piled high with posh crisps, carrot batons, dips, sliced fruit and olives. My mouth waters. I skipped lunch to mess with Ben earlier and now I'm eyeballing the food. David, sitting across the room, sees me and grins. I flip him a finger.

On my lap is a pristine copy of *Anna Karenina*. I read the first fifty pages and then watched the movie. I fell asleep during the movie and then read the Wikipedia page.

"Evening, everyone," Deepika says, pressing her hands together. She wears a creaseless plaid shirt and tight blue jeans. "Snacks are out, help yourselves! Oh, I've forgotten the wine." She trots out of the room on tiptoes.

My ears prick up at the sound of wine. I think I must have cocked my head towards our host, because David lets out a laugh. It's more of a bark. I roll my eyes at him and grab a samosa.

"Is it spicy?" Sophie asks, leaning forward.

I smile. "Not at all. It's very mild."

My mouth burns as I finish the delicious samosa.

Sophie latched onto me as soon as I walked into Deepika's house. Whatever Ben said to her at the café has made her clingy. He must have fed her some sort of sob story that's made her feel sorry for me. But Ben wasn't in a talking mood when he returned from his little outing. I think he was sulking about it getting cut short.

I watch Sophie spit out half of her samosa into a napkin and hide it in her handbag. Keeping the smile off my face is a challenge.

"What did you think of the book?" she asks.

"It was interesting," I reply. "Anna definitely got herself in trouble a few times there."

She laughs.

Deepika returns with what proves to be an excellent bottle of white. Beryl complains about the snacks. She doesn't like any of the choices. Sam, who I haven't properly spoken to yet, tuts at Beryl for being picky.

"I'm gluten free!" Beryl explains.

That makes me smile, remembering the pizza incident.

"Then eat the carrots," Sam retorts. "We're late as it is. I have to give my dog his medicine in two hours. Alex won't do it."

"Why not?" Beryl asks.

"He doesn't like touching the dog's... you know."

"Arsehole?" David suggests.

I bite into a carrot to hide my laughter as Beryl's eyebrows shoot up.

They discuss the medicine for five more minutes, which holds us up even longer. Deepika brings out more dips for Beryl. David and I exchange smiles as we eat almost all the samosas. Then, finally, we're ready to begin.

"Well, it's a classic, obviously," Sam says. "I like the strong themes about jealousy and love and—"

Beryl lets out a *pfft* noise.

"Sorry," Sam says. "Beryl clearly has something to talk about."

I dip a carrot stick into taramasalata.

"It's not a classic. It's about annoying, unlikeable people doing what they want at the expense of other people," Beryl says.

"I'm sorry but you don't get to pick and choose what is a classic," Sam replies. "This is *obviously* a classic piece of literature."

As the debate goes on, I find myself watching David. He's watching me. What is it about us that seems to fit? Whenever I'm with him, my body unfurls. Muscles relax that I didn't realise were coiled. He's handsome but nowhere near the same league as Ben. He seems bright and can hold a conversation, but he isn't brilliant like Ben. He's unlike Ben in lots of ways. He's kind. And for that reason, it could never work between us. He'd never accept my past, or my present.

"What do you think, Effie?"

I lift my eyes to Deepika, who's nodding enthusiastically.

"Well, I think this debate is more interesting than the movie. Honestly, I fell asleep. Did anyone actually finish this book?" I ask.

Sam appears offended. "Of course."

"Actually, I didn't." David shrugs.

"Me either," Sophie says.

"I gave up on chapter five," Deepika admits.

Sam throws his hands up in the air. Then he sighs. "Top up please, Deeps. I guess we may as well get drunk if no one finished it."

When our glasses are full, a few conversations break off

amongst the group. I'd rather be talking to David, but instead I find myself chatting to Sophie.

"I'm looking forward to our double date tomorrow night," she says.

"Same," I reply. Ben did remember to tell me about it so I'm not completely blind-sided. But I note that she doesn't mention her meeting with Ben in the town centre.

"I think it'll be just what Lewis and I need," she says. "Things have been tense recently."

I think about what I've seen through Ben's hidden camera feed and cringe, internally pitying her circumstances. Regardless of my feelings towards Sophie, she doesn't deserve what Ben is doing to her. This thought lingers and suddenly I realise something. When did I start sympathising with the marks?

"Well, I'm sure we'll have a lovely time tomorrow night. Maybe you two can begin to fix things. You make a lovely couple," I say.

"I hope so," she says. Her attention drifts over to the rest of the book club. "It's nice you're here. You really shake things up, you know? If you hadn't been honest, we all would've been sitting here talking in circles about a book no one finished."

"I think Sam finished it," I say.

She laughs. "See, that's exactly what I mean."

I watch Deepika leave the room and something comes over me. A desire to upend the status quo again. It's like a compulsion. A strange addiction.

"Deepika is such a good mother," I say.

Sophie nods, sipping her wine.

"I know some people would see it as a bad thing, but I think the fact that she bribes the school to give her kids better grades just proves how much she loves them."

Sophie gives me a sharp look. "Seriously? Wow, I knew she was competitive, but I had no idea she did that."

"Yep. She let it slip at the barbecue." I rotate my hand, mimicking lifting a glass of wine. "She had a bit too much to drink." Deepika walks back in, and I lower my voice. "Probably shouldn't say anything to anyone though."

"I won't," she says.

She will, I think.

THE UNUSUAL HISTORY BEHIND IVY OAKS

THE UNUSUAL HISTORY BLOG

Founded in 1926 by Reginald Jones, Ivy Oaks was designed as a living space for creatives. Painters, writers and actors were invited to this place of tranquillity. Jones even designed a wellness centre for the artists, a place to exercise the body as well as the mind.

The health spa, or the leisure centre that it is today, contained a sauna room, a massage room and, controversially, an enema room. Jones was certainly experimental with his ideas about what got the creative juices flowing. Ivy Oaks cultivated a wonderful reputation for nurturing good health and creativity and many artists flocked to the community.

After the war, due to a lack of space at Redfearn Psychiatric Hospital a few miles away, Ivy Oaks became a refuge for many patients. It was a disaster. Security couldn't cope with the sudden influx of complicated care. Many patients ran from the neighbourhood and never returned. The doctors and nurses adopted an authoritarian attitude and it became a place avoided by the local residents. And yet still patients were kept in Ivy Oaks up until the late eighties, when the terrible accommodations and horrendous treatment of vulnerable people was uncovered by investigative journalism. It was a national disgrace. Ivy Oaks then fell into disrepair after the hospital was closed down.

It reopened in the early 2000s completely renovated and revamped. Leaving the past behind, Ivy Oaks has successfully transformed into one of the most sought-after gated communities. With properties on the market for seven figures, Ivy Oaks attracts the rich and famous.

But there are rumblings of the old tempestuous spirit returning to Ivy Oaks. According to sources from within Ivy Oaks itself, there are petty feuds and bitter rows over hedge sizes and noisy pets. Indeed, there is a slew of unusual activities in this tiny cul-de-sac community.

In 2015, two pets went missing, a cat and a dog. It's thought the cat was mauled by a fox, the other was never found. That same year a couple moved into number seven and moved out six months later because they had a dispute with a neighbour about a tree. The angry neighbour played Black Sabbath loudly at 3am for a week.

In 2016 a toddler wandered away from Ivy Oaks but was found safe and sound outside the perimeter around three hours later. The little girl said a lady wanted to show her a puppy but then left her where she was. The family soon moved away.

In 2017 a man living in Ivy Oaks reported his car stolen. It was found ten miles away, burnt out. That isn't so strange on its own, but the man received threatening letters too. This started not long after he painted his front door yellow, something that was not approved of in the residential meeting. He soon moved away from Ivy Oaks.

In 2018 another pet died in suspicious circumstances. This time a noisy dog that couldn't be trained. The dog bit the daughter of a resident in Ivy Oaks and died not long afterwards. The owner of the dog blamed the mother of the child and there were extremely heated meetings at Ivy Oaks until eventually the dog owners decided to move away. They never found evidence of foul play. It was determined that the dog ate rat poison laid down by a professional a few days before the incident.

In 2019 another resident moved due to the hostility of their neighbours. Ivy Oaks' neighbourhood meetings are notoriously tense and difficult, especially when residents want to make changes. One family wanted to extend their house, but the other residents felt it would ruin the look of the street. The family then received death threats on their social media accounts from an anonymous source, and more threats were painted across their garage door. I spoke to this family, and they said it wore them down until they couldn't take it anymore. Even though they wanted to stay and fight, they didn't want to live there any longer.

In 2020, during lockdown, residents were reported by their neighbours for breaching lockdown rules. These included mild breaches, such as a resident taking an extra walk around the block. It was also reported that one neighbour saw another unload their car with an excessive amount of toilet paper for their own private use. The residential meetings took place via Zoom for most of the year, and there were many times when angry attendees would leave after vitriolic arguments. It sounds as though suspicions ran high during the lockdown period. None of the neighbours helped each other. Everyone was out for themselves.

There has never been any reason given for the strange kind of animosity that has spread through this gated community. A variety of families have moved in and swiftly moved away, without there being any unifying feature to explain why they may have been targeted by the strange goings-on.

Perhaps this is a case of snobbery—some neighbours don't "fit in" with the general ethos of Ivy Oaks. Or perhaps there's a sense of entitlement among the residents. Once someone gets away with one cruel act, they might be inclined to keep going.

It's hard to know whether there's one particularly mean resident at the heart of all these issues, or whether it's a group effort. But it's safe to say that this gated community is nowhere near as idyllic as it appears from the outside.

CHAPTER NINETEEN

EFFIE

Ben took the liberty of laying out a dress on the bed and pairing it with some high heels. A blue dress with a high waist and a full skirt. Designer, but not my style. I bought it specifically for a mark who wanted a modest woman. I forget his name now, I only remember that he didn't find confident women attractive, preferring those insecure in their own skin.

This outfit is designed especially for this couple. It's what Ben thinks Lewis will find me attractive in, and it's also something he thinks will endear me to Sophie. The lengths my husband goes to in order to gussy up his wife for the neighbours. And of course, Ben will have chosen his own clothes in the same manner.

I put Ben's choice back in the wardrobe and pull out a tight red low-cut dress. Then I grab a pair of patent black stilettos. I zip it up, put make-up on and admire myself in the mirror. With my hair long and voluminous, and my lips red, I'm the hottest I've looked in a long time. I feel great as I walk down the stairs towards my husband.

"Get changed," Ben says.

He stands in the hallway, the keys in his hand. He's been waiting for me for about ten minutes.

"No," I say.

When he grabs my arm, I press my red talons hard into the fleshy part of his hand.

"If you make me wear what you picked out for me, I'll tell her I had an abortion."

He lets go.

"That would be a big leap," he says. "I can't see you pulling that off."

I shake my head and laugh. "Are you sure about that? I'll wait until I'm alone with her and then I'll tell her all about it. I'll tell her you threatened to leave me and I didn't think I could raise a baby alone. I'll make it clear that it was your lack of support that forced me to make that heartbreaking decision. How would broody little Sophie deal with that? Don't you think there'll always be that sliver of doubt that maybe I'm telling the truth? Try making her putty in your hands after that."

A whistling exhalation emits from his flared nostrils. "Fine. Wear that. The point was not to outshine Sophie. But you look like a Christmas turkey, so I guess the effect is the same." He picks some lint from his shirt sleeve. "I suppose you'll just have to seduce Lewis another night because no one will want you in that."

I smile. His insults don't bother me. I know I look good. It's just his lame attempt at forcing me to back down.

It's just before seven and the evening air cools. There's a waft of jasmine floating down from Beryl's house. When I take my first step out of the house, my shoe lands on something soft. I exclaim, retracting my foot. What the hell?

Balancing on one leg, I lean forward to examine the foreign object. And then my stomach lurches.

"Ben," I say. "There's a dead dog on our front doorstep."

Backing away, I retreat into the house and place a hand to my mouth. There's something about hurt animals that I can't stand. Messing with humans is one thing, but it takes a true sadist to hurt an innocent creature.

"Should we cover it with a blanket maybe?" I suggest. "Or at least get it off our front step. The poor thing."

Ben steps around me and bends down. "Huh. That's weird."

We say nothing but exchange a look that speaks a thousand words.

"Who would do this, Ben? Who knows we're here?" He doesn't answer and I feel a stab of panic in my gut. "What if it's someone from the Beaumont?"

He looks away, his face dark. I wish I could see inside his mind right now because I know he's holding back. I think about those suspicious phone calls. Whatever else he's keeping from me, aside from the money, it could put me in danger.

"How the hell would I know?" he says. "Whoever it is is a twisted fuck."

I look at the sad creature lying there. "Maybe it was sick and crawled up here to find a peaceful spot to pass away?"

He laughs at the suggestion.

"Oh," I say, remembering what Sam said at the book club. "There is a sick dog on the street. Sam and Alex's dog."

He sighs. "Fine, well it's something to check out, I guess. We'll have to go over there. Maybe you should go and wait at Sophie and Lewis's while I tell them."

It seems surprisingly thoughtful for Ben. But then he adds, "You're too distracting with your tits out like that."

I roll my eyes. Ben moves the poor thing and I walk over to Sophie's. Of course, when I tell her about the dog, Sophie overreacts, pouring me a cup of tea and acting like we couldn't possibly go out now.

"I'm fine, honestly." I gesture to my outfit. "Plus, I got all dressed up. And so did you." Sophie is in a floral maxi dress with wedge heels and a cardigan.

She regards my dress. "You look... wow. I wish I had that confidence."

Of course, Ben was right about the dress I should have worn, I just didn't want to let him win again.

"Why don't we swap?" I say suddenly.

"Wh-what?" She glances behind her, as though worried Lewis would overhear, but he's washing the mugs from the tea.

I grab her hands. "Let's do it! Imagine the looks on their faces. Come on, it'll do Lewis good to see you in something new."

Her face lights up then. She bites her bottom lip. "Are you sure? I think you're a little smaller—"

"All the better," I reply. "You'll have more to show off."

We hurry upstairs, giggling like teenagers. I unzip her dress, purposefully allowing my skin to caress hers. Well, if Ben can seduce her, why can't I? And then I strip to my lacy underwear in front of her, parading around in my heels for a moment.

"Almost forgot," I say, bending down and slipping off the shoes.

She does the same, and then we swap. She's about half a shoe size smaller than me, which makes the wedges pinch slightly, but it's worth it to see her in my outfit.

"Hot," I say. "Like, scorching hot. *Incendiary*."

"You think?" She stands in front of the mirror, hands on her thighs. "Oh, I don't know, Effie. Can I really wear this?"

"Yes, you fucking can," I say. "And you fucking should."

Her eyes widen. "I've never..."

"Never looked this good?"

"I dunno," she says. "Maybe."

She really does look great. The red is slightly brash against her skin, but the dress hugs her body in all the right places. Lewis won't be able to keep his eyes off her. Ben neither. Maybe I'll be punished for this game later, but it'll be worth it.

When male voices swim up from downstairs, we decide to join them. I help Sophie negotiate the stairs in her six-inch heels. Silence falls when she walks into the room.

"Did you change?" Lewis says, stupidly, his jaw dropping open.

"We swapped," I say. "Sophie loved my dress so much I decided to lend it to her."

My eyes find Ben's, and I shine with triumph. His lips twitch, as though impressed, but I can tell by the way his chin angles down, flooding his eyes with shadow, that he isn't happy. I'm tampering with his plan and he hates that. Plus, I just reminded Lewis how sexy his wife is. Ben wants to drive a wedge, not push them together.

"Well, the dog was Sam and Alex's. Bailey. And he was definitely dead," Ben says, ruining the mood. "Sam cried and I helped Alex bury him."

"How awful." Sophie lifts a hand to her mouth.

"Sam left the back door open," Ben continues. "It looks like Bailey got out that way. The medicine they were giving him was for a urinary infection and they thought it was clearing up. They don't know why the poor thing died so suddenly. He didn't have any injuries though, so it must be natural causes."

I have a very uneasy feeling about this dead dog. It feels like too much of a coincidence that the poor thing died on the doorstep of the two venomous snakes living in Ivy Oaks. It must be a sign, surely. A warning perhaps. I look up at my husband. My partner. My co-conspirator. I know he's thinking the same thing. Someone did this on purpose.

CHAPTER TWENTY

BEN

Last night was a disaster. First the dead dog, then Effie dressing up Sophie. At least now I know for sure that Effie is messing with me. I'd had my suspicions, but she made it blatant when she swapped dresses with Sophie. All through dinner Lewis looked at his wife like she was the meal. I watched them fuck like wild animals when we got home that night.

Effie is disobeying me and I need to know why.

I also need to figure out why someone killed a dog and put it on our doorstep. Could it have been Effie? Sometimes she steps outside the lines and pursues her own form of revenge. If someone on the street, or even the dog itself, annoyed her, I wouldn't put it past her. Then again, why would she leave it on *our* doorstep? Effie is smarter than that.

Of course, there are other suspects. Standing in the kitchen window sipping coffee, I glance at my text messages. *I said tick tock...* An idle threat, or something real? Perhaps it's time to take action. The pictures they sent are not something I can ignore.

When I lift my head, I notice Sophie leaving her house. I

lift a hand and wave. She has an enormous grin on her face. No wonder, considering she got laid last night. Damn you, Effie.

Part of me wants to jog out there and find an excuse to talk to her, but I don't want to come across as desperate. Most women can smell a desperate man from a mile away. So, I just watch her leave.

There's movement upstairs and I hear Effie turn on the shower. I glance at my watch. It's just after eight. At least she isn't going to mope around the house all day again today.

I rinse out the mug and leave the house before Effie comes down. Once I'm in the car, I wonder: what is the endgame between me and Effie? Is there going to be a moment where our relationship naturally runs its course? I'm beginning to think so. The way things are headed, I may have to cut my losses soon.

I wave at Sophie one more time on my way out of the compound. I haven't decided about her yet. My instinct tells me that Sophie is someone to break, not make. Though if she showed even the slightest bit of potential, I could drop Effie and move on. Perhaps in time. Patience has never been one of my strong suits, but for the right woman I could make an exception.

There's just one snag. A huge one at that. Effie knows too much and cutting her loose would not be easy. She knows if she attacks me, I'll bite back harder, and that will keep her in check for a long time. As long as she remains clever enough to understand that. Perhaps it's worth reminding her every now and then.

But my marriage is a problem for another day. First, I need to deal with the idiot who insists on playing with a fire that's going to incinerate them. Today is going to be a long day. I fill up the car with petrol and glide onto the motorway heading towards London. Perhaps it would have been easier to get the train but I like to be in control. A few hours later, I reach my destination. I park in a space and cut the engine. As I exit the car, I walk towards the sign pointing me to the lobby of the Beaumont Hotel.

The place isn't particularly remarkable. It's an old hotel we stayed in for a while before coming to Ivy Oaks. While it wasn't a community like Ivy Oaks, the idea was the same. We worked on the other guests and staff, conning and seducing until we got bored. Only it ended abruptly. Frankly, it became a mess, and one that Effie can never discover the truth about.

Only one other person knows what happened. Anna. A maid. A sweet girl, just twenty years old, who believed we were in love. I worked my usual routine, took her out to dinner a few times, made her feel special, and she let me into guest rooms when I asked her. She thought I'd run away with her but eventually I told her I wanted to stay with my wife. In the end, I don't think she wanted to be with me anyway, I believe what she witnessed killed all of that.

If the threats are coming from her, then she's shown me teeth I didn't think she had. She kept something she wasn't supposed to keep. How else would she have those pictures? But she participated in what we did. She's complicit too. These messages are fighting fire with fire and she's going to get burned.

I hurry into the hotel and book a room, not sure how long I'll need to wait before I can see Anna. I don't know for sure that she still even works here but this is my best lead. She may well have left, after all she did break the law for me, several times.

On my way up to the room, I keep my eyes peeled for her. Yes, it's definitely risky being back in this place. But I'm willing to risk it to stop this harassment once and for all. Effie can never know what happened. She has her version of events and I need to keep it that way. I need to keep control.

If I go searching for Anna, the security cameras in the hotel will have footage of me walking up and down every hallway, so I decide to take a different tack. I spot a maid cart outside a bedroom and gently knock on the open door. A middle-aged, dark-haired woman pops her head out of the room.

"Hi there." I smile. "I'm Anna's uncle. Is she working today?" I ask.

"Fifth floor," the woman says, pointing up.

I thank her and head to the lifts, smashing the button. Easy. A sense of urgency washes over me, followed by indignation. Who does she think she is, trying to blackmail me? She has no idea what she's getting herself into.

The lift moves agonisingly slowly. I'm itching. I scratch my palms, the anger rising up. But I have to suppress it, there are too many people here. If I lose it now, I could lose everything.

The doors open and I sense myself exiting like a bull out of a cage. I flex my hands, forcing myself to calm down. There's a maid cart halfway along the hall. I stride purposefully towards it. Air whistles through my nose. And yet, by the time I reach the cart, I'm all smiles. The door is ajar and I push it open.

"You called, Anna-banana?" I say, leaning in the threshold.

She turns and gasps, staring at me in the same manner a deer would look at a car that's rushing towards it, about to pound it into tarmac.

CHAPTER TWENTY-ONE

EFFIE

The bastard snuck out while I was in the shower. He had a half-hour start on me before I could get dressed. By then I had decided not to bother following him. Instead, I watch the car on my phone via the tracker as it travels down to London. Whatever he's up to, he's in a hurry to get there. I make a coffee and wait. Finally, the car stops on a familiar street. I frown, zooming in. *The Beaumont Hotel.* What the hell is he doing there?

Pacing the lounge, I try to think what could have drawn him back to the scene of the crime. Even though I don't want to remember, blurry flashes filter through my mind. I push them away. Then I walk into the kitchen and pour a big glass of red wine. Anything to block those thoughts.

My fingers curl around the kitchen counter. The image of my bloody hands in the bathroom sink, red swirling down the plug hole. The body at the bottom of the stairs. I take half a glass of wine in one gulp. Ben manipulated the young maid he'd seduced into scrubbing the CCTV footage. That was definite, wasn't it? Why has he gone back there? No evidence can exist. There's nothing to show what I did, what I got away with.

A choking sob bubbles up in my throat. What happened that night at the Beaumont is the reason why I can never leave Ben. He'll tell everyone what I did, and I'll end up in prison. I slam the wine down on the counter and it sloshes over the side. *Stop thinking about it, Effie.*

Ben told me the same thing. He said to put it out of my mind and move on. Because what was the point in torturing myself. Ben fixed it for me as he promised he always would. He'd looked out for me. Maybe him stealing my money is payment. Maybe I should be thanking him instead of getting revenge. Maybe it's what I deserve after that night.

Restless, I grab my keys, shove my feet into a pair of sandals and get out of the house. I cross the street, knock on David's door and wait. A moment later, he answers. He's shirtless and shoeless. There are a few flecks of paint on his torso and jeans.

"Effie—"

I stride in. He shuts the door. I place both hands on his face and lean towards him until our noses almost touch. Then I wait. I need to know he wants this too. His eyes burn with intensity, scorching through me. Every part of my skin feels like it's on fire. My heart pounds so hard I can hear it. He doesn't look away and neither do I, and that's how I know he wants me.

When our lips meet, it's simultaneous. Our bodies close the gap between us. His hands are in my hair, then down to my waist. His skin is hot under my touch, and soft. He spins me, pushes me against the wall, fingers working at the straps on my dress.

This is very much against the rules. David isn't a mark. This is personal. But I can't trust a word Ben says to me anymore. I wrap my legs around David. I want him. I will have him.

The bed is comfortable, with cool, clean sheets under my skin. David naps, his breathing a soft snore that makes me smile. I can't sleep. Instead, I check the location of Ben's car, just to make sure he hasn't left London. Nope. It's still parked at the Beaumont. I wonder if he's going to stay the night. What's he doing?

Ben sometimes leaves for days, and I have to cover for him by telling people he's on a stag do or a golf weekend. When he returns, and someone asks him how his weekend with the "lads" went, he never skips a beat. The man is a master at staying vague and thinking on his feet.

I turn my attention to David, flat on his stomach, every muscle relaxed, and can't help but wonder how many times he lied to his wife when they were married. I know he was unfaithful but he still seems like a good man. And then I wonder how you can really tell. What is the moment you know someone is a good person? Are my parents good people? They fed me, clothed me, provided shelter for me. But they let the nanny do most of the work.

David stirs, breaking my thoughts. He stretches out his legs and rolls onto his side to face me. I run my fingers through his chestnut-brown hair, admiring those green eyes.

"Did you have good dreams?" I ask.

"The best," he says, tucking a lock of hair behind my ear. "What are you thinking about? You seem sad."

"Oh, nothing much."

"Liar." He gently strokes my cheek. "What we just did... I've wanted to do that since you moved here."

I smile but the words give me pause. Then I decide to be honest. I ask him, "Why? We hardly know each other."

"You seem so free," he says. "I guess I'm drawn to that."

I scoff. "I am anything but free. Trust me."

"Is that because of him?" He props himself up on one elbow. "Is he controlling?"

This is the point where I could paint my narrative. I could transform into the battered woman. Honestly, would it even be lying? There have certainly been... moments... between us. But I've always given as good as I got. What I can't justify are the many, many innocent victims who have been hurt by us. I participated in that willingly. I can never undo or explain it away.

I sigh. "No. But he isn't good for me. And yet I never manage to leave him."

Despite David's attempts to keep his face neutral, his eyebrows twitch and his mouth turns down. I place a hand on his cheek.

"Sorry," I say.

"Then I'm your bit on the side." He laughs. "That's a first. It's usually me doing the cheating."

"Is that okay with you?"

"Honestly," he says, "I don't know." He pauses, his eyes focused on the bed linen. "I do not like your husband. He seems like a grade A arsehole, and I don't understand why you're with him."

That makes me laugh. "He *is* an arsehole. But I'm no better."

David doesn't share the joke and looks at me with serious eyes. "You are."

I move away from his touch then. "No. Don't put something on me that isn't real. Don't make me into a better person than I am, because then this won't be real." I flick my finger back and forth between us to demonstrate what "this" is.

"Why do you keep saying things like that?"

"Because I spread a rumour that Deepika buys her kids' grades at school. I ordered a pizza to Beryl's house just to fuck with her. And I've done worse things I can't tell you about because they involve breaking the law. I... We..." I trail off. I was about to blurt out that Ben and I seduce couples to break them apart. What's wrong with me? I take a deep breath.

"Why do you do all that?" he asks.

"Because I'm bored! I'm always bored."

"Then get a job, Effie May." He starts to laugh. "Why do you live in this weird, effed-up world with your weird effed-up husband?"

"Because—"

"Do not tell me you're just like him because you are not. In any way. He's a..." He turns away.

"What?" I ask.

"Honestly, I think he's a sociopath. He gives me the creeps. I watched him at the barbecue. I saw his superficial charm and how he turns it on to people he wants something from. And then..."

"What?" I ask again.

"When you went into the house and Ben followed you. He came out and we talked for a moment. I was on my way home. He made this... ugly comment... about how you two had been having sex in the house because you just couldn't help yourselves. It was like a dog pissing all over his territory. He just *has* to be the alpha, doesn't he?"

"He said we had sex?" I don't know why I'm surprised. "We didn't." I shake my head.

David just nods.

"I should go." I step out from under the covers and search for my underwear.

"Wait," he says. "Sorry. I think I've upset you."

I hold up a palm. "You really haven't. I just need to go." I pull on my bra and pants, then grab my dress from the bottom of the bed.

David gets out of the bed and pulls on a dressing gown. "Please don't. Let me make you lunch."

"I can't," I say. I pause. I don't want to leave it like that. I want to say something poignant. Something that will make all of this right. But I can't think of a single word.

CHAPTER TWENTY-TWO

BEN

I watch as the thoughts race through the maid's head. She's considering what to do now that she's been cornered. Her furtive eyes glance at the doorway around me. She knows she can't get out. Then she looks at my face in an attempt to read my expression. Finally, she smiles. She walks over and flings her arms around my neck.

"Ben," she says. "I can't believe it. How are you?"

It takes every last ounce of willpower to stop myself putting my hands around her throat and squeezing tight. Instead, I grab hold of her arms and gently remove them from my neck.

"Don't play dumb, Anna, you know exactly why I'm here."

"Because you missed me?" Her voice is high, hopeful.

She's smiling. And I wish I could see that she's shaken and pale, but with so much make-up on her face, I can't.

"What is this game?" I say, taking a step back. "You've been messaging me. Threatening to tell Effie."

The smile fades from her face. "How is Effie? Is she okay?"

I narrow my eyes, searching for the lie. Why does she sound so genuine?

"She's fine."

"And you?" she asks.

"Also fine."

"I think I know why you're here," she says. She sinks into the folded sheets at the end of the bed, placing her hands on her lap. She looks tiny there, like she's barely a teenager. But I know better. She's twenty. Plenty capable of manipulation.

"Why am I here?" I prompt.

"You feel guilty about what happened. To Effie," she says. "But it wasn't your fault."

I don't say a word.

Her expression alters then. "Wait, did you say someone was threatening you?"

"Yes."

She stands. "And you think it's me?" She swats me playfully with a duster. "Come *on*, Ben. I think you know me better than that."

She walks towards me, her eyes on mine. The duster lands on the carpet at my feet. She invades my personal space and I want to push her away, but she smells like furniture polish and there's something oddly comforting about it.

"I would never do that to you, Ben." She lays her head on my chest and wraps her arms around me. "I've missed you. That day was crazy. I was worried about you. I swear I never told anyone. I even got the security cameras wiped. I did that for you."

"You're lying to me, Anna," I say. I grab my phone and scroll through the messages. "What does that look like to you?"

She glances at one of the pictures before tilting her face towards mine, showing me tears in her eyes. "That... It wasn't me, I swear. I promise I never kept anything from that night. I did everything you asked of me." Her eyebrows raise, pleading.

"Then how do you explain this photo? Because this is from the footage you promised me you deleted."

She grasps my hand. "I did! I swear. I... I don't know. Maybe Stephen found it somehow. Maybe he got to it before I deleted it."

"Stephen?" I ask.

"You know who I mean. My ex-boyfriend, the security guard you made me distract that night. Maybe he stole the footage. I... I don't know."

Something shifts in her demeanour. It's me, my expression. I can feel the rage burning through me and Anna certainly senses it. She backs away.

"Please believe me," she whines. "I wouldn't have stayed here if I wanted to threaten you. Would I? I would've run away. I don't know who it is, but it isn't me. Remember how I promised you I'd deleted it? And... and the police found nothing, did they? Let me see the picture again."

I show her the phone.

"Look, maybe I missed like a fraction of a second when I wiped what I needed to wipe. It might not have even been Stephen. What if someone else in the security office saw, like... I don't know, the briefest flash that the police didn't notice. It's so blurry you can barely tell it's—"

"Then how did someone in the security team know who to threaten?"

"I don't know," she says. "But I remember Stephen being jealous. He got a bit obsessed with you after we were together. He probably put two and two together."

"How does he know about Effie?" I ask.

She shakes her head. "I... I don't know."

"Where is he?" I demand.

"He got a new job up north," she says with a shrug. "I don't know where."

Heat rushes through me, prickly and uneasy. I grasp hold of her dust-blonde ponytail and pull.

"How is your mother?" I ask through gritted teeth.

"Wh-what?" she stammers.

I pull harder. Her head snaps back. Her hands are on mine, her eyes wide. I want to break her.

"Nice woman. What's her name again? Sandra, right? She lives in Dronfield."

"How do you know that?" she asks. Tears stream down her face. "Please, Ben. Please stop."

"I'm going to tell you what I want you to do. I want you to never threaten me again."

"I didn't!" she insists.

"I want you to continue working here. You're not going to flee, you're going to stay, be a good maid, and keep your eyes and ears open. I want to know where that security guard is, and I want to know where you are at all times."

"Fine," she says.

I feel myself leaning over her, drinking in the power of having her in my hands. I could wrap my hands around her slender neck and squeeze all the life out of her. But then I hear a voice inside my head, and I let go. Anna falls to the ground, crying.

The voice I heard is one I promised myself I'd never hear again and as soon as it's in my head, it's like the blood drains from my body. Shaking, I walk out of the room, following the twisting corridors back to the room I booked. Every part of my body thrums with adrenaline. But it isn't the good type. I've felt like this before. Maybe it's this place, I don't know.

Violence certainly came over me the last time I was here. I'm wired, and I hear *his* voice in my head again.

Why now?

My fingers fumble with the key card. I drop it twice before finally unlocking the door. He's back because I'm not in control anymore. Threatening messages. Dead dogs. Loose ends. This isn't me or how I operate. Droplets of sweat fall from my forehead onto the grey carpet as I stagger into the room.

I lock the door. The door needs to be locked. I check it twice. I'm safe now. I'm safe.

Here, boy.

When I touch my face, it's soaking wet. I blink, and my room transforms from the beige business suite to a wood-panelled study with a mahogany desk in the centre.

Come here when I tell you to.

But I won't go to him.

I fling open the wardrobe doors, move the coat hangers to the side, pull out the spare pillows and climb in. I slam the doors, shutting myself into darkness. My ragged breathing calms. The dark cloaks me. He won't find me here. I flex my hands and release. My father could never control himself, but I can control myself. I'm not like him. Quietly, in barely more than a whisper, I repeat to myself a mantra I have had since I was seven years old: *I'm not him. I'm not him. I'm not him.*

POLICE FIND "NO FOUL PLAY OCCURRED" IN THE DEATH OF ROBERT DINMAN

Four weeks ago, tech CEO Robert Dinman was found dead at the bottom of the stairs at the Beaumont Hotel in London. After an inquest, Mr Dinman's death has officially been ruled as accidental.

Mr Dinman had taken a long absence from his work after being diagnosed with bipolar one disorder. On the thirtieth of April, Regina Low, a guest staying on the third floor of the hotel, found Mr Dinman's body at the bottom of the fire exit stairs at the back of the hotel.

The autopsy revealed significant levels of alcohol in his blood, along with trace amounts of cocaine. It is believed that the tech mogul suffered severe head trauma during the fall.

There were some questions regarding CCTV footage missing from the time. But it appears to have been caused by system errors rather than any interference. A spokesperson for the Beaumont Hotel has released a statement to assure customers that a thorough investigation into their security will be made. It has been reported that the security guard working the night of Robert Dinman's death has been fired.

Mr Dinman leaves behind a widow, Julia, and two young

children. Collectively, with the new CEO of Leolane Ltd, Andrew Farrier, a statement has been made.

"We are heartbroken by the tragic death of our beloved Robert, taken too soon from our lives. But we thank the investigators for their thorough appraisal of this awful event. Every effort will be made to ensure the hotel is held accountable for its lapse in security and safety.

"We thank everyone for their love and support and ask for privacy during this difficult time."

It is unclear at the time of this article whether the Dinman family plan to sue the hotel for negligence.

Robert Dinman leaves behind a legacy in the tech world. The app created by him and co-founder Andrew Farrier is currently the second most popular wellness app in the world.

CHAPTER TWENTY-THREE

EFFIE

Unlike Ben, I've suffered from guilt for the things I've done. But that doesn't make me different to him. We're both terrible people. David doesn't know that I've washed blood from my hands and that I've woken up screaming, my body rejecting any goodness attempting to flourish inside me.

When I get back to the house Ben is still out. I don't want to be alone. I don't want to be in a house where there's a secret basement with all the names of the Ivy Oaks residents on the wall. I don't want to feel the oppressive weight of this place. So instead, I grab my swimming costume and a towel and head over to the leisure centre.

The changing rooms are quiet. I strip off in silence, place my clothes in a bag and wrap a towel around my body. Then I go to the sauna, enclose myself in its wooden cocoon and sit down on the bench. Leaning back, I enjoy the stark humidity and scorching temperature as it heats my skin. I wonder if it can burn away a few unwanted layers and make me good enough for David.

"Effie, hi!"

The peaceful quiet is interrupted by Deepika. She closes the door behind her and sits down on the other side of the bench.

"Hey," I say. "Nice day to sweat it out, isn't it?" I throw water on the rocks.

"Absolutely." She stretches out her toes and leans back. "The kids are at school, and I just want to *chill*."

"Hard day?" I ask, and then internally berate myself. Why am I prompting her for more conversation when I know it's usually all about her kids?

She nods. "Apparently there's this rumour going around that I pay for my children's grades." Clearly offended by the notion, she shakes her head in disgust. "We only donate to the school so that Kally isn't left behind. We don't get them to change hers or Danny's grades."

"Who would do something like that?" I say, more on instinct than anything.

"Sophie, apparently. She told Beryl. And, well, Beryl probably told everyone else. I happened to catch Beryl at it and confronted her. She was flabbergasted when I told her it was all a lie." Deepika laughs slightly. "I just hope it doesn't get back to the school. We're already on thin ice after..."

I cock my head towards her. Deepika flicks her eyes away. She was about to spill something important. But what?

I angle my body towards her. "Did something happen?"

Deepika is sweating profusely. We both are, but it's coming off her in buckets. I can tell she has something she wants to get off her chest. I need to make myself seem like the innocuous absorber of secrets.

"Nothing," she says. "Just school politics, you know." She laughs. "Sorry, I realise you haven't had to deal with these schools. At least not yet."

"Ben and I always said if we had kids, we'd send them to a

comprehensive school and nothing private." I tip my head back and laugh. "It's such bullshit. We'll obviously pay for the best. When I was a child at boarding school, I never appreciated the effort my parents put in to making sure I had a comfortable time. All the hoops they had to jump through to maintain good relations with the school. And the money they paid." I raise my eyebrows. "I just resented them for sending me there and I acted out all the time. I probably caused Mama so many problems."

Deepika smiles slightly, and then her lips thin. I can tell she's considering sharing.

"Oh, God. I don't know if I know you well enough to tell you this. But... well..."

I scooch over and place a hand on hers, ignoring the sweat. "Just get it out, Deeps." I hope I haven't overstretched this moment by using the nickname I've heard others from the neighbourhood call her. But it seems to work because she turns to me with a determined look in her eye.

Her shoulders release and she lifts her eyebrows. "Well, the thing is, Kally has a bully. A sturdy hockey player with a bad attitude. They have this competitive thing going on between them. The hockey player, Rebecca, gets better grades on every single paper." Deepika lets out a snort. "And then she rubs Kally's nose in it. She makes Kally feel like crap. And it's not like kids today can get away from the taunts, is it? It carries on across social media. Poor Kally gets tagged in horrible posts and videos about her, calling her stupid and ugly and worse." I see the tension invading Deepika's body. Her spine straightens, her hands ball into fists. "So, I did something. Something bad." She casts her eyes down, unable to look at me. "I was at the school art fair with Kally, who'd created this amazing display project of the rainforest. There was me, Kally and this Rebecca girl, who was at the back of the art room adding the finishing touches to her Notre-Dame project." She sighs. "Kally left to carry her project into the assembly hall, and I was about to leave, too, when Rebecca went to the toilet. I made an excuse to Kally, turned back, and destroyed Rebecca's art project."

I gasp. "Wow."

"It's my most shameful moment. But if I'm completely honest, it's the most satisfying thing I've ever done in my life." She wipes sweat from her forehead. "I wanted to smash that thing to smithereens, but I didn't. I played it safe. I made it look like a can of paint fell off a shelf onto the project. And do you know what?"

I shake my head.

"That bully cried her eyes out. She cried so hard you could hear it all the way down the corridor. And then, when her parents went to see what was going on, you could hear her screaming at them. Thirteen years old and throwing a tantrum like that." Deepika shakes her head. "I know she's a teenage girl, but I enjoyed every moment. Which is awful, isn't it? I'm a terrible, terrible person. Please don't judge me."

"You're a lioness," I say. "You protected your child. Honestly, I thought it was going to be something way worse."

Deepika laughs then. "I do like you, Effie May. We should drink wine together sometime."

"I would like that," I say. Who knows what else she might confess once the alcohol is flowing? "Ben and I have moved around a lot, but I'd like to put roots down in Ivy Oaks. It's such a lovely community."

Deepika lets out a harsh laugh. "Really? This place is full of beautiful houses, but there is no harmony here at all. I mean, sure, there is the book club, which is mostly fine. I started it because we'd had so much tension in the community."

"I had no idea," I say.

She nods. "Families move in and move straight back out. It's weird, actually. I swear there's some bad karma in this place or something." She fans herself. "But it provides a decent amount of status, living here. You know? At least until its reputation takes a nosedive."

It's getting so hot that I can hardly concentrate. "I think I need to cool off. What about you."

She stands, stretching out her legs. "I need a dip in the pool. But this was nice." She makes her way over to the door and pushes it. The door stays closed. "Um, Effie. The door won't open."

"What?"

I budge Deepika aside and try the handle. It won't depress, as though it's stuck.

"How the hell?" I mutter. I pound my fists on the wood. "Is it locked or stuck?"

"I don't know," she says. "Sauna doors don't lock, do they?"

"No." I regard the small space. "Maybe it's just jammed. This place is pretty old, right?" I shove my shoulder against the wood but it doesn't budge.

"I'm claustrophobic," Deepika says, backing away. "I can't breathe."

"Okay, just sit down for a moment. Take a deep breath. I'm going to figure out how to turn the heat down."

I find the control panel on the wall and adjust the thermostat. "It's down to the lowest level now, Deeps, okay? We'll be out of here soon." I bang on the door again, shouting at the top of my lungs. When I turn back to Deepika, she has her head between her knees. I bang harder, my voice rasping. "Where the hell is everyone?" I hurry over to Deepika and rub her back, trying to say something reassuring.

My eyes sting from the sweat and hair hangs in fat tendrils down to my shoulders. Even my towel is more damp than dry now and sweat trickles down my legs. I'm trying not to let it show, but I feel faint, and I can tell by how Deepika is slumped forward that she could collapse at any moment. I can't think what to do to cool her down. I pull her hair away from her face and neck, fanning the skin around her hairline. I help her lie down on the bench so that if she does lose consciousness, she won't hurt herself.

Panic rises. Where are the staff members? It's only a small, privately run leisure centre but there are a few members of staff here to make sure everything runs smoothly.

I fan myself, my heart is beating too quickly, too hard. There's no air and I can't take a full breath. How long have we been in here? A lot longer than the recommended time. When I get to my feet, I'm so woozy my backside hits the bench behind me and I slump forward, drowsy.

There's a thumping in my head. A dramatic migraine burgeoning at my temples. I close my eyes and when I open them again there are so many black spots dancing before my eyes that the sauna doesn't even look like the same room.

Ben shouts my name. He points down at the man lying at the bottom of the stairs.

"You did this," he says. "We're going to have to clean up after you. Get back in the hotel room."

My body hurts all over. Why is there blood on my hands? Why does Ben have to carry me? Then I feel like I'm on the hotel bathroom floor. Someone is removing my clothes. Not Ben. A girl.

"Effie?" A hand slaps my face. "Effie, can you walk?"

I nod, but when I try to put weight on my feet, I can't get up.

"She needs help too," says a voice.

I'm seeing double and the edges of everything flutter and swirl like I'm having a bad trip. But there's a man in a blue uniform putting his arms underneath my body.

"Watch out for the blood. You don't want to get it on your clothes," I say. Did I say it? The man doesn't react like I've said it. He certainly doesn't adjust me or his clothes to keep away from me. Instead, he lifts me up and carries me out.

That night on the bathroom floor of the Beaumont, covered in blood, with the hands removing my clothes. There'd been blood between my legs that hadn't come from the body at the bottom of the stairs. No, it had come from inside me. It had been my baby. My lost baby.

A life for a life. I took a man's life away from him and the universe stole my child in return. That's karma. That's what happens when you're a terrible person and you don't deserve happiness. And that's exactly what happened to me.

CHAPTER TWENTY-FOUR

BEN

Once the panic subsides, I climb out of the wardrobe and jump in the shower to wash away the sweat. It's always best to shake these episodes off.

I'm good at many things, but there are times when there is so much rage inside me, I worry it will just explode out of me, creating a path of chaotic destruction in my wake. What would be the point in that? Anything that involves me serving prison time is not worth doing.

My father still gets in my head even after all these years. Now, there was a man who lost control. Only ever with his family and behind closed doors, but fury would burst out of him, unchecked. I don't have that luxury, I remind myself. Not if I want to continue to live in the manner I so much enjoy. Perhaps that's the reason for my gambling habit. It's part of my father pushing its way through. Well, screw him.

I should go. Staying the night would only serve to torture Effie, not benefit me. I've seen Anna. I've scared her shitless. And if she isn't the one threatening me, I now have her eyes and ears looking for the missing security guard. Now it's time to get out of here before I properly lose control. Last time I was at the Beaumont it didn't end well.

My phone rings and I grab it from my trouser pocket.

"Ben? It's Sophie."

I would normally smile, but there's an element of panic in her voice that stops me. "Is everything okay?"

"It's fine. Well, it's not quite fine but there's no need to worry. Effie is in hospital but she's just being checked over, really. There was an accident at the leisure centre. She and Deepika ended up being trapped in the sauna. They're both dehydrated and woozy but they're okay."

"God," I say. "How did that happen?"

"Well, the door appears to have been blocked. From the outside."

"What? Someone did this on purpose? Okay, well, I'm in London but I'll drive back now. Which hospital is she in?"

Sophie reels off the address and I scribble it down on the hotel pad. Then I make my way out of the room, ready to check out. This is a bizarre turn of events. Could it be someone at Ivy Oaks? I don't actually know what she's doing with the residents in Ivy Oaks. She hasn't filled me in, and I've been too preoccupied with Sophie to care. But then, I remember the dead dog on our doorstep. What if that wasn't about me at all? What if the dog, and now this sauna incident, are all about Effie? And her being a target makes me feel strangely protective. Coldly possessive. Someone is messing with my wife and as an extension, they're messing with me.

I begin my drive back to London, switching the radio to something that will provide background noise to my whirring thoughts. Techno hums at a low volume while I try to think.

If we're being targeted by separate enemies, I need to figure out who is going after Effie, and why. But the potential pool of enemies is exhaustingly large. How many people have we screwed over the years? Some would say too many, but I would argue against that notion. The world is eat or be eaten. And I like to eat.

Almost two hours later, I park the car at the hospital and take a moment to find the right emotion of concerned husband. I pull down the rear-view mirror and examine myself in it. There are dark circles beneath my eyes. Sweat patches darken my shirt beneath my armpits. Good. All of this says worried husband. It will impress Sophie, which is the most important part. At least until I figure out who did this.

I make my way into the building and when I see Sophie in the waiting area, I let out a sigh of relief.

"Where is she?" I ask.

"This way."

Sophie leads me into a room filled with beds and Effie acknowledges me with a nod. She seems utterly miserable. Also furious. Her arm is connected to a drip, the bag almost empty, and she stares out, her eyes glistening with rage.

"How are you feeling, darling?" I ask, pulling up a chair.

"Like someone tried to bake me alive," she snaps. She gestures to the drip. "They needed to get my fluids back up. But I just want to go home."

"I know, honey." I take her hand and move my thumb up and down along her knuckles. She stares down at my thumb and for a moment I think she's going to tear her hand away. Then her gaze flicks over to Sophie and she thinks better of it.

I don't know why she's acting cold with me, perhaps she's annoyed I left for the day without telling her. It doesn't matter, because this is working in my favour. Effie acting distant will give me something to complain about to Sophie. We can bond over our unloving partners.

"They had to check for kidney damage and internal burns," Effie says. "Apparently it could've been bad. We were only stuck for a few minutes. And we turned the heat down." She sighs. "It felt like hours."

"I'm so sorry," I say, stroking her hair. "How is Deepika doing?"

It's Sophie who answers. "She's in the next room and she's doing much the same. Aaron and the kids are with her."

I nod. "Effie, when can you come home?"

"I've got to stay overnight," she says miserably.

"Then I'll stay with you," I say.

She turns to me, her eyes like two sharp knives. "You don't have to do that."

"I want to," I reply.

Her voice softens. "I'm fine. You go home. They won't let you stay anyway. Visiting hours are almost over."

I can tell that the smile she gives me is forced and costs her a lot of effort. When I frown slightly, she turns away. What is going on with her? Ignoring her mood, I lean over and kiss her on the forehead.

"I'll be back first thing in the morning. Is there anything you need before I go?"

She shakes her head.

"I lent her some pyjamas," Sophie said.

"Oh, thanks so much, Sophie." I pat her on the shoulder.

Out of the corner of my eye, I think I see Effie roll her eyes. Is she jealous? That's not like her.

"See you tomorrow, sweetheart," I say. I lay on the sweetness just to annoy her. She nods her head and smiles.

In the corridor, I turn to Sophie. "She's shaken, isn't she?"

"Yeah," she replies. "I think it was quite traumatic. She

was banging on the door and no one answered for a while. Luckily, Beryl was walking by on the way to the swimming pool and found a member of staff to open it for them."

"What happened?"

"Someone shoved a doorstop under the door and wedged it shut."

"What? What kind of person would do something like that? Have they checked the cameras in the building? Surely it would show up."

"There aren't any cameras in the leisure centre," Sophie says. "It's a small privately owned building so there isn't much security. The only parts of Ivy Oaks with cameras are the security gates and around some parts of the perimeter. Oh, and I guess most residents have doorbell cameras."

I nod. It occurs to me then that Sophie's doorbell camera might have recorded footage of the dog being moved to our step. Perhaps that will give me a clue as to who is behind all this.

Further down the corridor, I see a familiar man leaving the men's toilets. David. What is he doing here visiting my wife? And was he hiding in the toilets while I visited Effie? Perhaps Effie told him to stay out of sight. That means there's something going on between them. But Effie wouldn't break the rules, would she? No lies. No ties. Not telling me about a mark makes me suspicious. It makes me think it's personal. My seduction of Sophie is all business. If hers is personal, that's an issue. But maybe it's something I can use.

"Could I get a lift from you?" Sophie asks, interrupting my thoughts. "I came with Effie in the ambulance."

"Of course you can," I say. "And I want to thank you for everything you've done today. Being there for her..."

She holds up a hand. "It was no trouble. I was on my way over to the centre to work out when I saw the ambulance arrive. I just did what anyone would do. It's scary being in hospital like that. I thought she might appreciate a friendly face there."

"You're a good person, Sophie," I say. "I'm sorry Effie might not have seemed very grateful. She is really. I just..." I hesitate for dramatic effect.

"What is it, Ben?" Sophie asks.

We're passing the hospital café and I gesture towards it. "Have you got time for a coffee? It's a long story."

"Sure," she says.

I order us two decaf lattes and a tired woman pours them out for us. Then we grab a rickety table to slump at.

"I'm so sorry you got pulled into this drama." I stir the coffee, looking up and meeting her gaze. She shakes her head and her pretty red hair shivers around her face. Even tired she's very beautiful. "I wasn't going to say this, but I'm concerned about Effie. Trying to get pregnant has been hard on her. The truth is..." I pause, letting out a long breath. "The truth is, she's not doing well with her mental health. I think the stress of the IVF is taking its toll. She's said a few odd things recently. Sometimes she even accuses me of crazy things. And now someone has done... this. Could it have been a prank?"

Sophie lifts her shoulders. "I just don't know. Who would consider something so dangerous a prank?"

I sip my coffee and paint my face with worry.

"I feel so bad for Effie," Sophie says. "But I see things aren't easy for you either. What does she accuse you of?"

"It's usually based on jealousy. The accusations can be quite wild. God, I just can't believe that happened to her at the health centre. It's going to mess with her head and make things even worse." I sigh. "I really do love her. She's funny and smart and free, and I guess all of those good things have a negative. This is the negative for her. There are times when she... when she can't find reality anymore."

Sophie sips her latte, her eyes wistful.

"And..." I hesitate, dropping my eyes to the table.

"What is it?" Sophie asks.

"I think she wants to leave me."

"What makes you say that?"

"A hunch, I guess. When you've known someone for so long, you see these things coming. This has been building for a while." I shrug. "She wants out. I just don't know if she has the wherewithal to do it right now." I sigh, running my fingers through my hair. "Honestly, I think I'm just going to let her go. It might be the kindest thing for me to do. I'm just concerned about her mental state right now."

"Wow," Sophie says. "I can understand you wanting to do this gently if she's feeling a little off-kilter. Have you tried suggesting a therapist?"

"I've tried," I say. "But she won't listen." I reach out and take Sophie's hand. "Thank you so much for all your warmth and kindness. You have no idea how much you've helped me. I thought I was losing my mind before we moved here. I didn't know what to do. And you've made me feel so... so heard. You know?"

A charming blush spreads across Sophie's cheeks. I expect her to let go of my hand but she doesn't. Her sweet blue eyes continue to gaze into mine as our hands touch. This is it, I think. This is the moment when she falls for me. I should have known that pity would be the trigger for an innocent soul like Sophie.

Finally, she clears her throat. "I should get back. Lewis will be wondering where I am."

"Right," I say, retracting my hand. "Sorry, I didn't mean to—"

"Oh, don't be silly, you didn't," she says.

As we stand, our eyes meet again and we both let out a quiet giggle. We recognise it then, the flirtation, the way it makes us feel young. Even in this setting. Even with our respective partners hanging over our heads. Even with all the complications. Even with everything going on, I found a way to get through to her. She's mine now. I can feel it.

CHAPTER TWENTY-FIVE

EFFIE

Someone tried to kill me. I let that sink in for a moment as I lie here under the miserable strip lights. As I close my eyes, the sensation of hot, humid air burns my lungs. I think about the arms that circled me, pulling me out from that room. The towel barely covering my sweaty body. The memories that flooded my mind just before it happened.

Bitterness creeps up from the sour pit of my stomach. Whoever wants me dead knows the terrible things I've done. Maybe I deserve this, but would I have done any of those terrible things if I hadn't met Ben? Ben did this to me. It might not have been directly, but I'm almost positive it's because of him. Whatever shit he's got himself into, the consequences are falling down on me. I'm the one paying the price.

Something has switched in my mind and I can't turn back. I always thought I knew him, but maybe I've been as blinkered as everyone else. What I thought was *ours* is really *his*. He is the one pulling all the strings. I'm just one of those strings. What if *he* arranged for that door to be wedged in the sauna? What if he's had someone following me? Watching me and waiting for the best moment to strike?

I think of the last place I know he visited—the Beaumont Hotel. Perhaps he went back there to tie up loose ends. And let's face it, I'm also a loose end. My skin grows hot and I begin to sweat. I don't know what to do now. Tracking his movements, sabotaging his plans isn't enough. He knows too much about me. He has too much dirt on me. I have to get him out of my life.

My body is weak, and I drift off for a moment. When I next open my eyes, David is there. He brushes the hair from my face with gentle fingers. His green eyes gaze down at me, crinkling slightly at the corners.

"How are you feeling?" he asks.

"Tired."

"I got what you asked me to get," he says.

"Thank you," I breathe.

He hands me an envelope and I grip it tightly. Ben has dirt on me, it's true, but I also have dirt on him. And I knew I needed to get it out of the house as soon as I found out I'd be in the hospital overnight.

With me out of the house, Ben can search my things. And this is my one piece of protection. It is the only thing I know of that would be bad for him if it got into the wrong hands. I've had it for years and he has no idea. Ben thought he lost it years ago during one of our moves. It sent him into a downward spiral for weeks. Drinking, yelling, disappearing for days on end. I could've ended that spiral by producing the thing he wanted, but I didn't. I knew even then it would be useful to me one day. And I'm glad I made that decision.

"Why did you want this?" he asks.

I shake my head. I can't answer him.

David looks at me and then away. "Are you going to tell me what's happening in your home? Are you..." He lowers his voice. "Are you a victim of domestic violence, Effie? I could get a doctor right now, and you can tell them. We'll get the police, find a shelter—"

"No," I say.

I stare up at the flickering hospital light, letting my eyes sting. Maybe he's right in a way, but I feel too complicit, too ashamed to ever seek out help.

"Effie, are you all right?" he asks. "What happened at the leisure centre today was disturbing. Someone blocked that door on purpose, and with you asking me to get something from your house... Well, I mean, it's concerning."

I reach out and take his hand. "Thank you for getting me this, but don't try to save me, David. It won't work."

He squeezes my hand. "That's not what I'm doing."

"Isn't it?" I say.

"No," he says, his voice shaky and uncertain.

"You are, David. You're trying to save me because you think I can't possibly be as bad as I say I am. Respect me enough to listen to what I'm saying. I will chew you up and spit you out. I'm not worth your time and energy. Thank you for this, but you should just leave."

He drops my hand and backs away, like I've stabbed him in the chest. His expression hardens, then softens. He lets out a whistling breath from his nose and strides out of the hospital room, leaving me alone.

My fingers ball the starchy sheets as I watch him leave. There's an ache, somewhere deep at the back of my rib cage, like I'm trapped in a corset. I lean back and breathe in, stemming the tears that take me by surprise. And then I shake my head. The man was getting too attached. I can't have that if I'm going to win this game with my husband. He's a good man, I shouldn't be pulling him into the darkness with me.

And yet, I already regret what I said to him.

Pushing those feelings away, I open the envelope, tip the

contents onto the hospital bed and check everything's there. There's a train ticket dated December 2002, travelling from Paddington to Pewsey, a letter, and a photograph. In the photograph, a man in a tweed jacket stands next to a woman in a blue dress. In front of them is a boy about ten years old. He is the spit of his father. Even as a child his jaw is square and his hair is parted neatly to one side, just like his father. The boy scowls. The woman has a smile on her face that seems so tentative it may disappear in the span of a heartbeat.

The family stands in front of a vintage sports car. The man is closest to it, one hand resting on the bonnet. I wonder what makes him happier, the car or the people next to him? Actually, I don't need to wonder. I know the answer.

If Ben knew I had this envelope and the contents inside, my life wouldn't be worth living.

CHAPTER TWENTY-SIX

BEN

Back at Ivy Oaks, I watch Sophie walk into her house, and then I enter my own. Of course, I head straight to the laptop and listen to her conversation with Lewis in their living room. I check the window, surveying the typical married scene. Lewis is on the sofa, flicking through the channels. She sits down next to him. And then she begins to tell him everything that happened at the hospital. I listen carefully.

"Effie was so strange with Ben. It's like she didn't want him there."

"Maybe they're having problems," Lewis suggests.

"I think they are. Actually, Ben alluded to it a bit."

I notice that she doesn't tell her husband about our intimate chats. Another good sign that I'm slowly seducing her.

"I'm not surprised," Lewis says. "Those two have incoming divorce written all over them. She's too good for him."

Interesting. He clearly has a crush on my wife. So far, I haven't been able to get Effie to act on it. Usually, she'd have the husband eating out of the palm of her hand by now, but she's been too preoccupied messing with me instead.

Sophie's voice pitches higher, as though she's in shock. "Really? I don't think that at all. Ben seems very nice."

I smile. There's warmth to her tone.

"I guess so," Lewis says. "That advice he gave us about money seems to be sound, although it's early days. I just... I don't know. I was talking to David and he has such a low opinion of Ben that it really made me think. I mean, I have noticed he's charming, like maybe *too* charming."

Stop talking, Lewis, I think. That's enough now. Stop talking your wife out of loving me.

"David's just a bitter bachelor," Sophie says.

Yes, thank you, Sophie. You always have my back.

"I think David has a thing for Effie," Lewis says. "What if they had an affair? That'd give Beryl something to gossip about."

There's a brief moment of silence.

"So, who do you think blocked the sauna door?" Lewis asks. "I once read about someone dying in a sauna. The hot air burned them from the inside out. It was awful."

"Honestly, it's disturbing," Sophie says. "At best it's a prank that went horribly wrong. I guess it had to be either a member of staff or a resident of Ivy Oaks."

"Like Sam's dog," Lewis mutters. I barely hear him.

"What about the dog?"

"Well, don't you think it was strange? The dog wasn't on death's door, it was being medicated but seemed fine. Then suddenly it's dead on the Mays' front doorstep. And then Effie May gets trapped inside a sauna. It's like someone's out to get her."

"But it wasn't *her* dog," Sophie says. "It was Sam and Alex's dog."

"I dunno," he says. "Maybe it's a warning like that horse's head in *The Godfather*."

"That's so creepy. I don't like it."

"Don't worry," Lewis says. "I'll protect you." He reaches out and places an arm across her shoulder.

I move away from the window and close my laptop.

They're echoing my suspicions about Effie. I need to investigate the possibility that Effie is keeping secrets from me. What if *she's* the one with a stalker?

I need to clear my thoughts and think this through. Otherwise, I'll never get to the bottom of it.

Well, first of all, there's Anna and her security guard ex. Anna was at the hotel when the sauna incident happened, so I know it wasn't her. But could she have coordinated something with her ex-boyfriend? She'd need him to be staying close. I try to picture him sneaking in through the gate then following Effie into the leisure centre. You don't need a pass, but the staff do memorise faces. He'd have needed to choose a moment when the reception was empty.

It's possible, but it's not an easy method of getting to me. What does seem more plausible to me is that Effie has her own enemy. But who? I need more information.

I head upstairs to the bedroom, sit down on the bed and look at Effie's side. She has her own armoire, a bedside table, and we share a closet. I start with the armoire.

Moving systematically, I remove each drawer, dump the contents and then fold her underwear back up and replace it. Each one needs to be emptied so that I can check for anything taped underneath. I also search for secret compartments built into the furniture. Aside from an ultrasound scan picture, there's nothing in the armoire that gives me pause. I toss the photo back in the drawer without really looking at it. I had no idea Effie kept it.

The bedside table is a long shot, but I search it in the same systematic manner. There's only one drawer with nothing inside except a pair of ear plugs and a phone charger. Then I try under the bed. Nothing. I go through her closet, checking the pockets of every item of clothing. Still nothing. What I need is her phone. All her secrets are on her phone.

I'm still determined to find *something*. I check the floorboards for secret compartments. I search inside photo frames and behind canvasses. My investigation extends to the whole house, checking through every single cabinet until sweat drips from my nose. Nothing. Oh, she's clever, my wife. Too clever. But there must be something. There's no way we've lived together this long without her having some sort of secret.

Whatever it is, I'm not going to find it. Not tonight.

The house is quiet. I'm completely alone. I'm noticing things I've never noticed before. Like the settling groans of the building, the buzz of the fridge, and the hiss of a radiator filling with hot water. And then I notice something very out of place. I see a boot print on the tiles in the corridor at the back of the house. A man's boot print. Not mine, someone else's.

Who has been in this house?

CHAPTER TWENTY-SEVEN

EFFIE

When the doctor tells me I can leave, I'd much rather book an Uber, but that wouldn't be keeping up appearances. I call Ben. He's here in an hour, his face drawn. I notice the bags under his eyes but I know any sleep deprivation he had was nothing to do with worry for me. I'm sure that's how it comes across to others, though.

We leave without talking to each other. He's in a sullen mood and so am I.

Finally, halfway home, he breaks his silence. "Whatever you were attempting by being a bitch in front of Sophie worked in my favour. I told her you're leaving me. She's putty in my hands. I'll be able to get her even faster now."

"Good for you," I say.

"Why are you being like this?" he asks. "What was with the dress the other night? And then acting cold at the hospital?"

"This is the first thing you say to me? You're not concerned about the fact someone tried to kill me?"

He sighs. "Yes, I'm concerned about that too. But there's

nothing I can do. Not until the police find some evidence. Unless you know who did it?"

I chew my bottom lip. He's holding something back, I can feel it. If only I knew why he went back to the Beaumont.

"Why would I know who did it?" I snap.

He shrugs. "Perhaps you've been playing your own games this whole time, Effie. Because I'm not sure you're fully invested in what's happening in Ivy Oaks."

"Forgive me for not brimming with excitement over your sweet-natured redhead and her dim-witted husband. Maybe I'm tired of this life, Ben. Maybe I'm still waiting for you to fulfil your promises."

He laughs. "What? Get a cottage somewhere and settle down? We're too young for that, Effie. We're too fucking smart and we live free."

"Look, forget the cottage." I sigh. "I'm not the one who plans these games, you are. You're the mastermind. So, is there something you're not telling me? Is there someone from your past who might know where we are?"

"There's always a risk of that," Ben says. "But I doubt it."

I shake my head. "Maybe we didn't move far enough away. Considering what happened last time."

"Don't put all of this on me," Ben says. "We both have dark pasts. You know as well as I do, it could be anyone. Literally anyone. How many people have we scammed over the years? Dozens? More? I can't even remember their faces. Maybe someone recognised us but we don't remember them."

"Jesus," I say. "Then we need to leave."

He shakes his head. "We can't. We've only been here a month. How would it look?"

"We could invent a family emergency. I could say my mother is ill, leave on my own. Then you join me in a few weeks. After a while we send for our stuff and we're gone."

I watch his fingers tighten around the steering wheel. He hates that I'm right. And he hates it even more when I have a good idea.

"No," he says. "We'll just be more careful."

There's nothing more to say. With a few words, he's revealed his true feelings. He doesn't care about me, he only cares about winning. When he reaches across the handbrake to stroke my arm, it's as fake as him. I play along.

"Don't worry, love," he says. "I always keep us safe. Don't I?"

"Yes," I say.

A pause, and then he says, "This could be because of the Beaumont, couldn't it? And that was... well, it was you, wasn't it? It was your fault." His words make me shiver.

"Yes," I say, staring out of the window. "But I thought you'd dealt with all of that. You got rid of the evidence, right?"

"I did my best, darling. I always do." He smiles.

I smile at him because that's what he expects of me. "Thank you." But I don't like the way he phrased that. He told me all the evidence had been wiped away, including the CCTV footage, but now I'm not so sure.

"I love you, Effie," he says. "You're my soulmate. I mean that."

"I love you too," I reply.

He takes my hand and kisses it.

We're so broken I can hardly stand it. We pull into Ivy Oaks with what feels like all the residents watching us from their windows. Ben has a spider web pulled over this entire neighbourhood. But perhaps he's underestimating the people here.

THE UNUSUAL HISTORY BEHIND IVY OAKS

THE UNUSUAL HISTORY BLOG

Comments:

OliviaC: This place is wild. I feel bad for the pets. They don't deserve that. Whoever keeps doing it is a really sick person.

HarrietH: Who would want to live there knowing the history? It's obvious that the place attracts bad energy. People were badly mistreated there and it polluted the aura around the place.

TonyB: I'm not sure about any aura... But it is interesting that a community like Ivy Oaks went from a place for artists and creatives to a badly managed psychiatric facility and then seemed to attract the worst kind of people. I'd put it down to the management, personally. Chances are whoever ran the facility into the ground and allowed all those people to be abused then sold it to equally awful people who sell the houses to... well you get it.

Brian: Have any of you guys heard of someone called Eric Lansdown or Ben May? There are whisperings that he moved to Ivy Oaks and isn't a good dude... PM me on the blog if you have.

OliviaC: Did you hear the latest rumour? Two women were trapped in a sauna. They're okay but it sounds like it might have been on purpose! Maybe this is linked to your Eric/Ben, Brian.

Brian: It's possible. He's definitely capable of some dark stuff. But just how dark is what I'm trying to get to the bottom of.

CHAPTER TWENTY-EIGHT

EFFIE

Ben keeps looking at his phone. He's sullen, his expression tightly sour, and he's constantly staring at the damn thing while we're at a residents' meeting. I wouldn't usually care, but this one is an emergency meeting about the sauna incident, which makes me somewhat invested. You know, seeing as I almost died. I glance over at Deepika, guilt crawling through my veins. She's silently crying as Aaron reads out our report of what happened. We've also told all this to the police, but an email went around the neighbourhood to discuss it further in this meeting. There's one stark absence: David. I hoped to see him here but I think he must be avoiding me after what I said. I knock the thought out of my head and pay attention.

Our summary of what happened is this. I went to the leisure centre about 13:30. Deepika arrived about 13:35. She came into the sauna approximately seven minutes after that and I was already there. We talked for ten minutes or so and then decided to leave. We couldn't open the door, we banged on it, shouted for help. We turned down the thermostat, which helped make sure we didn't end up with third-degree burns.

Apparently, Beryl arrived at the leisure centre at 14:05 and, after getting changed, walked past the sauna on the way to the pool ten minutes later. She went to fetch a member of staff and we were rescued.

"I don't see the point of this meeting," Deepika says, her voice still gravelly from the burns. "It's not like the person who did it will admit to it."

Sam, the current chair, nods his head. "I agree. But that's not why we're here. It's to talk about whether we need to ask the security team to install cameras in the leisure centre. Now, this was voted on in..." He pauses to look through a binder. "September 2018, and the answer was no. Obviously, we may feel differently about that now."

There are a few murmurs around the group.

"Also," Sam adds. "We need to ask whether the staff were negligent that day. Do they need to be fired? If it weren't for Beryl, who knows what would have happened."

"I don't know, Sam," Alex adds. "Maybe we should hold off on that until the police investigation is over."

"But if one of them did this as a prank, then they're dangerous," Lewis says. "We can't live here with dangerous people working in our neighbourhood."

"Yeah, but if it was a resident, then we'll have to continue living with them until they're arrested," Alex replies. "We can't kick everyone out of their homes just in case. So, we can't fire people *just in case*."

"I don't think that's the same," Lewis says.

"Well, I do," Alex retorts.

"Guys." Sam lifts his hands to placate them. "Let's not go round in circles. Maybe we should vote. Those who think the leisure centre staff should be fired, raise their hands."

Sam, Ben, Lewis and Beryl raise their hands. I look at Ben in surprise. No doubt he cast his vote to cause trouble.

"Not passed," Sam says. "Moving on."

"We need to talk about Bailey," Alex says. "As you all know, our beloved dog, Bailey, died suddenly a few days ago." He pauses as though expecting a reaction from the group. "Now, he was poorly at the time, but it wasn't serious. And because of the history of pet deaths in this neighbourhood, we need to have a discussion about it."

"What are you saying, Alex?" Deepika asks, sharply. "Are you bringing up things that should stay in the past? Again?"

"Someone killed our dog." Alex leans forward in his chair, gripping the arms. "We all know that. There is a person in this neighbourhood who traps people in saunas and kills dogs. I don't know about you, but it doesn't feel very safe to me. We all know what happened to Sooty the cat." Alex starts counting on his fingers. "Loki the Labrador and—"

"That's enough with the conspiracy theories." Deepika is suddenly on her feet. "I know everyone thinks I killed Loki because he bit Kalinda but it's not true."

"I'm not saying you did, Deep—" Alex starts.

"Then why bring it up?"

"Because our dog died."

"Your dog was old and sick!" Deepika insists.

I lean back in my chair, forcing every muscle in my face to relax. Who knew residency meetings could be so damn entertaining. I glance across at my husband, whose eyebrows are high up on his forehead. The look he gives me is of pure glee, and for the first time in ages, we are back to being Ben and Effie May, feeding on chaos.

"And while we're at it," Deepika says, "I want to know who has been saying I buy my kids good grades at their school, because I don't. It's a lie."

There are a few eye rolls in the group. None of them believe her. I look away, guilt hitting me surprisingly hard.

"Okay, everyone. That's the end of the meeting," Sam says. "Well done. No punches thrown this time."

"That's because no one brought up lockdown," Lewis says, chuckling.

The group groans. I'm dying to know what this neighbourhood was like during the height of the pandemic. I make a mental note to ask David.

On the way back to the house, some of the excitement fades and I realise I'm back to living with a husband I don't trust. I'm back to plastering on a smile and being someone I don't want to be anymore.

Since the hospital, I've been so paranoid that Ben knows I'm hiding something that I've kept the envelope David stole from the house in the lining of my dress. Before the hospital, I hid it in the pocket of a jacket in my closet. The temptation to touch the fabric where the envelope sits proves to be difficult to ignore. But I know he's constantly watching me like a hawk.

I can't help but wonder if David went downstairs into the cellar while he was in the house. I doubt it. He had no reason to and he wouldn't be expecting anything sinister to be lurking there. Would he? No. I don't think so. But if he did, part of me might be relieved he finally knows how awful I am.

I keep picturing his face after I made him leave the hospital room. He didn't deserve to be treated like that. I was cruel and for once I feel terrible about it.

"They make us look like amateurs," Ben says as he opens the door to the house.

"I wasn't expecting to hear about so many dead pets," I admit.

He loops an arm over my shoulders, guiding me into the corridor. "Maybe we could settle here. The constant drama would keep us entertained." He shuts the door behind us, locking it.

"Probably not, if you're going to fuck the neighbour's wife and then con them out of money."

He grins down at me. "That's a good point, Euphemia."

His use of my full name makes my skin itch. He hasn't called me that for a long time, and it's usually during moments of true intimacy. Back when that equated love. At least, I think it was love. Ben is the only man I've ever wanted to be with. My dark half. And that's exactly what he always said to me. David, on the other hand, is too light to ever be my match. I'd never be able to be the person he wants.

As Ben holds me close to him, I consider stealing his phone. That's my next step, but I'll need to plan it carefully.

I'm at the point now where I need to know exactly what's going on. Everything Ben does has a knock-on effect on me. If he owes money to bad people and they retaliated by locking me in a sauna, I have the right to know. If one of his ex-lovers is seeking revenge, I need to know in order to protect myself. And most importantly, I need to know what evidence he has of that awful night at the Beaumont Hotel. I need to know if he can prove I murdered a man.

I don't put my plan into action for another two days. I need Ben relaxed, but that never happens. He's always guarded, eyes observant, his mind processing every possible threat. Ben needs a distraction, and that's where Sophie comes in.

I can tell that he's frustrated things haven't moved forward with Sophie at the speed he'd like. To put it bluntly, Ben would usually be fucking his mark by now. The cameras are already installed, waiting to capture him with his conquest.

And I would be watching at home. Like the diligent wife, I'd sit at home watching my husband have sex with another woman.

The first thing I do is bump into Sophie while she's taking some recycling to the bin. I make sure I'm looking unkempt, that I seem frazzled. It fits with the tales Ben has already told of my instability.

"How are you doing, Effie?" Sophie asks, pity dripping from her voice. "Have the police got any leads yet?"

"No," I say. "There's not really any evidence. They took fingerprints on the door but there were so many it was impossible to determine who might have done it."

That's all true, and I'm not surprised the police are stumped. A security camera would be the only lead aside from a confession or a witness. They interviewed a lot of the neighbourhood but most had alibis. The last I heard from Deepika, she was convinced it was Sam or Alex because she thinks they suspect she killed Bailey.

"I'm feeling a lot better though. How are you and Lewis doing?"

"I got my period last week," she says, her chin wobbling.

"I'm so sorry." I reach across to rub her arm.

She lowers her voice. "The worst part is that Lewis wasn't even sad."

"Seriously?"

She nods. "I don't think he even wants a baby anymore."

"I don't think men understand the ache, do they? It's hard work for them and they lose interest."

"I'm starting to think that might be right about Lewis at least." Now her lower lip joins in with her chin and one tear escapes, which she promptly brushes away. "At least he's away for a few days. He's gone on a stag do. Maybe some time apart will help us."

"You deserve better," I say. "You deserve someone who wants a baby just as much as you do."

"Oh, don't say that." Her eyes widen.

"Why not? It's true."

"I can't leave him. He hasn't done anything wrong," she says.

"You don't need to wait for your partner to do something wrong, you know," I point out. "Sometimes people just aren't in the right place with each other." I touch my lips with my fingers. "Sorry, I'm overstepping. I'm projecting my own relationship problems onto you. I think my marriage is over."

"Oh, Effie. Are you sure? I'm so sorry."

Copying her chin wobble, I look up to the sky and then back to her. "I'm pretty sure. I mean, we're staying together in the house for now, but it feels like something has died. And can't be revived."

Yup, I think. Dead. Dead. Dead. Now please go and fuck my husband so I can steal his phone and get his secrets.

I smile sadly, watching her, hoping she's buying it. I'm pretty sure she is. Then she leans towards me and pulls me into a hug.

After we say our goodbyes, I head back into the house, striding into the living room, where Ben is lounging.

"She's warmed up for you," I say, throwing my handbag on the sofa. "Go get her, tiger."

Sleepily, Ben's eyes turn to mine. "What are you talking about?"

"I saw Sophie on the street and told her we're over. Now, when you talk to her, make sure to emphasise about how much you want a kid. You want it more than anything. You ache for a child."

"I thought you were sabotaging me?" His eyebrows are raised in confusion.

"I was just having some fun." I shrug. "I got bored and wanted to mix things up. You can't have it too easy, can you?"

I walk over to the sofa and sit on his lap, leaning into his chest like I used to. This used to be my happy place. I'd breathe him in, the woodsy musk of him, and I'd feel safe.

Pressing my body against him, we kiss, and my hands roam his chest. When I touch his thighs, I can tell the phone is in his pocket. I leave my hand there on his upper thigh as I tell him Sophie is all alone in the house for the night.

"Seriously?"

I nod. "Maybe you can tell her I'm going to meet some friends tonight. And maybe I'll leave so that it's true." My hand squeezes his thigh. He's distracted, his gaze fixed on the computer screen on the arm of the sofa. He's watching her fold laundry on the bed.

He kisses me and I run my hand higher until his phone slips out of his pocket. I whisper in his ear, telling him to go to her. The phone drops onto the seat next to him and, staring into his eyes, with one hand on his neck, I push it under the sofa back cushion with my other hand. My eyes flick down to check the phone is safely out of view. Then I slide sideways off his lap, and offer a conspiratorial smile. He gets up at the same time and steps over to the mirror to check his hair. Then he walks straight out of the house.

CHAPTER TWENTY-NINE

BEN

I love the smell of Sophie's house. She must spray her perfume in every room. Her heady scent intoxicates me as I follow her into their homely kitchen. She pours out two cups of coffee, tucking a lock of her strawberry hair behind her ear.

"I'm so sorry to barge in like this," I say, rubbing my temples. "Effie just came home and told me she's leaving me."

She turns to me, her mouth making an "O" shape. "Jesus. I'm so sorry." She spills the coffee on the kitchen counter and swears.

"You okay?" I ask, rising to see if she burned herself.

She smiles. "Fine. Sorry. You caught me by surprise then. I wasn't expecting you to say that." Sophie grabs a wad of kitchen roll and wipes it up. "I'm glad you came. You shouldn't be alone right now." Smiling sadly, she passes me the coffee. "God, what an awful thing. I ran into her not long ago, and she did sound like... like maybe she'd reached that decision."

I stare down at the table, remaining wistful. "The worst part about all of this is that I'm not surprised or particularly sad. I guess I knew this was coming, you know? It's like when you're about to crash a car. You can see it happening but you're powerless to stop it, and then you just have to hold on tight and accept it."

She nods, gripping her mug with both hands.

"The truth is, I mourned for this relationship a long time ago. I think I'm most upset that..." I clear my throat, imitating the thick-sounding voice someone gets when they're upset. "Effie may have been my last chance to have a child. Now that dream has been taken away from me."

"No," Sophie says, her hand shooting out to grab mine. "Don't say that. You still have options."

"I doubt it," I say. "I'm in my early forties. By the time I'm in a serious relationship, I'll be even older."

Sophie shakes her head. "No, men have a much longer window to have children. You've still got plenty of time. Trust me."

I allow that to sit there for a moment. Then I look up at her. She returns my gaze as I say, "Lewis is an idiot." Then I shake my head like I didn't mean to blurt that out. "Sorry, I shouldn't have... I... It's just I had this conversation with him the other day." I didn't, but she doesn't know that. "He said something to me, and I think you have the right to know."

"What?" she asks. Her expression is furtive, like a squirrel searching for a nut.

"He's tired of trying. He's given up."

Her posture slumps. "I know. I can tell."

I move around the table until I'm sitting close to her. "Listen to me, Sophie. You are the most beautiful, kind, sensitive woman I've ever met, and you deserve to be a mother with someone who cares. I think you're amazing." I brush a lock of hair from her face and tilt her chin towards me. She's compliant. Desire stirs within me. My heart is pounding. I hope hers is too.

I let my hand run through her hair. Women like that. It's comforting and arousing at the same time. Then my thumb trails the line of her jaw. I lean forward and kiss where I touched, moving softly up to her ear. She lets out a gentle moan. I say her name, then pull her closer, our mouths meeting for the first time.

She's mine, I think. All mine. I knew I could do this. There's no woman I can't possess if I want to.

Her arms circle my neck. Our kisses deepen. I pull her onto my lap, so that she's above me. So she feels powerful. My fingers work the buttons on her shirt, but when her bra is exposed, she breaks free, backing away.

"I can't do this," she says. She pushes herself up and away from me.

Fuck.

I thought I had her. It was too soon. We needed to be drinking alcohol on the sofa, not coffee at a table. Following my instincts, I get up from the table and pour a glass of water to drink. Moving around her house might stop her leaving the room straight away. The last thing I want is for her to kick me out.

I turn to her, resting my back against the sink. "I'm so sorry. I can't believe I did that."

She's buttoned up her shirt while I was turned away. "I... I reciprocated." She seems surprised she did.

"I have to be honest, Sophie," I say. "I have feelings for you. Strong feelings. This isn't... This isn't me getting back at Effie or anything like that. It's not me reaching out because I'm hurt. I swear, I've had feelings for you since we first met."

Her expression softens. "You have?"

"Yes. But the question is... do you have feelings for me?"

I hold my breath. This is a Hail Mary pass right here. If she says no, this is all over.

"Yes." A hand flies to her mouth. "And I hate that I do, because I still love my husband and I like your wife a lot."

"She's not my wife anymore," I say.

Sophie shakes her head. "No, she is until you're divorced."

"Not to Effie. She's already moved on. And, honestly, I'm relieved, because it means in my head, I'm free. That's all I want now. To move on and be free." I take a tentative step towards her. "I know this is intense, Sophie. But I can't stop thinking about you. Every time I think about having a child, I think about having a child with you." I take another step and she doesn't move away from me. "You'd be the perfect mother. Do you know that? I can't think of anyone better. You're so special." I run my hand through her hair again.

This time she melts into me as we kiss. There's no resistance left. Now all I need to do is gently manoeuvre her into the bedroom. I want to be able to watch it back later.

CHAPTER THIRTY

EFFIE

After the front door shuts, I wait a few minutes. Then I reach underneath the cushion and grasp the phone. I walk over to the window and see him in Sophie's kitchen. She's making him coffee. My heart pounds. Any minute now he's going to realise he doesn't have his phone with him. Any minute...

I need to get out of this house. This is it. This is the best opportunity I'll ever have. I put the phone in my bag and think for a moment. I told myself I was going to keep David out of this, but I need help. I need a safe space. My eyes drift over to his house across the street. Will he let me in after what I said in the hospital? Am I even doing the right thing trusting him with this? My heart pounds as I leave the house and stride straight over to David's. When he answers the door, I'm breathless.

"I have his phone," I blurt out. "I've finally got it and as long as he doesn't realise until after he's slept with her, he'll think he's lost it at hers. He won't even know."

David leads me through to the lounge and I flop down on a sofa.

"What are you talking about?" he asks.

"I need to store it here," I tell him. "I'm sorry to ask, but it's the only place it'll be safe. If I'm going to get away from him, I need to see what he's keeping from me. But I don't know his passcode."

He's silent for a moment. "You can leave it here," he replies. "But I don't think you can get into it without erasing all the data."

"There's a trick with Siri," I tell him. "It doesn't work all the time, but if it does work, I can get in without erasing the data."

I start fiddling with the iPhone, holding down the home button to activate Siri, then pressing more buttons to get into a text message, copying and pasting random words into a text. It's a weird system but one I found mentioned on a few websites.

"Effie, do you want to explain exactly what's going on, because the last time we met, you said some pretty awful things. And that was after I had to sneak into your house to find an envelope, which is not particularly normal behaviour."

I look up at him. "I'm sorry about that. I didn't want to get you involved but I need to be somewhere safe."

"Why? Every time I've asked if you're in a bad situation with Ben you've brushed it off."

I glance down at the phone, which is restarting. There's adrenaline coursing through me, which, if I'm honest with myself, gives me a thrill of excitement. But there's heaviness, too. Deep in my bones and my heart.

"Maybe I'm more afraid than I thought I was," I admit. "The truth is, I want to get away from Ben, and he's not going to let me go. Not easily anyway. And I suppose I've never been in this position before and I don't know how he's going to react."

David pushes his hands into his pockets and stares down at his feet. "Do you think you're in danger?"

I nod my head. "I think maybe I am."

"Okay," he says. "I'll make us some tea. You can stay here as long as you need."

Some of that heaviness subsides, though the adrenaline continues to pump around my body. Is this what it's like to have an ally? Ben is many things to me, including partner in crime, but has he ever truly had my back? Something flickers on the phone screen and I watch it as it reloads. Nothing happens. I keep staring. The screen clears. I blink. I'm in.

The first thing I check is the text messages. Someone has been threatening Ben, though admittedly not getting very far. *Tick tock. I'll tell your wife what you did. You don't have much time left...* The messages don't seem to have a point. There are no demands. It's like they just want to keep him unsettled and on his toes. Ben doesn't care much about an empty threat. I look when the last one came in and check it against the car tracker. The day Ben went back to the Beaumont. So, the threats are related to that? My stomach turns.

Why would this person send *Ben* threatening messages when *I* was the one who killed that man? He loves to remind me that what happened at the hotel was all my fault. Ben enjoys rubbing salt in the wound. It's why I'm afraid right now, because he's had this hanging over my head like a sword ready to drop.

In order to protect myself, I've pushed those memories away. That night is a sickening blur. But now I need to face up to what happened or I'll never be free. I need to remember.

My heart pounds against my ribs. I'm back in that hotel bathroom with someone standing over me, pulling at my clothes. There's blood in between my legs and on my hands. I close my eyes, accepting the pain that comes with the memory. As it always does, shame washes over me like cold water. I push through. There's a chance I'm missing something from that night. Missing a vital detail that could help me.

"Effie? Are you all right?" David's voice sounds concerned.

I nod my head. "Yes... sorry, David, I'm just... thinking." He squeezes my shoulder and leaves the room.

I have to concentrate. What came before? Me in Ben's arms. The body at the bottom of the stairs. Ben carries me up the same stairs and the maid's there. What was her name? Anna. She's young, but I know she's besotted with Ben. She'd do anything for him.

Ben asks Anna to go to the security office and distract the guard there. He wants her to erase the CCTV footage from the stairwell.

What happened on the stairs?

I'm staggering and my hip bumps into his. Robert. His kind smile. He laughs, and a giggle bubbles up from my throat. It's strange that there's no fear or animosity in my thoughts.

I can't remember where we're going. Down to the lobby? The hotel feels quiet in my memories, like it's the dead of night. Robert places a hand on my shoulder. It's friendly. Warm. I like it being there.

And then what?

Everything changes. There's pain in my abdomen, my shoulder crashes against a hard surface. The next moment is a blank space, like I'm in a pitch-black room. I blink. And that's when I see the blood, and I see Robert lying at an awkward angle. Dead on the ground.

Ben said no one would find out what I did because he'd

been drinking. We were going to leave him there so someone would find him. We wanted it to look like an accident. But we knew there was a security camera on the stairs and that was where Anna came in. Without the video footage of me pushing him, it was just a tragic accident of a man who drank too much and fell to his death.

Robert Dinman had been a mark we'd chosen carefully. He drank in the bar every night where Ben liked to watch him. Ben noticed his new shoes, new watch, tailored suit and knew that Robert had recently acquired his wealth. So, I was sent to the bar each night to talk to him. The usual game of seduction and blackmail.

I check through Ben's files. There aren't many photos. We occasionally take them of ourselves for appearance's sake. Neither of us are sentimental. There are a couple of pictures from the double date with Sophie and Lewis. Then a few from a different date night. I scroll back. Ben is diligent about deleting photographs taken with people we've scammed. He only keeps the videos of him having sex with those women, those victims, and he crops his face out of those. And he stores them in encrypted folders. Fuck. I realise then that if there's any existing evidence of me pushing Robert down the stairs, it'll be in one of those files.

I take myself back to the hotel bar. There I am sitting next to Robert. Ben and I had realised at this point that he liked to drink a few bourbons every night. I'm with him, and while he drinks, we talk. He tells me that he's taking a break from work to escape the pressure. A few years before he created a popular app and made quite a bit of money. But as the company grew, he found it harder and harder to deal with the responsibilities of being CEO.

"Look," he'd said, removing his phone from his pocket.

"This is how many people have called me over the last few days."

I'd seen the alarming number of missed calls and imagined his second-in-command tearing their hair out, wondering why their creative genius had disappeared.

"But I need time away. I just need to breathe." He'd let out a long, sad sigh.

I had felt sorry for him in that moment, and I'd said something earnest. "Why don't the people in our lives give us time to find out who we are?" That was it.

I gasp, surprised those words have come back to me. It's the first time I remember saying them. I stare down at Ben's phone in my hand, willing more memories to the surface.

"Exactly," Robert had replied.

"It's like we're playdough, and... and someone has us in their fist. They keep squeezing until there's nothing left." I'd lifted my arm and squeezed my fist to demonstrate.

His eyes had brightened. "Exactly. You get it, Fi. You get it."

That's right. I was Fiona to him. Fi for short.

We'd stumbled up to his room and made love on the floor next to his bed. I'd known I was pregnant with Ben's baby throughout all of this, and I'd already decided I'd be a terrible mother. And yet, at the bar, I'd decided not to drink. When Robert was distracted, I'd ordered mocktails. When he'd bought me a drink, I'd taken a few pretend sips and then figured out a way to get rid of it when he wasn't looking. I'd wanted him to think I was as tipsy as him.

That night was the only night we had sex. I'd slept in his bed afterwards and we'd ordered room service. Ben wanted me to take photos of him naked so we could blackmail him—we'd already established that he was married—but I didn't do it. I'd enjoyed our chats and I was starting to feel different.

The fun of robbing and tricking people was fading. I wanted out and I assumed it was the baby giving me those good thoughts. *The goodness growing inside me.*

Those days in the Beaumont are such a blur. It's almost like I'd been drinking heavily, but I hadn't. Early pregnancy made me woozy and I'd fainted the day I took the test. No one knew that. I'd never told Ben. It wasn't a secret; I just hadn't thought to tell him.

David returns. "Have you found anything?"

"Only that he's gambled away a lot of my money and most of his," I say, giving him a nugget of truth. Of course I already knew this and didn't *just* stumble upon it.

"Fuck," he says. "What are you going to do?"

What *am* I going to do? I've come this far. I can't fail now.

"I'm going to try making some calls," I say. "Is it okay if I go upstairs?"

"Sure," he says.

As I walk out, I try not to think about the worry on his face. But what he doesn't get is that I'm not a wounded bird who needs saving. I'm a vulture.

In his bedroom, I sit down on the edge of the bed, fond memories of what we did the other day drifting into my mind as I scroll through Ben's phone. I need to find the number of the maid. Anna. She removed my clothes when I was in that hotel bathroom. She wiped the CCTV. I need to know exactly what she knows.

Ben would have kept her number under another name. He has a system for useful people. They are a service. So, a maid from a hotel would be under a cleaning service. I check through his contacts. *AB Cleaners*. That could be it! A for Anna? And the B for the Beaumont? It makes sense. I call the number.

A female voice answers on the third ring. "What do you want?" She's not happy to hear from Ben.

"It's Effie," I say. "Don't hang up. I just want to talk."

"You've got his phone." She sounds surprised.

"That's right."

"He won't be happy about that," she says. "Are you calling for him? He told me to stay where I am."

"When did he tell you that? Did he come to see you?"

"Came to threaten me, more like," she says.

"It's Anna, isn't it?" I ask.

"Yes."

"Can you tell me what happened that night, Anna?"

She pauses. I can hear her breathing.

"It's okay," I say. "We can take it slow. Maybe I could meet you in London for a cup of coffee?"

She's silent again.

"I'm not him, Anna. I'm not like him. I can help you."

"How do I know that?"

"You don't," I admit. "But I know you're still working at the Beaumont and that must be hard. You had to watch the aftermath, didn't you? You saw them take Robert away. You had to give a statement. You made that video disappear. You broke the law."

"Shut up," she snaps.

"I'm grateful for that, you know. What did Ben give you? Not enough for you to start somewhere new?"

"No," she says. "I had to give it to my mum. She's struggling."

"I understand," I say. "I can help you with more money, you know. I can make it so you never need to work at the Beaumont again. Wouldn't that be a weight off your mind?"

She sighs. "I'm sick of dealing with both of you. Sick of it."

"I understand," I say. "If you just tell me everything that happened that night, I'll never bother you again."

"I can't," she says. "I can't. He'll kill me."

"Please, Anna. I need your help..."

Before I can say another word, she hangs up. I'm left staring down at the phone, out of options.

CHAPTER THIRTY-ONE

BEN

I can tell Sophie regrets it as soon as it happens, but by then it's too late. She rests her head on my chest, but the expression on her face says it all. Her eyes have that thousand-yard stare of a person contemplating their terrible decisions. Once she makes her excuses and heads to the bathroom, I get up and pull on my clothes. I can't wait to head home and discover what the camera recorded.

A toilet flushes and she returns, dressed in a robe. "I... Um..." she starts.

"I'll go," I say. I close the gap between us and plant a kiss on her forehead.

"Yes, I think that's probably a good idea. Lewis might come back early, or..."

"Don't worry, Sophie. I get it. And I meant everything I said, but I know you love your husband. Call me if..." I let it hang for a moment. "If you want to choose me."

She nods. "Okay."

Her body is tensed and her arms wrapped tightly around her chest. She can't wait to get rid of me and that's fine as far as I'm concerned. I leave, cross the street and open the door.

It's empty. Good. Effie decided to go out and that gives me ample time to do what I need to do.

First, I watch the footage of me and Sophie in the bedroom. Then I sift through it methodically, editing it to crop out my face and remove any identifying marks. Sophie needs to be in full view, otherwise it won't work.

And then I watch myself dress and I realise something. I don't have my phone. It must be at Sophie's house. Fuck. I'm usually careful, but this evening happened so fast.

I can't go back to Sophie's because she asked me to leave. Instead, I use our landline to call her mobile number and she tells me she'll search for it and get back to me. While I wait, I check my email. To my delight, there's one from Lewis. He must have sent it while on a stag do, which I find quite interesting.

Hi mate,

Just a quick question about that investment. Is it normal to lose so much money in the first month? Only I have lost quite a lot and because the investment was so big, I'm a bit concerned. Will it then grow over a long period of time? Because this doesn't seem normal. I know I'm not an expert like you, but...

And so, it continues. Poor Lewis. He doesn't realise that money is already in my account. He's quite slow on the uptake and I wonder if I can eke more out of him. Ivy Oaks is an interesting place to stay for a while longer. On the other hand, I now have everything I need to destroy them both. A shudder of power works its way through me. How can Effie consider giving all of this up? That's what she wanted to do, after all. She wanted to stop, to have her baby, to be a mother.

It was never meant to be. People like me and Effie should never bring children into this world. That was my parents' mistake. The same reason they left this world, too, because they'd made too many mistakes, hurt too many people. There was no more fitting end for my father than the one he suffered. Mark my words.

The landline rings and I snatch it up.

"Sophie?"

"I've looked everywhere," she says. "I'm afraid I can't find your phone."

"Everywhere? Are you sure?"

"Yes," she snaps. "I wouldn't want my husband to find it, would I?"

I can already tell there won't be a second time with Sophie and I'm a little disappointed the rose-tinted glasses came off so quickly. I wonder if she's analysing how it happened. The small manipulations that forced her to drop her guard. Once I threaten her, she'll see everything crystal clear.

"All right," I say, diffusing her frustration. "Can you let me know if you do find it?"

"Yeah, sure," she says.

"Sophie. I just want you to know that what... what happened meant something to me. I don't regret it and I hope you don't either."

There's a slight pause. The landline muffles slightly, like she's exhaling close to the receiver. "It meant something to me too. I just don't know what to do about it right now."

"I get it," I say. "No pressure. Okay? Take your time."

"Okay," she says. Her voice is warm again. I smile to myself as I hang up the phone.

But now I need to deal with the other issue. If my phone isn't at Sophie's, that means I must have lost it before I left the house. My eyes trail over the living room. I picture myself sitting on the sofa, watching my cameras—which I need to uninstall soon if my affair with Sophie isn't going anywhere—and then Effie came over. She was different. Flirty. Encouraging.

Fuck.

Effie stole my phone. Of course she did. What with the calls from loan sharks and the threatening text messages, I've spent far too much time staring at it in front of her and she wants to know why. She got a taste the day of the barbecue when I left the phone in the bedroom. The question is—has Effie found a way to get in without the passcode?

I pace the living room, wondering how bad this is. She'll find out about the threatening text messages. I deleted the pictures so she won't find those. But she might even guess that I don't have footage of her murdering the man at the Beaumont. Though for all she knows, I could keep that file on a flash drive somewhere. The threats are bad, because now she'll think I'm the reason someone locked the sauna door.

I've always been able to manage Effie, ever since I first met her in that bar. She keeps me on my toes, which I like. Even back then, when she stole my watch. But fundamentally, I'm the one in charge. While she thinks she's a free spirit, I know how to get her to do what I want. But something changed that night at the Beaumont. Things have been different. It feels like we're no longer playing on the same side. I thought she was just sulking but there's a chance that I've lost her for good. I need to figure out if she's on my side or if she's my enemy. If she is my enemy there's no turning back. There's a whole new me she's about to meet.

CHAPTER THIRTY-TWO

EFFIE

I lean into David, feeling the warmth of his torso beneath me. He has a different scent to Ben, which is something I've never noticed about the men I seduce before. David smells fresh, like orange peel or cut grapefruit. It isn't quite as masculine as Ben's aftershave, and I like that. I like David. Which means this is doomed.

"What are you going to do now?" he asks, echoing my thoughts.

"I don't know."

"You're going back to him, aren't you?"

Instead of answering him, I roll from his chest and place my cheek against the cool pillow. Next to his bed, an alarm clock tells me it's after midnight. At some point, I'm going to have to go home. And Ben will be there, waiting for me. Will he have guessed that I stole his phone? And what will he do to me if he knows? But first I need to know more, I need to make Anna talk. I need to go back to the Beaumont.

Before I leave, I'll find somewhere in David's house to hide Ben's phone.

"Well, you're a grown woman and you can do whatever

you want," David continues. "But you can do better than him." Before I can open my mouth to counter that, he carries on. "Don't you dare tell me you're as bad as him. Because you're not."

I roll over. "How do you know that? You don't know me."

A sharp puff of air whistles through his nose. "I do know you."

I want to tell him I'm a killer. But he'll run away.

"Okay, you know me," I say. "But you don't know what I've done. It's something terrible. It's just... I don't know *why* I did it."

"You don't know why?"

I wring my hands. "It's like my brain has fudged all the details together. I know *what* I did, I just don't know why. Ben knows. He chooses to keep it from me." I bite my lip. "But there's another way to find out. Can I borrow your car?"

"What?" He looks at me with an incredulous expression on his face. "Now?"

"Yeah," I say. "Now."

It's a relatively big hotel with a 24-hour reception. I can book a room as soon as I get there and catch Anna in the morning.

"Then I'm coming with you." He's out of bed in a flash, his naked body moving over to the ottoman where he left his clothes earlier.

I'm also out of bed, grabbing Ben's phone out from under the pillow. "No. I'm going alone."

"Then you don't get my car. Care to sneak over to your garage and get yours without your husband noticing? I saw him leave Sophie's house about an hour ago, by the way."

"You are infuriating." I shake my head as I grab my underwear.

"That's what my ex-wife told me." He's smiling now and

it's infectious. "By the way, what is going on between your husband and Sophie? Are you and Ben in some competition to see how many neighbours you can sleep with?"

"Pretty much," I deadpan.

David pauses for a moment, and then laughs. "Seriously?"

I shrug. "Almost. He wanted to seduce Sophie." I walk over to him and pinch his cheek. "I wanted you."

"You have an open relationship?"

"Not completely open, no," I say. "He wouldn't approve of this."

"What is this?" David gestures to the two of us.

I pull my dress over my head and pull my hair out the other side. "The fuck if I know."

He regards me, his eyes slightly narrowed.

I sigh. "All right, fine. I like you, okay? Ben wouldn't approve of this because I like you. It isn't part of the game. I'm not supposed to be with someone I actually like. We go somewhere, we split people up, mess with their heads and then we move on. Are you happy now? That's the truth, we're terrible, sociopathic people."

My shoulders slump forward and for half a heartbeat my body is lighter. There. I said it. I was honest with him.

He's quiet for a moment, and then he says, "How long has this been going on?"

"Since I met him in a bar and he tried to con me. I stole his watch instead."

"How old were you, Effie?" His voice has changed. It's become quieter, more intense.

"Old enough to make my own decisions." I raise my eyebrows to signal that this conversation is over. We walk through to the kitchen and David starts making coffee for us to take on the journey. I have no qualms with that. We'll need it.

My attention drifts over to mine and Ben's house. The downstairs light is still on but the curtains are closed and I can't see him in any of the windows. Why didn't he stay the night with Sophie? Did she kick him out? She hasn't been the easy mark that Ben expected her to be. But also, he's less patient than he used to be. He doesn't have the same touch. He's getting older and can't rely on his looks as much as he used to.

That'll happen to me too. In fact, it'll happen more quickly. The thought is oddly comforting. It brings with it a sense of relief.

"Come on," David says. "I guess you need to tell me where we're going if I'm driving."

"I'll put it in the satnav." My eyes never leave the house across the street. I can sense my husband seething from all the way over here. The house breathes with his rage.

Ben knows. He's figured out that I took his phone. Otherwise, he'd be asleep, and all the lights would be off. No, he's waiting for me to come home and that means he *knows*. I'm his enemy now. All these years, I've only known Ben as my partner in crime. I've never known him on the other side of that. A shiver of fear runs down my spine. I follow David out to the car, and we drive away.

David's questions are probing as we drive to London, and I feel I owe him some answers. I don't want him to know how terrible I truly am, because I don't want to lose him, but if I say nothing, I'll lose him anyway.

"If you really want to know," I say, somewhere along the motorway, "we con people for money."

"Why?" he says. "Aren't you both rich?"

"Yes. Born rich."

"Then why?" he asks.

"Ben likes power," I say. "He grew up powerless in his childhood home. His father was a violent man who controlled every inch of his wife and child. What Ben needed was therapy, but instead, he developed a method of controlling others."

"And you're part of that," he says. "You know that, right? He controls you as much as he controls everyone else."

I don't answer. I'm not sure I believe him.

"Why do you do it?" he asks.

My fingers grip the arm rest. "I like games. People are puzzles to me and I have a knack of understanding them."

"Why?" he asks again.

"Would you stop analysing me?"

"No," he says. "I won't. Someone needs to. Forget Ben, Effie, you're the one who should've gone to therapy and saved yourself all this."

I rub my temples. He's right, but it still hurts to hear him say it.

"Tell me why you do it," he says.

"I don't know." I lift my hands and slap them down on my thighs. "I guess it's the only thing I'm good at. You've probably seen my mother in magazines, right? She's very beautiful and enjoys being beautiful. Her whole persona is all about being *admired* for her body. She thought I'd want the same, even though I'm not as beautiful as her. So, I was sent down to London when I was about sixteen years old."

"On your own?" he asks.

"Yes. Sort of. I stayed in her old flat. Another model lived with me." I can't tell him about Kathy or Louisa. Not yet. "I went to casting interviews and walked a few runways. I posed for editorials, blah blah. But I didn't have what my mother had. It didn't come naturally to me. I was so bored." My hands ball into fists. "I started messing with the other girls, figuring out how to manipulate them."

"Why?"

"Oh, would you stop asking that?"

"You need to dig deeper," he insists.

I rest my head against the glass. His questions make me feel like I'm ten years old. My eyelids close.

"Don't you dare pretend to be asleep again." He pokes me in the arm. "We're doing this. We're getting to the bottom of it."

"Fine," I say. "I was in competition with these girls. I competed with them, and I needed to find a way to win." I'm quiet for a moment. I glance at David, wondering if that's enough, if he's finally appeased. His eyes are on the road, he seems to be waiting for more. When I turn my head, the landscape is a blur of lights filtering through rain tracks on the window. Then I go somewhere I haven't allowed myself to go for years. I focus on the lights outside and I begin to talk. "None of them warned me about him. They all knew, but they never said a word. I walked into that shoot after hundreds of girls had been before me, and no one said what he'd do to me. And from then on, I hated them all. But that will never excuse the... the cruelty I inflicted on some of those girls. Because I was hateful. Hateful."

David lets out a long sigh. "I'm sorry, Effie."

"Don't be sorry for me. I can't stand pity."

"I know," he says. "I don't pity you. For one thing, I care about you. And for another, you have my understanding, not my pity." He taps the steering wheel. "And now you know why. You can see how you've got here. Now you understand everything. Did you know before?"

My shoulders rise, I hold them there, my body tense. "I

don't know. Does it matter? Nothing excuses the things I've done. This isn't a movie. I won't have a redemption arc."

He glances at me. "How do you know that?"

"I should be in prison. I probably will be soon."

"No, you won't," he says.

But he doesn't know about the man at the bottom of the stairs in the Beaumont. He doesn't know what I did.

How am I going to speak to Anna without David hovering around me? I need to see her alone. He can't know about the worst thing I've ever done.

It's almost 2am by the time we walk into the hotel and ask for a room. The man behind the reception desk asks no questions. We're not carrying bags so we can't have had a late flight. We're not dressed up from a night out. It must seem strange to him, but then I'm sure he's used to anything.

When we're alone in the room, David lies down on the bed and stares at me. "Are you going to tell me why we're here?"

I bite my lip. "I can't."

"Why couldn't this wait until morning?"

"Because he knows," I say.

"Ben?"

I nod. "He knows I have his phone. And now I can't go back. Not without answers anyway."

David props himself up on one elbow. "What will happen if you go back?"

"I don't know, but it won't be good," I say, walking towards him.

He opens his arms as though to fold me into them and I feel safe.

I fall asleep with ease but wake up with a tight chest. When I check my phone, there's a WhatsApp message from Ben. He must have sent it using his laptop. I almost don't want to open it, but I do.

All went well last night. I got what I wanted. And then I came home to discover something dear to me had been stolen. What a shame. If you can't find what you're looking for, it's because you're searching in the wrong place.

He sends a picture file and I open it, my fingers trembling.

It appears to be a screenshot taken from some sort of video footage. The CCTV from the Beaumont that night.

There I am, standing over the body. The quality isn't great. I'm a fuzzy shape, but it's definitely me. Below me, there's blood on the ground. I squint, making the image bigger. In the picture my arms are outstretched, and I seem to be gazing at my hands as though in shock. My hands are red with blood.

I close the image before David wakes up.

TEXT MESSAGES TAKEN FROM ANNA HENNESSY'S PHONE

30th April 2021

Anna: It's done.

Ben: Thank you, Anna-banana.

Anna: How's Effie?

Ben: Sleeping.

Anna: Won't she remember what happened?

Ben: I'm confident she won't for the reasons we discussed earlier.

Anna: K.

Anna: Ben, I feel really bad. Can I come and see you?

Ben: Not right now but let's meet tomorrow. Can you bring your phone and laptop? I trust you, but also need to make sure there's no trace of the task I gave you tonight.

Anna: Are you sure you trust me? Because it sounds like you don't.

Ben: Don't get shaky on me now, sweetheart. You know I trust you. And I know I've asked for a lot recently but I swear that's all over now. Everything is going to be okay. Once we're together properly, it'll make all of this worthwhile. I promise. I love you.

Anna: I love you so much. I know you'll take care of me.

Ben: I always do.

CHAPTER THIRTY-THREE
EFFIE

David is still asleep when I slip out of the room. I leave him a scribbled note to tell him I'll be back soon, and then I head down to the foyer. First, I walk tentatively down the stairwell, stopping where I think I remember the incident happening. Was it the third or fourth floor? I can't remember. All I know is that the blood has long since been scrubbed away. There's no trace of Robert Dinman. I open the message from Ben, enlarge the picture, and stand in the exact same place I was standing over the body.

Unfortunately, seeing the spot Robert died doesn't magically bring back all my memories from that time. I don't linger. I make my way to the reception desk, hoping I can find out if Anna is working today. Ben certainly spent a lot of time with her when we stayed here, which makes me think she worked full time. It's almost 8am so there's a chance I can catch her before she begins her cleaning rotation. She could be in the staff's quarters or a laundry room.

There's a young woman on reception, who seems surprised when I ask for Anna. I mumble some lie about being a school friend. She's younger so it doesn't make much sense but it's all I can come up with after being so shaken by Ben's text.

I find Anna outside the hotel smoking a cigarette, chatting to another maid. When she sees me approach, her face pales. It surprises me that I recognise her right away, considering the blurry memories I have from that time. The moment in the bathroom must be clearer in my mind than I thought. She's a pretty girl, with thick eyebrows and her hair pulled back into a tight bun.

"Can I talk to you?" I ask.

She hesitates and looks to her friend. "Okay," she says before ushering me towards the car park.

"Look, I'm sorry to turn up like this," I say.

She smirks. "Are you sure about that?"

"Yes." I stop and turn to her. "Do you think I want to relive what happened that night? Because I don't. But the thing is, I need to get away from him."

Her expression softens then. "You mean Ben?"

"Yes, Ben. He's... he's not a good person."

She rubs her upper arms. "I know. Trust me, I've learned all about that lately."

"Did he do something to you?"

Anna's fingers flutter up to her hairline. She seems to be considering saying something, but then she doesn't. She shakes her head slightly but won't meet my gaze.

"Anna, you're the only person who knows what happened that night. I don't remember. I wasn't drunk. I remember not touching alcohol. So why is my memory blurry? Can you explain that to me?"

Her eyes close slowly and then open again. "I can't talk to you, Effie. It isn't safe for me."

"Because he came here threatening you?"

"Yes," she says, the word hissing between her teeth. "And..." She glances back at the hotel as though expecting Ben to emerge at any moment.

"You said something over the phone about Ben wanting you to stay here. What did you mean?"

She bites her bottom lip and brushes a tear from her cheek. "I... I can't..."

"Anna, I can help you."

She shakes her head. "Are you sure about that? Because you seem just as fucked up as me and it's all because of him. He's a monster. You married a psychopath, do you know that?"

"Yes."

"So why should I trust you? How do I know you're any better?"

"I'm not the one threatening you, am I?" I say. "Look, I understand your concerns, but I'm not like him. As soon as you share what you know, I'll be gone. You'll never see me again."

She throws her cigarette on the ground, crunching it under her heel.

"I'll pay you, Anna. I really need your help."

She sighs. "How much?"

"A lot." I glance down at my finger, to the large diamond I made Ben buy me. I remember the ruddy-faced man in the jewellery shop, the way I'd asked to look at the clarity of the stone myself. I know what this ring is worth, and I also know I don't want to wear it anymore. "But I can't pay you in cash, and an online transfer can be tracked. I do have this though." I hold up my hand. "You should get at least twenty thousand for it."

"How do I know it's real?" she asks.

I remove the ring from my finger, along with the band,

and move closer to her. I turn it over to show her the markings on the band, and then I show her the stone. "Maybe you'll have to trust me, because I don't know what you know about diamonds. But it's real. Ben wouldn't have me walking around with a fake stone on my finger. It wouldn't look good. The people in our world know when something is fake."

She nods. "I just need enough to make sure my mum's safe. Ben threatened her. And me. And my ex-boyfriend. He wants me to tell him where Stephen is, but I won't."

"Why does he want that?"

Her chin wobbles. I grab both of her arms and make her look at me. "Anna, tell me."

"I... I did something stupid. I was going to ask for money, but he guessed it was me right away and then he came here. I got scared so I stopped. He threatened my family so I made it seem like it could have been Stephen. But it wasn't."

"Jesus," I whisper. "Tell me everything. Now. I need to know what happened that night."

"He made me inject you with something that night and that's why you can't remember. You were already out of it before I did it. Then afterwards you practically passed out."

"He made you administer a sedative?"

She shrugs. "I guess so. I... I didn't want to, but everything happened so fast. You... you had so much blood on you, and I was scared. He said it would help you."

"It's okay," I say. "What did you see on the CCTV footage?"

"I saw you and Robert Dinman together on the stairs, and then suddenly you're both on the floor. You *both* fall. Then you try to help him, but I guess you see that he's already dead. You stand up. You have blood on your hands and you're freaking out, so you call Ben. I've seen it a million times and I've never seen you push him."

"What?"

She takes a step towards me. "He made you believe you killed that man. But you didn't."

The ground beneath my feet seems to shift, like an earthquake just rippled through the Beaumont Hotel car park. *I didn't kill Robert Dinman.* All this time he made me believe I had blood on my hands and all this time he was lying.

No lies. No ties.

He told the worst lie he could possibly tell.

"I lost my baby." The bitter words escape through gritted teeth. "My baby died that night."

"I'm sorry," she says.

I pull myself back from the brink of darkness. "Did you send Ben a copy of the CCTV footage? He sent me a photograph of me standing over the body."

She shakes her head. "No. Just some screenshots from it. He met me the day after and made me prove I'd wiped everything from my phone and computer. But before I met him, I saved everything onto a USB stick. He doesn't know that. Well, he might suspect it but he doesn't know for sure."

"Is it on your phone? I need to see it."

"No, it's on a USB stick somewhere safe. But I have this." She fumbles with her phone and shows me a blurry picture. I look at it again. Ben in the stairwell. It's so strange, I don't remember him there at all, and yet he was.

"You need to send me everything you have," I say. "But not to my phone number." I grab a pen from my handbag, take hold of her hand and scribble an email address onto her palm. "This one should be safe." It's an old email address I haven't logged into for years. The password is still etched into my mind from my modelling days.

"I don't know. I can't," she says. "What if he finds out?"

I shove the engagement ring into her inked hand and

pocket the wedding band. "It's my turn to trust you. Send me that video and then go somewhere far away from here. Never come back to this place again. Don't message Ben anymore. Stay away from him."

She seems hesitant.

"Anna, you owe me this after everything you did to help Ben."

A moment of silence hangs between us. She hugs me then. It feels strange. I should be resentful of a girl who slept with my husband. But she was only young, easily manipulated by him, and could have ended up in a lot of trouble. I'm the one who knew what he was doing. I didn't stop it then, but I can protect her now.

"There's something else," she says, as I'm about to walk away. "I think he was drugging you while you were here. Not just the injection he gave you when you were hysterical. I think he drugged you the whole time."

My hand rises to my mouth. "Are you sure?"

She nods. "I saw him put something in your drink. I'm sorry I didn't say anything. He made... he always seemed to make everything seem okay, like there was a good reason."

I nod. "I know. It's okay."

Her face crumples. "I'm sorry."

I should hate this girl. I should want to destroy her. Ben pulled her into our game and then he corrupted her, and I know exactly what that feels like. When I look at her, I feel a strange sense of peace wash over me. Giving her that ring feels like cleaning up some of the messes I've made. Even if she screws me over and never sends that video, I've done something to help her.

"It's okay," I say. "I'm going to go now. Use the money from the ring to get yourself far away from here."

I walk away on shaking legs. Ben drugged me here in the

Beaumont but as far as I know he's never drugged me anywhere else. Why here? Why did he want me foggy-brained in this place in particular? Unless making me foggy wasn't the goal. The only difference between that time and any other was that I was pregnant. What if he did it to poison me? What if he did it to make me miscarry the baby?

Back inside the hotel, I make my way to the bar and sit down in one of the armchairs. There's a lot to process. My abdomen is tight and sore, like I'm going through it all over again.

When I told Ben I was pregnant, he didn't react. We were in a quiet suburb in Wiltshire and Ben had just seduced a neighbour. He played his usual tricks, only this time he hired a private investigator to "find" him and the wife and take photographs. He pretended to work with the woman to stop the photographs being sent to her husband. What was her name? Susannah, that's right. She paid him a lot of money to get him to fix it. He pocketed all that money and then we moved away.

Before we moved, I put the positive pregnancy test on the coffee table and made my announcement. He stared at me with a blank face before eventually coming to life.

"How did this happen?" he asked.

"Well, it was probably that time we did it on all fours outside—"

"No," he interrupted, not appreciating my joke. "I thought you were on the pill."

"I am," I said. "But it isn't foolproof."

He stood. Pacing the room with his hands in his pockets, his eyes fixed on the test. He shook his head. "How do I know it's mine?"

The air left my body. How could he say that to me? He was the one who sent me out to other men in order to take part in his games. And now here he was, throwing it in my face. "Trust me. It's yours."

"Trust you?" He laughed. "We can't trust each other. How are we going to raise a child doing what we do?"

"Well," I said. "Maybe we stop doing what we do. Ben, I'm tired. I'm sick of seductions and tricks. Haven't we done it enough? Don't we have plenty of money to live our lives?"

He softened after a while. Now, when I think back to that moment, I can pinpoint the very second he decided my baby had to die. After pacing back and forth for a few minutes, Ben walked over to the fireplace and rested a hand there. I'd been talking about us buying a cottage somewhere and settling down. He'd been extremely quiet and still. Then he seemed to come round to it. We spoke for a long time.

Lies. So many of them. Every single time he told me we'd quit, it was a lie. As he talked about a cottage in the countryside, he'd already begun to plan a way to kill my baby.

After that, Ben said Susannah's husband was obsessed with revenge. He convinced me we weren't safe and we moved into the Beaumont for a few weeks while we decided which cottage to buy. It was during our first couple of days he persuaded me to play one last game. According to him I needed to do it while I was still attractive, before the bump started to show. Before I became a "mum". I should've noticed the derisive tone he used for that word. I should've seen this coming.

He drugged me. No doubt he gave me something dangerous for the baby, something illegal. He kept me just groggy enough that I didn't notice the change in myself. And then he snatched everything away from me. I need to see that recording for myself. What if Ben followed us that night? With me dizzy from drugs and Robert drunk, we were no doubt easy targets. Maybe he'd lurked in some shadowy corner, waiting to shove us both and watch as we tumbled down the stairs. Perhaps the risk of killing me was worth it to make sure I never had my baby.

I've known Ben is capable of murder for a long time. I just never thought he'd try to kill me.

CHAPTER THIRTY-FOUR
BEN

After what happened at the Beaumont, I thought getting Effie back into the swing of things would be the best way to move on. I thought she only wanted to stop and settle down because of the baby. Perhaps I misjudged that. Clearly, she hasn't moved on at all, otherwise she wouldn't have stolen my phone.

Through a crack in the curtains, I see David's car pull out of his drive. What is he doing up at this time of night? And where is he going? I move through the house, thinking.

It's clear that Effie is in a relationship with him now. Their flirtation was obvious from the start. Effie is a flirt in general, but this was different. I remember his pathetic face at the barbecue when I talked crudely about her, how uncomfortable he was. It was all a test, of course, I just wanted to see his reaction. Whenever I go to a new place, I like to sniff out the threats, and David is a threat.

It's a shame I went to the lengths I did at the Beaumont. I hate that I had to use such drastic measures to bring her back on track. But Effie and I as parents would never work. Besides,

I saw the look in her eye. There was no convincing her to do the right thing, so I did it for her. I had no choice.

I thought the Morgans would provide a nice distraction, for her as much as me. Only I was the one who became distracted. Effie has one singular focus, it seems. She's determined to dredge up the past no matter how harmful it might be.

As the headlights fade, I use our landline telephone to call Anna. Effie will have seen the threatening messages on my phone by now, and I'm sure her mind will have gone back to that night in the Beaumont. I should have deleted them. Of course I got rid of the pictures, but I'd kept the messages in case they proved useful later. In case I needed the number they came from. As the phone rings out, I grit my teeth. It's the middle of the night but I still expect better from a girl who should know to bend to my will.

Instead, I get my laptop and open up a messaging app. I send one asking Anna to respond as soon as possible. If Effie has been in touch with her, I need to know.

I get some sleep, because I'm going to need it. Then I take my time going through the next stages, thinking about what I'll need and how I'll need to look. After I've decided, I grab a travel bag and throw in some essentials. I'll need my laptop, gloves, dark clothing, and so on. I take my keys on the way out of the house, lock up, and make my way out of Ivy Oaks.

There's a strange sensation lying low at the bottom of my stomach. Not dread, so much. Certainly not fear, I got rid of that long ago. No, it's more like the sense of an ending. The acceptance of what is to come. When a man's life begins to spiral out of control, he's forced to do everything in his power to right it. Effie is pulling my life away from its natural orbit, and I have to correct that path by any means necessary. She shouldn't have crossed me like this. She knows the consequences. After all, she's the only person in this world who knows what I did to my father.

CHAPTER THIRTY-FIVE

EFFIE

I order a room service breakfast and get into bed with David. I'm surprisingly ravenous, despite the knowledge I uncovered while speaking to Anna. After we eat, I lean back against the pillows, strangely serene. Then I check my bag for the envelope, just to make sure it's still there. I do this fairly often, making sure I still have those few things that Ben should have burned long ago. He didn't though, he allowed them to fall into my possession. Always underestimating me. His one mistake.

"Where did you go earlier?" David asks. I can tell he's broaching the subject carefully. He clearly wants me to tell him everything, but he's prepared to go slowly with me.

I take a deep breath. I didn't kill Robert, which means I can tell him everything. But do I want to? I'm not sure.

"I went to meet a maid. She was working here when I stayed in a suite at this hotel with Ben. We'd been in a suburb a lot like Ivy Oaks prior to this hotel, and Ben ended up blackmailing one of the neighbours—"

"Wow," he says. "You say that so casually."

"Well, that was our life. It was what he—we—did." I grab

the bed linen and work the fabric between my fingers, insecure all of a sudden. "Are you sure you want to know about all this?"

He nods. "I really do. I'm sorry for interrupting you."

"Okay, well, we came here because we needed to hide out and gather our thoughts before moving on." I push my fingernail into the cotton. "I'd just found out I was pregnant and I didn't want to play these games anymore."

David leans forward slightly, but he doesn't interrupt.

With one deep breath, I carry on speaking, and I don't stop until I reach the point where I'm in the hotel bathroom with blood on my hands after Robert's death. Somewhere in all this, David gets up from the bed and paces the length of the room, his hands balled into fists.

"We need to go to the police," he says. "That man cannot get away with this."

"But what about me?" I reply. "How am I going to explain my involvement in all this?"

"You didn't do anything." He pauses. "Don't you have the video?"

"Not yet."

"And we're on the same page here, right? Thinking that he pushed you both down the stairs?"

I remain very still, letting those words sink in. "I can't know for sure. Anna would have told me if it showed him doing that. She said we both fell, but... I don't know. I feel like... like he wanted the baby gone and was willing to do anything to get rid of it, including killing me."

David lets out a long breath. "Fucking hell."

"I know," I say. "Anna's going to send me the video. I gave her a payment."

"What payment? Something that can be tracked? Effie—"

I hold my hands up. "Don't panic. I gave her my engagement ring."

His eyebrows raise. "Wow. That feels final."

I nod. "It is."

"What are you going to do when you get the video?"

"I don't know," I admit. "All I know is that I need to see him do it. I need to know for sure what he's done to me."

"Are you going to go to the police?" he asks.

"No." I say the word firmly, like I'm putting my foot down. "It's too big. It's too complicated. David, I've broken the law a hundred times since I met Ben and all of that will come spilling out."

"So, you'd rather save your own skin than put a murderer behind bars?" he asks.

"Yes," I say, ignoring the shame that creeps over my skin like a thousand ants. "Besides, it's not just me. I don't want to bring Anna into this. She broke the law too. She was barely more than a teenager. It's not fair on her."

"Like it or not, she's involved," he says.

I shake my head. "She's going to disappear and start a new life."

He glares at me.

"It's what she deserves for dealing with *him*."

David shakes his head in disbelief.

"This is it for me, now. This is my opportunity to get away from him. I finally know the truth about what happened to Robert Dinman. I know I'm not a killer. But Ben isn't going to let me go. Not without a fight."

"So now what?" David flops down on the bed. He looks exhausted and guilt floods through me.

"Now I leave. Just for a while. For long enough to figure out what I'm going to do next. I need to wait it out and let him get past this moment."

"Where?" David asks.

"I don't know. Maybe I should leave the country." I sigh. "Shit. I forgot my passport. Well, maybe I'll hide out on a Scottish island or something."

"Okay," David says. "But what about your finances? Does he have access to your bank accounts?"

I shake my head. "We only have one joint bank account. Most of my money is in my name. I have enough to last me for a long time."

"Jesus, Effie. How did you pull me into this?"

"Sorry." I reach out and rub his back. "But it's okay. You can go home. You can go back to your life and carry on like you never met me."

"Can I?" he says. "Or will your psycho husband torture me for information?"

"Torture is not his style. Threats, stalking and blackmail are more his thing."

"Oh, well, that's okay then," he says.

"Check your house for hidden cameras and microphones. Check your car for trackers. Keep your phone and laptop password protected. Don't give him any ammunition. I'll be his focus, but you're right, he may look to you as a way to get to me. I'm sorry, David. This is why I said those horrible things to you in the hospital. I thought it would end... us... But then I dragged you back into this because I needed someone. I hope you know how grateful I am you're here."

I lean back on the bed, exhausted. He strokes my forehead and hair. Then he kisses me.

"So, I guess it's time to leave here. You need to go somewhere far away from him. Shall I drive you to St Pancras?"

Tears well up, threatening to spill. "Yes."

"Have I got time for a shower?"

I nod my head.

He kisses me once more and makes his way through to the bathroom. I roll over on my side. As the water runs, sadness spreads through me. This will be the last time I see David. The one man I've told everything to. The one man I can trust. I'm letting him go because survival is more important and there's no way he could come with me. He has a daughter.

I'm resting on David's pillow when it begins to vibrate. He must have left his phone underneath. Almost instinctively, I reach under and pick it up. The notification on the front is a text message from someone called Billie. The message reads: *How's the story coming along? What have you learned about the con man and his wife?*

Electricity surges through me. I sit up straight. Story. Con man. Wife. *Fuck*. My heart sinks as the pieces fall into place. Oh, Effie, how could you be so stupid?

I don't want to read more, but also, I do. With the sound of water still running in the background, I tap in David's passcode, something I watched from over his shoulder and memorised long ago. I always do. It's a habit I can't switch off. His screen unlocks and I open his text message app. There are dozens of messages from Billie. I scroll through them and pick some out to read.

DAVID: *I think I have a better story than the pettiness at Ivy Oaks. This couple just moved in, and I'm pretty sure he's a con man. I recognise him from somewhere. Do you remember years ago there was that blog post that made its way around the paper? About the fake pharma CEO and how he scammed women out of money? The guy who claimed he was going to cure cancer. I think it's him!*

BILLIE: *That's a good angle. Try doing both for now. Ivy Oaks is notorious for weird pet deaths and arguments so it's still a good story. But find out what you can about this guy.*

DAVID: *I can always use the Ivy Oaks stuff for my Unusual History blog series.*

BILLIE: *Sounds good.*

There's more, but it's mostly the same. David gives his boss plenty of updates via text message, but none of them mention me. They certainly don't mention our relationship.

Before my heart breaks in two, I grab my bag and walk out of the room. I close the door quietly behind me, trying not to look back.

CHAPTER THIRTY-SIX

BEN

It's just past 6am when I buy a train ticket with cash. I walked here, not daring to get an Uber. It took me an hour and I stuck to side streets without cameras. I'm wearing glasses and a blonde wig. I've shaved away the stubble that usually defines my jawline and I'm wearing a baseball cap pulled down low. Even my clothes are different, from the old trainers on my feet to the puffer jacket making me sweat.

Even if I show up on CCTV, the police will have a hard time identifying me. As long as I keep my head down.

While I wait for the train, I log in to the station café's WiFi and check the messaging app on my laptop. I get the confirmation I needed, and I allow myself a small, triumphant smile for knowing my wife so well.

Anna: *She called me yesterday. I don't know what's going on though.*

I reply back: *What did you tell her?*

Anna: *Nothing, I swear!*

Ben: *Keep me in the loop. If you see her in the hotel, I want to know immediately.*

She doesn't respond to that. But if she knows what's good for her, she'll behave.

The train is ten minutes late and a spike of annoyance shoots up my spine. I can control everything in my life except for public transport, it seems. But coming this way was better than my car being identified leaving Ivy Oaks.

I have a loose end to tie.

The first step is buying a cheap second-hand car with cash and getting a new phone. The second is tracking down my wife, though I'm confident she will have now checked into the hotel to see Anna. What happens after that will be determined by Effie's behaviour, but I have some options in mind.

It has been a long time since I allowed myself to live this recklessly, to commit the kind of crimes I usually avoid. But they are not beneath me. I have no qualms going to these extreme lengths when they are necessary. Me first. Always.

The train finally arrives. I choose a seat next to the window and pretend to read a book. I don't want to run my laptop battery low and I don't have a phone to stare at. When the train gets into London, I disembark and make my way down into the tube. The wig and baseball cap are no good for the Beaumont Hotel. I ditch both, along with the jacket, and grab a pair of sunglasses from my back pocket. Half an hour later, I'm outside the hotel. There's a group of tourists heading inside, so I walk quickly alongside them, hurrying through to the bar. There I grab a seat and get out my laptop.

I send a message to Anna: *Is Effie here? Which room is she staying in?*

It's still early. I order a tea and try to look like a guest killing some time before checking out. But it's bothering me that Anna isn't responding. Fifteen minutes go by. I send a follow-up message.

Where are you? I need to see you.

When another ten minutes go by without a response, I slam the empty cup down on the saucer in frustration. I could walk around the hotel looking for Anna or Effie, but chances are I'll be noticed. And it's not like I can walk straight up to the reception desk and ask if my wife has checked in.

This time I try starting a video call with Anna. She cancels it. What the hell?

Heat spreads through my body. That confirms it. Anna has gone rogue. And now I'll never find out where she sent the CCTV footage, or what's going on with my wife in this hotel. I clench and unclench my fists, thinking.

All is not lost. I have a good view of the foyer from my seat. Maybe all I need to do is sit back and watch, and wait. Surely Effie will appear soon. It's just after ten. I wonder what her next move will be. Has she seen Anna? Does she know everything?

Obviously, there's a chance I won't see her. I could end up here all day, though I won't because I'll begin to attract attention eventually. But that's okay. I'll find another way to get to her. She'll never escape me. Not now that I know we're no longer on the same side.

One way or another, I'm going to win. It's just a matter of time.

CHAPTER THIRTY-SEVEN
DAVID

It comes as no surprise to me that Effie is gone when I come out of the shower. I can't imagine she's one for sentimental goodbyes. But I am surprised to see my phone in the centre of the bed, not under the pillow where I left it. When I pick it up I idly check my texts, I see there's a new message from my editor, Billie, asking about the piece. Shit. It's marked as read which means Effie got into my phone and saw it.

I slump down on the bed. She'd be half right about it all and I wish I could have told her before she walked out. The thought of her reading these texts before she left... It leaves a sour taste on my tongue.

I never worked in finance; I just tell people that out of habit. Even after I gave up investigative journalism, I suppose I couldn't stop thinking that there might be a story around the corner. And I've always uncovered more stories by being obtuse about what I do. The vaguer the better. Not many people ask questions about the financial sector. It's boring to ninety per cent of the country. And while David, my middle name, is the name I generally go by, my first name is Brian, and that's the name I've always used for my articles ever since I started.

When I moved to Ivy Oaks, which was for my daughter (that part was true), I did the same thing out of habit. Everything else is relatively true. I did retire from my profession early, though the vast majority of the money I live on came from my divorce, not my savings. Journalism doesn't pay that well.

I told Effie a lot of truths about my background, but I also left a lot out. My ex-wife, Rachel, was just as dirt-poor as me when we met at Sheffield University. We both lived on our student loans and overdraft. But Rachel was studying business, which proved to be much more useful than my English and journalism focus. During our engagement and the early years of our marriage, she set up a skincare company all on her own and we moved down to London. Sure, I helped a little. We lived on my income when I was copywriting. I kept the flat clean when she worked long hours and travelled the world to find the right distribution service for her product. And the business grew from strength to strength.

Rachel, my smart, hard-working wife, blossomed while I dried up. When she became worth millions, I, regrettably, struggled to cope with her success. When Lori came along, we got a nanny, Rachel cut back on her hours, and somehow, despite our mutual love for our daughter, it all fell apart. I did drink too much and cheat on my wife. I never lied to Effie about that. And Lori does go to school with Deepika's kids. All of that is true.

We moved out of London so that Lori could go to an excellent private school. Rachel has been running the business from Oxford for over a decade. But it was during this time everything fell apart for us as a couple. Soon I found myself needing somewhere else to live.

I'd heard the rumours about Ivy Oaks before I moved there. Lori told me about how her friend's mum, Deepika, was accused of killing a dog and then listed off all the strange goings-on Kally had told her about. Perhaps on a subconscious level I wondered if this warring neighbourhood would be a good story. Perhaps that factored into my decision to purchase a house there. But it wasn't until I saw a council meeting for myself that I became invested. The pettiness. The squabbling. The people relocating again so soon after moving in.

I joined the book club. I went to the leisure centre. I jogged up and down the street. I thought I might have a lead when I heard about Deepika's run-in with the dog that died and at that point I called my old editor, Billie, and mentioned it to her. She thought it might be an interesting article if I could find out who the pet killer was.

But I didn't know. There was no one I felt comfortable accusing of being an animal murderer. Many of them had motives. None of them left any clues. I'd all but given up when I saw Ben May moving into the house across the street.

At first, I thought I recognised him from TV or something. He has a daytime TV type of face. Handsome, but not striking enough to be a movie star. I folded away my recognition for a few days and I sat with it, letting it percolate beneath the surface. It wasn't until the barbecue, when he showed his teeth, that it hit me.

Years ago, while I was at *The Herald*, I'd come across a blog post about a man called Eric Lansdown. The post had been written by a young woman about twenty years old. She included a picture of herself next to this Eric, and the post was a warning to stay away from him. He'd chatted her up at a bar, taken her on a few dates, including one very expensive sushi restaurant, and then he began acting strangely. His lies about working for a top pharmaceutical company included the government blocking his cancer drug. They seized his assets, and he was homeless. He desperately needed money. She'd wire transfer him small sums, a few hundred here and there, until it added up to several thousand. And then nothing. He cut her off.

I'd tried to find Eric Lansdown, but I had no leads. She'd met him in Manchester, and he was apparently there for a conference. After their initial meeting, they'd met in other cities, including London, Leeds and Bristol. All of this made it impossible to track him down. The more I dug, the more elusive he was. Eric Lansdown was obviously a fake name.

I put out a call asking for more information about him. Another woman contacted me to say she'd met a Peter Flynn who'd done something similar. But then no one else came forward. I always suspected that there were dozens of young women out there, tricked by him. Maybe some of them saw my call but felt too embarrassed to come forward. All I know is that the story never got off the ground.

Until he walked into Ivy Oaks.

To my surprise, when I looked up Ben May, I realised he was using his real name in Ivy Oaks. As was his wife, Effie. His aliases seemed to be reserved for his earlier scams. I thought then that he might have changed his ways, but I still thought he deserved to be held accountable for what he did. I decided to keep an eye on him.

I watched him and his wife grow closer to the Morgans at number two. Ben always seemed to be isolating Sophie from her husband. He'd turn on the charm, smiling, nodding, listening. I followed him once, and I saw him bump into her. The slimy fuck was orchestrating "meet-cutes" with his neighbour to seduce her. All the while I felt powerless to stop it. All I could do was observe and research, try to form a story to expose his lies.

But there was Effie. Clever, acerbically funny, beautiful and sad. I met her before I even saw Ben and I liked her right away. Sarcastic with a sparkle in her eye. That "don't give a fuck" attitude which is damn sexy. When I looked her up online, I felt a sense of sadness wash over me. She was as bad as him. There were posts on model forums talking about how Effie used to cause chaos when she was a model. One girl had a breakdown because of the awful things Effie did. They were in it together, I thought. They tear people down. They love chaos.

I didn't want to believe it of her, and for that reason, I got to know her. Perhaps it was my bias, but deep down I was convinced she was different. But later, as she talked to me, opening up a little at a time, I realised how young she'd been when Ben swooped in and made her his pet. I realised she carried guilt from what she had done when she was a model. And it was clear that whatever scams she'd been running with Ben were starting to eat her alive. Sociopaths don't feel that much guilt. She was never as bad as him.

The more she told me, the worse it got. Until, finally, she told me about the baby. I wanted to tell her how this all started. How much I already knew. How despite it all I want to help her.

I toss the phone onto the bed and sigh. If I'd been honest with her, she might still be here. I was contemplating doing just that in the shower. She'd been so honest with me it was my turn to come clean. I wanted her to know there was another way that didn't include her running away, that we could take him down together. But I wasn't sure what would happen to her. She broke the law with him. Maybe she deserves to be punished too. My brain grappled with it all and I probably spent too long in there. But it's done now. Now she's gone. It's too late.

PART 2

NEWS AT TEN LOCAL NEWS REPORT

The daughter of supermodel Isabella Dupont has been reported missing. Thirty-year-old Euphemia May was last seen in London, where she was staying at the Beaumont Hotel with a friend. Metropolitan police have said they are concerned for the former model after she had been displaying erratic behaviour at home.

Euphemia, known as Effie May, was hurt in an accident in a sauna room just a week before her disappearance. Her husband, Ben, is deeply concerned for her safety. He spoke to Susannah Hart about this devastating time.

Susannah Hart: "Effie May has been missing for two weeks now, leaving her parents and husband desperate for answers. She was last seen exiting Coutts bank on the Strand in London. She is believed to have withdrawn enough cash to live on for several weeks."

Ben May: "I just want her to come home. She's the love of my life and the house is so cold and empty without her laugh."

Susannah Hart: "How have you found the police's response to your wife's disappearance?"

Ben May: "Underwhelming. It's like she disappeared into thin air after leaving that bank. There has to be something, some trace of her. With all the cameras in London, you'd think she'd be seen somewhere. I don't understand why the police haven't found anything. I feel like they might be looking in the wrong place. Like they're distracted or don't see my wife as a priority because of her wealthy background."

Susannah Hart: "What would you say to Effie if she is watching?"

Ben May: "That I love her and I just want her to be safe. Effie, please pick up the phone and call. Even if you don't want to come home, just let us know you're okay. Your parents and I miss you so much. We adore you and we just want what's best for you. If you need time, that's fine. But please tell us you're okay."

Susannah Hart: "Our hearts go out to the May and Fitzalan-Dupont family who are asking for privacy during this difficult time. Back to the studio."

CHAPTER THIRTY-EIGHT

DAVID

I grab a beer from the fridge, take it over to the window, and stand there, watching the house across the street. His lights are on so he's probably home. He's always home these days. The man barely does anything or goes anywhere. Knowing Ben May, he's bored out of his brains, but he knows what's good for him. He knows he needs to keep a low profile.

Where is Effie May? Did she get away or has he done something to her? She's been gone for over two weeks now. I've tried calling her but her number doesn't work. I've emailed her but she hasn't replied. I've tried every contact I've ever made as a journalist to see if I can get more information on Effie's whereabouts but there've been no sightings of her. She walked out of our hotel room, went to the bank, and then no one saw her again.

The last thing she did was read my phone and figure out who I am. I can't help but wonder if that influenced her decision to leave. If something happens to her, will it be my fault? She certainly seemed capable of staying one step ahead of her husband. Effie is someone who can hold her own. I have to believe she's OK. In my emails to her I've tried to explain everything. I've been completely honest about who I am and what I was doing. But I think it's too little too late.

I sip my beer. He's watching me. I don't know how I know it. I just do. It's the prickle at the nape of my neck, the identification of a predator, something primal. He has been watching me since Effie's disappearance. He searches my face for clues every time I see him on the street. We don't make small talk. We don't interact at all. We pretend we don't know the game we're both playing.

I step away from the window and walk around the house. The daily inspection. I remember what Effie said to me in that hotel room. He installs cameras into his victim's homes so that he can watch them. He thrives on the power. I've found three so far. Every time I find them, I wordlessly deactivate them and throw them away. I believe Ben has given up breaking into my house to try and spy on me, but I still check just in case. I won't be blackmailed by him.

No doubt he's trying to dig up dirt on me too. He must know I used to be a journalist. Perhaps he's found my call for information about him, though I took great pains to scrub that from the internet. But there's always a trail on the internet. Nothing goes completely away. I know that.

I don't dare keep any notes on my laptop. Instead, I handwrite them and place them in a locked security box in a locked desk drawer. Maybe it's overkill but I'm not taking any chances. Perhaps I should report the times he broke into my house—I once caught him on a security camera—but I'd hate for him to only ever receive justice for breaking and entering. He needs to go down for murder.

Potentially more than one. As much as I don't want to think it, I do have a bad feeling about Effie's disappearance. She hasn't contacted me once. And I feel like she would have.

I can't shake the feeling that he's done something to her. Every time I see his face on a BBC article about Effie's disappearance, or a local TV news segment, I see the evil lurking behind his eyes. But then again, I did lie to Effie. Why would she want to contact me? She's not the kind of woman to put her trust in a liar, not after so many years being married to a man like Ben May. I'm probably deluded.

Still, Ben needs taking down, and if Effie won't do it, I will. I'm going to finish what she started. I'm gathering together a dossier of evidence. Everything I know about Ben May and his crimes. First, I went to see Sophie, because she told the police that Ben had been to see her on the day Effie disappeared. Sophie admitted they were having an affair, and then two days later, she and Lewis moved out of Ivy Oaks. It was, frankly, bizarre. Their house isn't even sold yet. My guess is that Ben blackmailed Sophie into admitting the affair to provide him with an alibi, and then she fled Ivy Oaks to protect herself and Lewis. And why would he need an alibi? It's one of the strongest reasons I believe Ben has hurt Effie in some way.

Sophie and Lewis left without a trace, but yesterday, I may have made a breakthrough. And it came from my daughter of all people. Lori mentioned in passing that Kally had talked about her mum visiting Sophie. Deepika and Sophie are still in touch. Now I just need to get Deepika to spill.

I'm about to wander back to the kitchen window when I hear the letterbox rattle. I take a last swig, toss the beer bottle into the recycling and make my way over to the door.

There's an envelope sitting on the doormat, upside down, the same shape and size as a regular household bill. As I approach, I can see there's no return address on the back. I pull out the contents and my heart soars. A written note from

Effie. I read it again and again, clasping the piece of paper that she has held. She's okay. I am smiling.

And then my attention turns to what else is inside. Hurrying back into the kitchen—but remembering to shut the curtains first—I dump it all onto the table, spreading everything out. There's a photograph, a longer written letter and a train ticket. The photograph catches my attention first. A dour little boy stands in front of a stern man and a thin woman. No one in the photograph looks particularly happy, even though the mother is attempting a smile. Behind them I can just make out the shape of some sort of sports car. An expensive one. I'm not a car aficionado, but I'm pretty sure that's an MG logo.

But what's more important is the fact that the boy is almost certainly Ben May.

The train ticket is from December 2002, from London to Pewsey. There must be a connection between these three things. Lastly, I read the long letter.

Dear Mother,

The deed will soon be done, and I hope you know that all of this is your fault. If you'd believed me when I told you what he did, then I wouldn't have been forced to stoop to this level. But as Father grows older, he becomes even meaner. I'll be damned if I'm going to be the son of the man who kills his wife. This is better. Cleaner. I've sorted it for you because you couldn't do it for yourself or even me.

Do you even remember what I said to you all those years ago? I told you what he did. And you said I was imagining it. I still remember the expression on your face. It was disgust. It wasn't disbelief or annoyance, but disgust. In that moment I knew you'd never want to face up to it. Doing that would mean you'd have to acknowledge your own failings, and we both know that would never happen.

I hope Father is dead when you read this. I certainly laid out a plan in the hope of killing him. There, I said it. You're welcome, by the way.

Now I have to try not to become him. It's there, though, you know, always beneath the surface.

Perhaps I'll make do with my games. They really do seem to keep me in check. Each time I adapt to whatever challenge I face. It's thrilling. I learned from the best, Mother, because we both know you're rather skilled at manipulation.

You know, as I write this letter, I realise I can't send it. However, saying these words is bringing me the most wonderful sense of catharsis. Perhaps in the future when you're on your deathbed, I'll give this to you, so you know the way I felt on the day I killed Father for you.

Your loving son,
Ben

I put the letter down as my legs give way and drop into a chair. Fuck.

EMAIL FROM DAVID HOLT TO EFFIE MAY

Effie, I know you read my messages, which means you know I used to be a journalist. And you must know that I was working on a piece about Ivy Oaks when I recognised Ben May.

I just need you to know that I'm sorry and I want to tell you my side of everything.

First of all, I hate the way you found out. I was going to tell you, but I needed to find the right moment. And secondly, not everything I said and did while we were together was a lie.

I did, and still do, want to take Ben May down. And I have to admit that at first, it seemed that you were as bad as him. But once I got to know you, I began to understand everything. What first struck me was the heavy weight of guilt you carry every single day.

Before you left the hotel you insinuated that you only care about yourself. That isn't true. I think you want to atone for what you've done.

And, yes, I'm sure if you were here with me you'd give me one of your wry smiles and tell me I'm overestimating you, that I think you're a fragile little bird who needs taking care of. You're wrong. I don't want to fix you. I want you to do that yourself because you're quite capable of it.

Wherever you are, I needed you to know that.

I know you probably won't reach out to me, but I'm always here when you need me.

David

Written Note from Effie May to David Holt

Okay, fine, there's a redemption arc. The contents of this envelope tell you exactly what kind of man Ben is and I'm sure you'll figure out what to do with it.

Remember our talk at the Beaumont, before I found out who you really are? You need the video we discussed. Find the maid. She has it.

Most importantly, don't come looking for me. You know I'm not one to be saved.

Don't let him win the game, David. I don't like losing. —E

CHAPTER THIRTY-NINE

DAVID

Ben May killed his father.

I frown, staring at the letter. Would this be enough proof for a conviction? It's a confession, but how could anyone validate it as Ben May's confession? I look at the envelope which held this treasure trove and check the postmark. It's from York. Effie won't be there anymore, I'm sure of that much.

Even though I've already checked the house for cameras, paranoia spreads across my skin like goosepimples. I collect up the evidence and take it through to my desk, locking it away in the box with the rest of my notes on Ben May's crimes.

When I first contacted Billie about the potential story, I researched both Effie's and Ben's parents. Effie's mother lives in Rome while her barrister father continues to practise law in London. Through the grapevine, I heard Isabella Dupont was a bit of a diva. Someone with exacting standards who didn't like it when her daughter failed to be a superstar. And a friend who's a lawyer told me Graham Fitzalan is a ruthless, amoral man hated by the majority of practising solicitors and barristers who cross paths with him.

Ben's father, Nicholas May, owned a successful haulage company before he died. I've done my research into the "accident". The accident took place three miles away from the Mays' stately home. His father was driving his vintage MG around the country roads as he did every Sunday, only this time the brakes failed, and the car tumbled down a steep cliff into a patch of forest. It was not a sudden death. He was trapped under the car for several hours, slowly dying of blood loss. According to the news report, Ben was at his place of work in London, clocking in some extra time on a Sunday. Or establishing an alibi.

This train ticket shows that someone travelled from Paddington to Pewsey the day before Nicholas May died. It has to be Ben's ticket, but how could I prove it? There's no way anyone would remember him on the train from twenty years ago. Effie has sent me this evidence but it just isn't enough. I sigh.

A few years later, Ben's mother died of cancer and he inherited everything his parents owned. He became rich overnight, and yet it wasn't enough for him. There are people all over the world whose circumstances would vastly change if they inherited this money. But Ben was quite happy to fritter it all away. The man is a vampire. He's evil incarnate. He must be stopped.

I'm not sure what I'm going to do with this latest development. While I consider it, I decide to carry on with the plan I had in mind. I need to track down Sophie first.

After all, she is Ben's latest victim, and she chose to disappear for a reason. It's time to talk to Deepika.

To say Deepika has never liked me would be an understatement. The problem with being a journalist is that you can occasionally give off what others would call a "bad vibe". Intuitive people like Deepika sense my motives aren't always pure. And they would be right, because I'm always looking for a good story, even when I don't realise it.

Most of the residents of Ivy Oaks don't like me, but they don't know why. I'm also a single man who keeps to himself and rarely dates, that's always a red flag. Though the reason I haven't dated much is because of Lori, not because I don't want to. Effie got under my skin. I wasn't expecting that.

I find Deepika smoking a cigarette in her front garden while the kids are at school. She hides it behind her back when I approach.

"Don't tell Aaron," she says, with a sheepish grin.

I laugh. "Your secret's safe with me." I'm about to keep walking, not sure if now is the right time to talk, but then I change my mind and wander over to her wall. "Can I ask you something?"

She nods.

"Don't mention this to anyone else, though. I'd hate for it to run around the neighbourhood." I pause. "Do you think it's odd that Sophie and Lewis moved out so quickly after Effie disappeared?"

There's a change in Deepika's demeanour. It always happens when Effie is mentioned in her presence. I think she re-lives the sauna moment. I know after their shared trauma in the leisure centre, Effie's disappearance affected her more than she'd be willing to admit.

"They couldn't stay though, could they? Not after Sophie had an affair with Ben."

"But it was so fast," I say. "And it's weird Lewis even wanted to stay with her after that."

She shrugs. "I guess they didn't want to throw the marriage away." She takes a slow drag of her cigarette and exhales. "And what about you? People talk, you know. Some say you did the same thing as Sophie did, admitted to your affair with Effie during the police investigation."

I nod. "I did. Effie and I were together."

"Wow," she says. "I didn't expect you to be so honest." She pulls in some smoke. "So, what do you think happened to her?"

My eyes drift over to house number one.

"You think he's hurt her?"

"Honestly, I don't know what to think," I admit. "I don't trust him though. And I don't trust that alibi Sophie gave him the night she disappeared."

"Me neither," Deepika says.

So, Sophie did provide him with an alibi, I knew it.

"The police never found out who blocked the sauna door," she continues. "And then less than two weeks later, one of us goes missing. That's weird. The only person with a motive is her husband." She steps towards me, lowering her voice. "If she dies, he'll inherit Effie's money, won't he? Maybe that's enough motivation for him. Maybe the affair was a distraction?"

"Do you know where Sophie is?" I ask. "I want to talk to her."

She nods. "She left me a forwarding address. But she won't be happy about me passing it on."

"I get that, but this is important. I think you're right about Ben May. And I think you're right about the alibi."

She grabs her phone from her pocket. "Good luck getting

anything out of her. That girl is tight-lipped. Here. I typed her address into my phone."

She holds it out and I copy the address into the notes app on my phone.

"Thanks," I say.

"Let me know what you uncover," Deepika says, her eyebrows raised.

"I will."

I walk away. And as I make my way back to my house, the familiar prickle runs across the back of my neck. I look up. Ben May stands in the window, watching.

CHAPTER FORTY

BEN

How many favours do you have to call in to catch a wife? Effie has successfully melted away somewhere. First, she slipped out of the Beaumont without me noticing—though I'm not sure how, perhaps she took a back exit—and then she somehow evaded the police as she withdrew money from her private bank.

But I'm working on it. I have friends in horrible places that can do things the police can't.

As I'm watching Brian David Holt, a pathetic excuse for a journalist, walk back to his sad little bachelor house, my phone rings. I sigh and reluctantly hit accept.

"It's Graham," he says tersely. My father-in-law still hasn't figured out that his name appears on the screen when he calls, not that he calls often. "Is there any news?"

"Nothing. Like I said, I'll be in touch as soon as I hear anything."

"It's fucking preposterous," he snaps. "Listen, pay attention to everything you hear from the police, won't you. If there's any chance to take them to court, I will. And what are you doing?"

"I have things I'm looking into," I say.

"But you're not doing that now?"

"Not right now, no," I say. "I'm at home. The police are watching me as well, you know."

"I thought you had an alibi? A rather unfortunate one."

He's referring to the fact Sophie covered for me, revealing our affair. "I do, but they're still wasting their time coming to the wrong conclusions about the husband as they usually do."

"Ah yes. Well, I suppose they always have to check the husband," he says stiffly. "Your house in Oxford. Could you give me the address again? I can never keep up with the two of you moving around all the time. It's most peculiar."

I reel off the address.

"Ivy Oaks, how strange," he says.

"Why?"

"Oh, nothing. I just had a to-do with an old institution in the same location. It's nothing of interest," he says.

"Right, okay," I say, bored of this entire conversation.

"What are the police focusing on now?" he asks. "Did they investigate the neighbour from across the street? The one she was in the hotel with?"

"Yes. But he was seen leaving without her. And he came straight home. So, unless she's still in the hotel somewhere, he had nothing to do with it."

"Unless he went back," Graham suggests. "And moved her."

"That's highly unlikely."

I listen without interest as Effie's father spouts various other conspiracy theories about what happened to his daughter. It's all delivered in an unemotional tone, and his one moment of distress comes from when he considers the "family name". I'm not one to judge a man on his morals, but even I'm impressed by his lack of feelings.

He finally hangs up, and I walk back over to the window. So far David has found every camera I've hidden in his house, and I've failed to find any evidence of Effie contacting him. I had hoped he'd be a helping hand to finding my wife. But I underestimated her again. She's too smart for that. She obviously warned him about my tactics.

It's time to regroup. To put my plans into action. Effie isn't the only person I need to track down. There's Anna and her pesky security guard ex. Seeing as Effie was at the Beaumont the day she disappeared, I'm sure they're involved in this somehow. And anyway, I need to track down the video from that night in the Beaumont. I don't care which one of them has it, the maid or the security guard, but whichever one it is is in trouble. I will find them and silence them.

CHAPTER FORTY-ONE

DAVID

I'm parked outside a regular semidetached house. It's in a nice neighbourhood, but nowhere near as fancy as Ivy Oaks. There's no security gate, no perfectly pruned rose bushes, and no leisure centre. Just a road with a few cars parked outside their houses, and attractive matching porches with stained glass windows.

A man steps out of the house, and I duck down. He doesn't see me. He gets in his Volvo and drives away. I've been sitting here waiting for Lewis to go to work, and finally, he's gone. I wait a few minutes, to be sure he doesn't return, and then I exit my car and walk over to the house. My heart is racing.

Sophie's jaw drops when she answers the door. Then her eyebrows bunch together, and I can see she's annoyed.

"I made Deepika promise," she says.

"I know. I forced it out of her," I reply.

She lets out a *pfft* noise. "No one can force Deeps to do anything. Why are you here, David?"

"We need to talk about Ben May."

She immediately pales. I see her intention to close the door in my face before she pushes it, and I jam my foot over the threshold.

"Sophie, I know that on the day Effie disappeared, you claimed Ben was with you in Ivy Oaks. But I don't think that's true, is it?"

She glances away.

I press. "What does he have on you? Is he blackmailing you? If you tell me, I can help you."

Her eyes fill with tears. She pushes the door hard against my foot, but I hold steady.

"Go away," she says. "I don't want to do this. I can't."

"Yes, you can."

She places her head in her hands, letting go of the door. Then she backs away, and I take that as a sign that she's letting me in. Slowly, I close the door behind me and follow her through to the kitchen. Still crying, she leans against the counter.

"Jesus, Sophie. What did he do to you?" Her tears make me feel like an inconsiderate oaf standing there, not sure whether to pat her shoulder or pass her tissues.

Sophie wipes her eyes and straightens her spine. "I can't tell you." She shakes her head. "You shouldn't be here. He could be..."

"Watching?" I suggest.

I see the shiver run through her. She wraps her arms around her body. It's only then that I see how thin she is. Even the perfectly applied make-up fails to hide dark shadows beneath her eyes.

"I know a little something about Ben May and the methods he employs," I tell her. "So far, I've found three cameras in my own house. Do you want me to check for you? I know what to look for. I've researched it."

She nods eagerly. "We check too. But I keep worrying I've missed something."

We spend the next hour systematically going through her house checking for anything unusual. I show her pictures online of the kinds of spy equipment Ben might use. We unscrew light fittings and replace them. And at the end of it all, we find nothing.

"I doubt he knows where you are," I say, back in the kitchen.

Sophie flicks the button on the kettle and watches the water heat.

"But regularly check your car for any tracking devices," I say. "Does he know where Lewis works?"

Sophie pours out the tea. "Not anymore. Lewis has a new job. He lost his old one. Ben stole money from us, and he gave Lewis terrible financial advice that led to him being demoted. He was so embarrassed he found a position elsewhere. We're lucky he wasn't fired. Getting a new job after that would have been a problem."

Now I understand the house downgrade. She walks over with two mugs of tea, and I accept one, placing mine on a wicker coaster.

"I have to ask, Sophie. Why haven't you been to the police about Ben?"

She pales again. "He has videos." Her fingers tighten around the scalding mug of tea.

"A sex tape?" I ask.

She nods her head quickly. "He has so many. Not just of me and... him, but me and Lewis too. He says he's going to release them everywhere. Send them to my family, friends, upload them to revenge porn sites, send them to Lewis's place of work, his family... It's... it's horrible." Her hands are shaking. "I know it's just... bodies. I know we're only doing things other people do. I mean... celebrities have these things leaked, don't they? And it's horrible but people move on afterwards. I just can't face the humiliation. I know my circles. I'll be shunned. My dad... well, he'd be devastated."

"I understand," I say. "No one wants this."

"There's more," Sophie says. Her eyes drop down to her hands. "I'm pregnant. And it's his."

I blow out a long breath. "Oh, Sophie, that's... I don't know what to say."

"There's nothing to say," she replies. "It is what it is. I've wanted a baby for so long. Lewis and I have tried for years. And then *he* comes along and... I wanted it, but I didn't want it like this." Her right hand slips down to her stomach. "But it isn't the baby's fault, is it? She, or he, deserves to live."

I shake my head and sip the hot tea. "My God, what a mess. Effie discovered something harmful about Ben before she disappeared. I won't tell you what because I don't want to put you in any more danger than what you already—"

"Tell me," she says. Her expression hardens. "If my family is in danger then I need to get us away from here."

I contemplate this for a moment. But there seems no reason not to tell her, as long as I keep it vague. "Effie found evidence that Ben killed a man."

Her hand flies to her mouth. "What?"

"It's worse than that. He made Effie think she was responsible and he..." I rub my chin. I don't want to tell her the worst part but she needs to take this seriously. "Ben found out Effie was pregnant and gave her drugs to try and create a miscarriage. When that didn't work... we believe he pushed her down the stairs."

She drops her head into her hands. "He's deranged." Trembling, she straightens her back and picks up her mug. Her eyes have the faraway look of someone lost in thought.

"And now he's killed her. Hasn't he? And now he'll be coming for me. I should get Lewis and go. It's the only way. I'm sorry, David, I definitely can't help you now."

"I don't know what's happened to Effie but if you recant your alibi, he might end up in prison. He can't do anything to you from prison."

"He can still release the videos of me," she says. "I'm sorry. I know it's selfish. I liked Effie until I realised she was in on his schemes." She wipes tears from her cheeks, her hands flicking angrily across her translucent skin. "She knew who he was, what he was capable of."

"She did," I say. "But she wasn't like him. She made some horrible mistakes, but for a lot of it she was under his influence. He's a master manipulator."

Sophie nods. "I can understand that. He's a monster." She screws her eyes tightly shut. "I want to help, but I don't know if I can. What if I go to prison myself?"

"I can't know for sure. But it seems unlikely to me. You were being blackmailed by a murderer. I can't imagine a judge demanding you serve time."

She shivers and pulls her cardigan more tightly around her shoulders. I decide to call it a day because she grows even more upset. Sophie is a good person, and she doesn't deserve this.

"Think about it," I say. "That's all I'm asking. You can call me anytime. Okay?"

Her gaze trails out of the window. "I'll think about it." When she turns back to me there's a flash of anger in her eyes. "I hate him so much it scares me sometimes. It kills me that he has so much power over me."

"I can't even begin to understand how that feels," I say.

She nods. "No, I suppose not. But I'm not the only one, am I? There must be so many others who feel this way." She shakes her head. "I'm sorry, David, I think you should go. But I will consider what we've talked about."

I thank her for talking to me and make my way out. If I'm not mistaken, there was steel in her voice. Sophie is much stronger than she lets on.

CHAPTER FORTY-TWO
BEN

I've been cautious up to now, letting a few of my contacts put out feelers for Effie's whereabouts. But that was when I felt the police weren't buying my alibi. The longer they investigate, the more they lean towards the idea that Effie just wanted to get away. They're stretched, and the press haven't jumped on this story as I thought they might, what with Effie being the daughter of Isabella. Aside from a short interview I gave with local news reporters, the fact that Effie is rich and privileged and probably fine means the public soon lost interest.

The kid leaving a scruffy terraced house in Oldham has a neck tattoo and a shaved head. I never forget a face, but I would've struggled to place him had I not followed him here. Stephen Foggarty, the security guard. The bastard who may be blackmailing me.

I watch him get into a scratched-up Nissan and leave. Since I found him, I've learned that Stephen still works as a security guard for a supermarket three miles away. He's about to start a long shift, giving me plenty of time to poke around his house.

I'm in the second-hand car I bought on the day I was last at the Beaumont Hotel, the one I intended to stuff Effie into. I've been keeping it in a garage just outside Oxford. It's an old Volvo, the kind with a huge boot. It's also dented enough to not look out of place on this street.

I climb out, grab my bag of tools, and make my way over to the house, slipping down the alleyway between Stephen's house and his neighbour's. Then I make my way into the garden at the back of the property. This is the tricky part. It's early morning and still dark, but this is a built-up area with plenty of neighbours around to see me breaking and entering.

A quick glance around the area doesn't reveal any faces peering through net curtains. So, I pull on a ski mask and approach the back door, listening carefully. From what I've seen, Stephen doesn't live with anyone, but this entire operation has been rushed. The house is quiet. I run a gloved finger down the UPVC door. I try the handle just in case. It's locked.

I grab the crowbar from the bag and get to work. It's louder than I'd prefer but not as bad as smashing the window. I work on the frame, hammering the crowbar into place and then wrenching it as hard as I can. Sweat gathers beneath my ski mask. There's a crack, and the door opens. I swing it into the kitchen and walk in.

There's no time to waste. I'm here to grab his laptop, install a few cameras and get out. But almost as soon as I'm in the property, there's a low growl coming from behind me.

Fuck.

Stephen has a dog. I turn around slowly, to see the mutt snarling at me, its hackles raised. A big dog, too. A mongrel most probably, but I can't be sure. I pull off the ski mask, deciding to try out the easy solution first. I crouch down to the dog's height.

"Hey boy." I hold out a hand. "Are you a good boy? I bet you are a good boy, aren't you?"

The dog regards me carefully, its head moving one way then the other. One ear twitches as he weighs me up. My eyes roam across the room searching for some sort of dog toy. There's a chewed-up, saliva-darkened teddy. I grab it and throw the thing across the room. The dog bounds away, happy as Larry. I shake my head and get back to work.

For the next ten minutes, the dog, who I've now named Larry, returns with his toy, wagging his tail happily. I throw it, watch the dumb dog chase it, and install another camera to keep tabs on Stephen. Then I grab his laptop, every USB stick I can find inside a messy desk, wire some listening devices into a few strategic places and leave. The one thing I don't have is his phone, but hopefully there's a way into a back-up programme through the laptop. If this yields nothing, then I'm on to Anna next. Or maybe Effie if I get any leads.

Larry sits on the doorstep whining as I leave. Stupid dog. And then my phone starts to ring on the way back to the Volvo.

"Make it quick," I say.

"I think I found the taxi driver," comes the reply.

"Tell me what you know."

I smile to myself. I'm closing in on Effie at last.

CHAPTER FORTY-THREE

DAVID

Calling up the Beaumont Hotel manager and asking for Anna's surname and address isn't going to work. There's no way in hell I'm going to sound like anything other than a creepy stalker guy. I decide to take a different approach. I drive down to the last place I saw Effie alive and check into the hotel. Then I spend a few days there as a guest. I read my book in the lobby, have a drink or two in the bar. What I'm actually doing is watching when the shifts end for staff members.

It's Friday night, and there's a little more buzz amongst the receptionists. At about ten, there's an obvious shift change, and I casually follow the finished workers out of the hotel. Just as I thought, three or four head to a pub nearby. I go into the same pub, and I order a drink. I don't sit too close to them, instead I hover over at the bar and pretend I'm lost in my own thoughts.

Just before last orders, one of the receptionists orders a glass of white wine at the bar and looks at me strangely.

"Aren't you a guest at the Beaumont?" she asks.

I smile. "Guilty."

"Guests don't usually come in here," she says, not suspiciously, more like she's impressed.

"It looked like it had decent atmosphere." I extend a hand. "I'm David by the way."

"Jamelia," she replies.

She stays after the handshake, sipping her wine. "Some of the staff fancy you." Her eyes twinkle. She's tipsy, but in a cute way.

I laugh. "Really?"

She nods, laughing into her wine glass. "You pass the vibe check, David. You kept eye contact with all of us, and you said please and thank you for everything."

"Isn't that common decency?" I ask.

"Yes," she says. "But you'd be surprised how few people have it." She shakes her head slightly and glances towards her table.

She's about to leave, sensing she's overstepped, and I don't want her to do that.

"Can I ask a favour, Jamelia?" I say.

"Sure," she replies. "Unless it's late checkout because I don't have my computer." She mimes using a computer and then giggles.

"It's actually kinda serious," I say, rearranging my features to something I hope is sombre.

Jamelia climbs up onto a bar stool and places her wine glass on the bar. "Oh no. What's happened?"

"It's my younger brother. He got involved with a maid at your hotel and she... well, she stole some money from him. He doesn't care about the money. He's more concerned about her welfare. She disappeared, you see. She has some problems with drugs, and he's concerned about her. I stayed here for a couple of days to see if I could find her, but I can't exactly ask any of you probing questions about a young woman, can I? I'd look like a creep."

"Oh, my God, are you talking about Anna Hennessy?"

"Yes!" I say, widening my eyes. I hadn't expected it to be this easy.

"I do not know how she managed to keep her job for so long because that girl was messy. There were rumours about her sleeping with hotel guests. She definitely slept with someone on the security team. And a few months back she started to act really weirdly." Jamelia leans towards me, lowering her voice. "She didn't turn up for a few shifts and her work got really sloppy. She got very thin and always looked very tired."

"Hmm yeah, that fits with what my brother said. Do you know what happened to her?"

Jamelia shakes her head. "She's gone. She left without giving notice just over three weeks ago. The hotel manager even went to her flat to ask if she was coming in, but all her stuff was gone. She didn't have a lot of friends around here, honestly. But I chatted up her ex a little. He said she didn't say a word to him before she left. Though he did mention she would send money to her mum. Her mum was pretty sick apparently, maybe she went to stay with her? She still should've handed in her notice though. Selfish bitch. She left us in a right mess. We had customers complaining because their rooms weren't ready on time."

"Sounds like I need to find her mum," I say.

Back at Ivy Oaks, I get to work figuring out where Anna's mother lives.

It takes a lot of poking around on social media to work out

what Anna looks like. Anna is smart enough to have deleted all of her social media accounts. But I do find one photograph of her on a Beaumont Hotel blog post. Someone posted a photo of her posing with a bartender at the staff Christmas party. The caption reads *Anna Hennessy, maid extraordinaire, with Sam Harris, master mixer*. Finally, I know what she looks like. Then I have to trawl through the many Facebook accounts for women between the ages of forty and sixty with the last name Hennessy.

Sandra Hennessy's account is set to private, but a few details, like her profile picture, banner photo and profession, are all public. Sandra is retired, due to illness, it says. Then at the side of the banner photo, I see Anna. Bingo.

I use an AI composite photo of a woman in her fifties and call her Carol. Then I set up a profile and add a few friends in my pretend age group. I need more photos, so I use stock images. They can't be too well done. An off-kilter sunset. I crop the pictures to make them seem more natural. Then I share a lot of memes. When my profile is ready, I send Sandra a friend request. As soon as she accepts, I go through her friend list and add a few of them as friends. Not too many, I don't want to arouse suspicion. Then I check out Sandra's groups and add the ones that seem important. *Dronfield school survivors '86*.

A few days later, I send Sandra a message asking her if she was in my year at school. I mention how I'm looking for an old friend. By this point, I've spent a lot of time scrolling through the school group, internalising as much information as I can about the teachers and the school itself. She doesn't suspect a thing when I complain about Mr Johnson the science teacher and his explosive rages, or the pink custard in the cafeteria.

And then she says: *All the kids on the Fielding estate got treated badly by him. He was a snob, that man. We all thought so.*

You're right, I reply. *I never liked him because of that. I ended up moving to London for a while though. What about you? Are you in the same area or did you move?*

I still live here, she says. *And my health isn't too good these days.*

I'm so sorry, I say as Carol.

We continue chatting for a while, but now I have a lead. Now I know where to go next.

CHAPTER FORTY-FOUR

BEN

Stephen Foggarty is not the man I'm looking for. His laptop is clean. I check through the entire thing, sifting through hazy nightclub selfies, a sea of "tattoo inspo" pictures and many more intimate photos of himself that I assume he sends to prospective lovers. If this generation continues the way it's going, I'll have no one left to blackmail. These twenty-year-olds give away their nudes to each other for free.

I'm able to check his phone files on the back-up that links to his laptop. There's nothing. The USB sticks are mostly old college files and some attempts at graphic design.

I'm pretty sure this guy knows nothing, but I'll keep an eye on the devices I set up just in case. But in terms of his laptop, I'm able to toss the thing out after a couple of hours. There's a chance I destroyed it before he even realised it was missing.

This confirms that Anna is working alone. I just need to figure out where she is, because she's no longer at the Beaumont.

I pull the Volvo into a multistorey before walking another

thirty minutes with my head down, dropping a jacket and hat on the way to meet my contact. If I do end up a suspect at some point down the line, I don't particularly want there to be a trail of CCTV camera footage from the car park to the location.

Once I'm there, I check the address on my phone and enter the café I agreed to meet them in. Dominic nods to me on his way out, saying nothing. At the back, seated in a booth, is the man I want to speak to.

Dominic is someone I met at a poker game who turned out to be well connected in the criminal world. And, no, I didn't borrow money from him, I loaned *him* money back when there was more of it available to me. I sized him up as someone useful to have in my pocket. And now he's repaying me.

The taxi driver is older, probably in his late fifties judging by the grey hair and laugh lines, and sits low in his seat, practically huddled down. He regards me with a wary expression.

"Hello," I say. "Thank you for meeting me. Has Dominic ordered you a drink?"

"Yes," he says.

"Good."

"I don't want any trouble," he says. "I told your friend that."

"There's no trouble here." I flash him my best smile before pulling a photograph from my jeans pocket. It's Effie, taken three years ago. I removed it from a photo frame to carry around like I'm a caring husband. "I think you might have seen this woman about two weeks ago."

He nods. "Your friend says she's missing. I'm sorry about that. I don't watch the news or I would have gone to the police."

He's lying, I think. I wonder what Effie paid him to keep

silent. "Actually, I'd rather you didn't say anything to the police. The thing is I'm her husband and I'm concerned about her. She's not in her right mind and I think the police approaching her would just scare her away. My wife is well-off and she can live by her own means for a long time."

He nods. "She paid me a lot of cash that day."

I tilt my head, interested. "And where did you take her?" The man is hesitant so I press harder. "Like I said, my wife is well-off. But so am I, and I'm willing to pay you even more than what she gave you that day."

He pulls in a deep breath. He's ready to tell me everything.

CHAPTER FORTY-FIVE

EFFIE

I'm tired of letting my husband win. I'm tired of letting anyone win. From now on, there's no one I care about other than myself. The game is about to end, and I intend to be on top.

The pain took me by surprise. I never expected David's lies to pierce the armour I've been wearing all these years. But after he coaxed out so much honesty from me, the fact I wasn't awarded the same from him really hurt.

Returning to the Beaumont revealed lots of truths. Not least the truth that my own husband is prepared to kill me. Anna has no evidence of me pushing Robert Dinman down the stairs. I'm not the murderer I thought I was. The thought is freeing. But how did we both fall? I think I know. I think my husband is perfectly capable of killing me.

I was on edge as I left the Beaumont, checking over my shoulder at all times. Even with a hat pulled down low I felt eyes watching me. But I left the hotel through the kitchen and went down a back alley. There I made my way through the city, taking as many side streets as I could, until I reached Coutts bank.

I have an account there and I needed a lot of money. Most banks can't handle that without warning, but Coutts is a private bank with exclusive clients who handle large sums on the regular.

After my handbag was stuffed full with as much cash as I could carry, I ditched both of the trackable phones and bought a cheap one. Next, I needed somewhere to stay. Really, what I needed was to leave the country, but I didn't get a chance to grab my passport.

My heart was pounding as I made my way through London. With cameras on almost every street, I ducked down alleys, made my way down side streets, and slipped in and out of groups of people. I ditched the hat and my coat, tying my hair back and putting on sunglasses. I need new clothes, but heading into a store would get me on camera.

Somewhere near Hyde Park, I flagged down a taxi. It was about the only place I could think that might allow me to slip away without the taxi showing up on CCTV. With there being fewer shops and plenty of wide-open space, I had a chance.

"Can you drive me to the north?" I asked him.

"North London?"

"No, the north of England. Off the books."

"What are you on, lady?" he snapped, shaking his head.

I pulled out a wad of cash.

He sighed. "You'd best not get me in any trouble."

I shook my head. "You'll be fine. I need to get away from my husband, that's all."

He put the taxi in gear and I sank back in my seat. It was a start. Everything I was doing helped keep me one step ahead of Ben, but for how long?

The countryside opened up around me, as I left the city behind. Ben couldn't possibly know where I was, and yet I made up impossible scenarios in my head. Ben was in the red car behind us. Ben knew the taxi driver and had found a way to follow us. Ben was omnipotent, floating above us, watching my every move.

Three hours later, I checked into a small B&B in Whitby. I asked the taxi driver where was nice, and he chose here. The room was small, overlooking the sea. I had no luggage. No change of clothes. Nothing but a bag full of money and an expensive wedding band in my jeans pocket. But for once I felt free. I felt untouchable. I was going to take my husband down, it was the only way I could be free forever.

CHAPTER FORTY-SIX
DAVID

I'm on the road. It feels good to be out here, doing something, chasing leads. After a few hours up the M40, I finally reach Sandra's council estate. There are no perfectly manicured lawns and rose bushes here, but there are cosy gardens filled with plastic kids' outdoor games, bed sheets flapping on washing lines, caravans on bricks and "beware of the dog" signs. My new BMW stands out like a sore thumb, which is something I probably should have considered. I've lived too long in Ivy Oaks.

I have fond memories of the estate where I grew up. The place felt different depending on which street you lived on, some were friendly with a sense of community, others were harder, colder. I lived on a street where everyone knew each other. My mum struggled with five kids, but she always did her best.

It seems there's only one way in and out of the Fielding estate. But I have no idea if Sandra or Anna will leave the house today. I glance warily at a couple of houses who definitely wouldn't let me use their toilet.

My phone rings and I tap the accept button.

"Hey, Dad," Lori says. She sounds breezy but there's an edge to her voice, like the nonchalance is forced.

"You okay, Lor?" I ask.

"Yeah," she says. "It's just I thought we were going for lunch today. But it's one and you're not here."

"Oh, no. I'm so sorry, chicken, I forgot."

"That's okay," she says. Her voice is so soft and sweet. My stomach clenches with guilt.

"No, it's not, honey. I'm so, so sorry and I promise I'll make it up to you. The thing is I'm not in Oxford right now."

"Where are you?" she asks.

"I... I can't say. But I'll explain it all soon."

"Right." The edge is harder now. I picture her straightening up, annoyed. She has the same expression of annoyance as her mum.

"Sorry, sweetie. How about we go for lunch next weekend, and you can get whatever dessert you want. We can go wherever you like. Somewhere fancy, or a burger, whatever. Think about what you want."

"And I want that dress from Urban Outfitters," she adds.

I'm about to protest when I see a woman about fifty years old walking down the pavement. "Sure. Whatever you want."

"How about—"

"Don't push it, Lori. I have to go, chicken. I love you."

"Love you too, Dad," she says.

I'm out of the door as soon as we hang up. The woman is a few feet away now and I wave to her. She glances at me and then over her shoulder, thinking I must be waving to someone else.

"Hi," I call. "Can I have a quick chat?"

She stands still, her expression like a deer caught in the headlights. I notice her glance back towards the estate.

"What's this about?" she asks.

"I'm so sorry to bother you. I'm looking for Sandra Hennessy."

"Sandra," she says. "She doesn't live here anymore.

"Oh, did she move?"

"Who wants to know?" Her eyes look me up and down, clearly unimpressed by what she sees.

I grab a fake pass from my back pocket. It's a sneaky method, but sometimes works. "Sandra's won the lottery and we can't get hold of her."

The woman rolls her eyes. "Typical. I use my numbers every single week and she plays once and wins. How much did she win then?"

"Sorry, that's confidential."

"Oh, it's like that is it? She's won a load of money. Well, I don't know where she is. She and her daughter moved out before they even sold the house."

"You don't know anything?" I prompt.

"Well, there was something."

"Anything you know could be helpful," I say.

"I picked it up off the drive because it was littering, I wasn't snooping," she says. "It was one of those leaflets for a house. You know, the kind estate agents give out these days. Well, it was a flat for rent. I don't remember the address though."

"Do you remember the street? Mrs Hennessy won't get her money otherwise."

She sighs. "All right. I'll tell you."

I make a note of the street and thank her when she tells me.

"I hope you come again," she calls, as I make my way back to the car. "For me next time!" She laughs.

As soon as I'm in my car, I put the name of the street into RightMove and look up flats for rent in that area. There's one no longer available that looks just the right size for a mother and daughter. It's still in Dronfield but about a fifteen-minute drive away. Anna must have been concerned that Ben knew her mother's address. But perhaps her mother didn't want to leave the area, not without an explanation.

I put the car in gear. My heart is pounding. I'm going to make sure you get that redemption arc, Effie.

CHAPTER FORTY-SEVEN

EFFIE

I do all the things people usually do when they're running away. I cut my hair and dye it black. I buy wigs and sunglasses, different clothes and change the way I walk. Most importantly, I move between towns and cheap B&Bs. There's no part of Effie May left now. Instead, I'm Gemma and Claire and Becky and Tina. Names that don't stand out, given in establishments that don't check ID. Soon I'll need to pick a name and buy some form of identification. A fake driver's license maybe. A passport might be harder.

My life is boringly terrifying. Fear runs through each day. There's always that fear of him coming up behind me. It seems inevitable that maybe in a day, or a year, he'll be there. Waiting. The only way to stop that is to stop *him*. And I'm not sure I can.

But I have to try.

I have to hope.

The weather is warm. I move down the coast to Bridlington. It's pretty here and I like watching young women on hen parties have fun stumbling around the bars. Though I also spend a lot of time in hotel rooms. I move from one to the other regularly.

Long-term plans seem impossible but I'm putting feelers out. I'm making moves towards it, using the library computer, making sure nothing can be traced to my location. It's in Bridlington library, in the middle of the afternoon with a story time session for children going on at the other end of the building, that I finally watched the CCTV video from the Beaumont Hotel. Anna kept to her word. I watch it over twenty times. Robert and I are walking, and then we suddenly fall. My hand reaches out to grasp his, but instead I knock into him. We're tumbling together, a tangle of limbs.

It takes my breath away. This is me watching myself miscarry. It's me watching Robert die. A man I actually liked. And all the while I can hear the sound of children's voices at the other end of the room.

I go back to the library the next day with the intention of watching the video again. I also want to save it to a USB stick. But instead, I find an email from David.

I read it. And then I dismiss it. There is no one I can rely on in this world except myself. But what's wrong with that? I'm good at it, aren't I? I'm a survivor.

Yet I read it again. At night, in a dirty little B&B, I find myself reciting that email to myself. Over and over and over.

Eventually I buy a train ticket to York, remove the envelope from the lining of my jacket and stare at it for a long time. Then I regard the USB stick with the video on it. Turning it over and over in my fingers I wonder what good it would do to send it. There's nothing on the video to implicate Ben in Robert's murder. And then it hits me. Ben isn't on this video at all. So where did Anna get the screenshot of Ben in the stairwell? When she showed me the screenshot on her phone,

Ben was there. She must have another video from a different angle.

I scribble out a note, seal the envelope and stuff it into a post box. That's it, then. Decision made. I'm keeping the USB stick with me for my own protection, to prove I didn't push Robert. But I send David everything else I have. He is free to gather the evidence we need to put a stop to Ben. I'm anything but free. But hopefully I will be soon. I don't want to linger in a city so I move again, to Saltburn-by-the-Sea, taking trains and buses, using the cash. After a night there, I move up the coast to Redcar, not sure when I might finally stop. Maybe at John O'Groats.

There's someone in Middlesborough who might be able to help me get out of the country once and for all. I'll be starting again from nothing. Most of the money I have left will go towards getting me out and forging a new identity. But I can't meet my contact for a few days yet. So I wait. The nights are lonely. I've taken to talking to myself.

I have one last task I want to do before I leave. I buy a cheap laptop. There's more to tell David. But he can't know until I'm safely away.

I slept in this morning before heading out to a place I found that does a decent brunch. For some reason the butterflies in my stomach won't stop fluttering. Maybe I made a mistake trusting David with that evidence. I feel like his email was sincere but then he fooled me before. No, I have to stop doubting myself, he wants to stop Ben playing his games as much as I do. That's one thing I know for sure. I can't trust that the man ever cared for me, but I can trust how much he hates Ben.

After some eggs, I head into the bathroom to freshen up. With a slick of lip gloss, I feel more like myself than I have for a few weeks.

"Hiya, I'm Gemma. Nice to meet you," I say to my reflection in the mirror, practising my Yorkshire accent. It's not bad but still needs work.

"Hi, Gemma."

I freeze. The blood drains from my face. Ben. His grin widens in the reflection, gurning so widely he shows teeth. Before I can scream, he grabs me by the throat, fingers digging into the soft flesh.

"You'd better be quiet," he says. "You messed up, Effie. You went to the maid, didn't you?"

I shake my head.

"Yes, you did. You went to her not knowing I have control over everything she does. And now I have her in the boot of my car. Bound and gagged. Now. I'm going to tell you exactly what is going to happen next. I'm going to let go of you. And then we're going to walk out of this bathroom together and you're going to come with me. If you run, Anna's blood will be on your hands."

He releases me. I turn and face him. I wonder how I could have ever loved such a monster.

"How do I know you're telling the truth?" I ask.

Slowly, we begin to walk out of the bathroom. "You know me, Effie. Do you want to risk it?" When I say nothing, he smiles. "You're not like me. You won't go to the lengths I will. I knew that when I saw you crying over that lost baby. You're too soft. Maybe I should have let you leave, but then I'd have to find someone else, wouldn't I? And who's to say you wouldn't come back to ruin things for me?"

I look at my husband, horrified. Throughout, he maintains

an easy smile as he speaks, as though we're having a conversation about the weather.

It must seem strange, us both walking through the café at the same time. My heart beats a fast tattoo against my ribs. The woman at the counter says nothing about Ben by my side as I pass her a few notes and tell her to keep the change. She must sense something is wrong. Surely. She must know. I'm rigid, like someone has set me inside concrete. I have to concentrate to make myself walk away.

"Anna will die if you try anything," Ben whispers into my ear as we make our way to the café door. He grabs my arm, looping his through mine in the same way we did when we were in love.

"What if I kill you first?" I say through gritted teeth.

We're soon out in the sunshine. The seagulls squawk above us, swooping and diving for discarded chips along the pavement.

"Okay, sure, let's pretend that's a possibility," he says. And then he laughs.

He loves this, the ownership. He loves that he's won. I cringe away from him. His arm is like iron looped around mine. There's nowhere to run. Can I believe his claims to have Anna Hennessy trapped in his car? I don't know. What I do know is he's capable of anything. "It's a shame we can't have an ice cream on the beach. Maybe next time, eh? Come on, the car is just up here. I found a nice quiet spot where no one will be looking."

"How did you find me?" I ask.

"With great difficulty," he says. "I had a friend interview dozens of taxi drivers in London. One of them got very cagey about a certain customer. It took Dominic a while to get him to admit he'd driven a woman all the way to Whitby in exchange for cash. And from there, I managed to track a few sightings of a woman paying cash in small B&Bs. Once the police got bored of looking for you, I was finally free to put up a real chase. I spent yesterday driving around the coast checking small hotels. You're very smart, you know, it's one of the reasons I married you."

My palms itch. I keep looking over my shoulder, searching for an opportunity. A saviour. Anything. But it never happens.

"What are you going to do?" I ask. "What's all this about?"

"It's about punishment, Effie," he says. "You conspired against me." He raises an eyebrow. "For a wife, you're not very loyal."

"You killed my baby," I hiss.

The look he gives me could have been carved from ice. It's such a sudden change that I recoil, like I've just seen a snake in the grass. He steers me up a steep incline towards a car park overlooking the craggy coast. The car park is empty.

Dread sinks like a stone in my stomach. I can't trust this man. But there's nowhere to go. I stop. He tries to pull me forward, but I stay where I am.

"If you have Anna, you must know I paid her for the video. How much did I give her?"

He looks at me for a long time. He knows I'm testing him.

My eyes roam the car park searching for someone, anyone, to see me. A family getting ready for their day out. An old couple enjoying their retirement. But it's empty.

"You gave her jewellery," he says. His eyes glance down to my hand. "Your ring."

I turn to run. He figured it out, the bastard. He knew I wouldn't have enough cash on me before I left the hotel, and he knew my engagement ring is the most expensive piece of jewellery I wear daily. But as soon as I try to escape, his arms are around my waist. When I open my mouth to scream, he blocks it, and I taste the salt on his palm.

He drags me kicking all the way over to an old Volvo.

"Stop," he hisses in my ear. "It's pointless, Effie."

He throws me against the car and pain explodes through my hip. While I'm off balance, his fist pounds into my nose, and I stagger back. Warm blood trickles down to my mouth. He wraps an arm around my waist and lifts the boot lid. The space is empty. Anna is not bound and gagged in his car, she's somewhere else, probably safe. But I'm not. I throw myself at him, hitting and kicking, but he's stronger, and he pushes me into the car with ease.

There's a jab in my arm before he closes the boot, and I'm thrown into darkness.

CHAPTER FORTY-EIGHT

DAVID

The flat is small, above a chip shop. I park across the street and then head into the shop below. I need to be sure this is the right place. The man behind the counter nods when I walk in.

"Hi, mate. Does Sandra live upstairs?"

"Dunno, mate," he says. "But there were two women moving boxes up there about two week ago. Young lass about twenty and her mum. The mum didn't look well."

"That's Sandra. Thanks." I nod and leave the shop.

Effie told me to find the maid and I'm almost there. So close. I walk around the back of the buildings and hit the buzzer for the flat. My heart is pounding. As I wait, I half expect Ben May to emerge from the shadows, a gun clutched in his outstretched hand.

"Who is it?" The voice is young. It must be Anna.

I lean closer. "Effie sent me."

There's a pause. A face briefly appears at the window, sizing me up.

"Go away," Anna says through the intercom.

"Anna, I need to talk to you. It's important."

"There's no way I'm letting you in this flat."

"I understand," I say. "I know you're worried for your safety right now. But I swear I'm just here to help. Effie disappeared a few weeks ago. She sent me something in the post that led me to you. Look, I was there in the hotel the day she gave you her engagement ring. I don't know how you sold it, but if there's any kind of paper trail, you could be in trouble. The police are investigating Effie's disappearance right now—"

"God, would you shut up," she snaps. Then I hear a sigh. "Fine, come in. The rest of the street doesn't need to hear this shit."

Sandra goes to make me a cup of tea while I sit down on a black pleather sofa. Then Anna walks in, her head low. She sits down on an armchair, frowning. She says nothing. She's young and pretty. But there are dark circles under her eyes and she hasn't smiled once. She holds herself stiffly, as though she's afraid to relax.

"How are you settling into the new flat?" I say, glancing around the living room.

She leans forward. "How did you find me?"

"Well," I say, "you might want to tell your mum to delete her Facebook account."

Anna sighs.

The flat is clean and tidy to say they've just moved in. It reminds me of my parents' home. From the covers on the sofa to the dog ornaments lined up along the windowsill. The only mess is the stack of medication boxes piled high on a bookcase. Anna notices me looking at the pill packets.

"Mum has cancer," she says. "She had a hysterectomy a

few years ago to get rid of it, but it's back. She starts chemo next week."

"I'm sorry," I say.

Anna runs her fingers through long, dark hair. "The last thing I need is Ben May turning up at the flat. But if you found me then so can he. What am I going to do?"

"I know it's hard," I say. "But if I were you, I'd move again as soon as I could."

She stares out of the window at teenage boys kicking a coke can around. "I guess you're right. But why are you here? What do you want?"

"Well, I know you spoke to Effie the day she disappeared. And I know you gave her some proof of Ben May murdering Robert Dinman."

Anna sucks in a long breath. "Shut up!"

"Sorry." I decide to cut to the chase. "Look, I know you have evidence that can put Ben May in prison. Hell, you as a witness would be a lot for a prosecution case. I'm working on collating as much evidence against him as I can. Just give me a chance. Please?"

She regards me, her eyes moving up and down, weighing me up. "You're not just a friend of Effie's, are you?"

"I'm a journalist. I know Ben May has been conning women for years and I wanted to break that story. Only at the same time I got to know Effie and I fell in love with her. I'm doing this for her. But I'm also doing it to stop Ben May."

She sighs. "The last few weeks have been hell."

I can see it on her face. I know she means every word.

Sandra comes into the room, carrying a tea tray, still eyeing me with suspicion.

"Mum, I don't know if you should be here while I talk about this," Anna says. "Maybe we should go to the kitchen, David?"

"Absolutely not," Sandra says. "Anna, I need to know what's going on."

The daughter stares at her mother, biting her lip. I can see the tears gathering in her eyes. She brushes them quickly away and helps her mother into a recliner chair.

"I really messed up, Mum. I got involved with bad people and I did stupid things. I don't know how it ended up so bad."

"Oh, Anna," Sandra says softly.

"Mrs Hennessy, a man called Ben May manipulated your daughter. He's done it many times to a lot of other women. He has a way of making regular people make bad choices." I turn to Anna. "You need to remember that you weren't your usual self. You were under his influence."

She sniffs. "I guess so." But I can see she doesn't believe me, that she blames herself.

"Tell me how you met Ben," I say.

"I was cleaning a room like always. I had the door open, and the cart parked outside. I think I was stripping the sheets. Ben stood there in the doorway and asked me questions, like he was interested in what I was doing. I don't remember what he said, but I know he made me laugh. I didn't think much of it, I finished the clean, he went off somewhere. Then the next day I ran into him again. And then the next day. And then he asked if I wanted to get a coffee." She lets out a shaking breath and wipes her eyes. "I met him after my shift ended. To be honest, I didn't know what to expect and I really didn't know what to wear. He took me to this really fancy place with, like, a mural all along the wall. I had this dessert that was all shiny on the outside and creamy on the inside. And a green latte." She pauses, wringing her hands together. "It was the best date ever. And then I guess he dialled it up a notch." She glances at her mum. "We started meeting for dinner, which was always at a fancy place, and then I... had sex with him."

"It's okay, Anna," Sandra says.

"Everything got worse after. He had this... this hold on me. He'd bring me gifts, little romantic gestures like chocolate for after my shift. I'd think about him all the time, from the moment I woke up, to when I went to sleep at night." She sniffs away tears. "I started doing things I'd never normally do. I let him into rooms if he needed something. Ben wanted me to stay close to my... boyfriend, Stephen. Well, he wasn't really my boyfriend. We were hooking up for a little while before I met Ben."

"The security guard?" I ask.

Anna nods. "He must have thought we might need him in the future. I can see now that he values contacts. He uses people."

"Oh, Anna." Sandra dabs a handkerchief at her eyes. "He sounds horrible."

"He was. But I would never have said a bad word against him until after the accident." She screws her eyes shut. "I'm calling it an accident again, but it wasn't, was it?"

"What do you mean?" I prompt, hoping she'll open up.

"I didn't show Effie everything," she admits. "I... I wanted to keep something for protection." She pauses, staring out of the window again. Then she looks back at me. "Do you swear you can end it?"

"I swear." I say the words without hesitation. I hope I'm right in thinking I can end it all.

"He pushed them," she says. "And I know that, because I have two videos of what happened that night." She wipes her palms on her thighs and takes a deep breath. "I kept them on a USB stick just in case I needed leverage. But then... I don't know. I did a stupid thing. I got angry with Ben for leaving me like that. He blocked my number. I'd stolen for him, and he didn't even check in on me. Not once. He was so sure I wouldn't go to the police and that made me so angry. Because he was right. I would never have gone to the police because I'd done something awful. I'd stolen and lied for him. And worse, everything I did that night made Effie think *she'd* pushed Robert down the stairs. But she didn't. So... So I tried to blackmail him. I sent him two images. One from each video. I wanted him to know that someone out there could take him down." She shakes her head. "I was so stupid. When Ben confronted me I was so scared I didn't even ask for money. All I could do was try to throw him off. I even threw my ex under the bus."

"It's okay," I say. "I think you were probably in way over your head. Can I see the CCTV footage from that night? Both videos."

She nods and disappears into another room in the house. Sandra dabs her eyes again. She doesn't say anything. I think she's processing Anna's words.

Anna returns with a laptop and a USB stick. She plugs it in and boots up the computer. I regret not bringing my Mac now, because this thing is slow. The fan whirrs, gaining momentum like a revved car engine. Anna taps nervously on the keypad, like she's willing it to go faster. It takes a good couple of minutes and my tea is drained. Finally, Anna gets her video app working and angles the screen so I can see it.

The fall happens in a flash. It's over almost as soon as it starts. The camera is positioned between floors so that one set of stairs is visible above, and another set is visible below. You see two pairs of feet walking down the top set of stairs, and then their torsos come into view. Then there's a blur and suddenly the two of them take a tumble. I wince when Robert smacks his head on the corner of a step, landing awkwardly, snapping his neck.

After the fall, Effie climbs to her feet. She's unsteady and clearly dazed. But she drops to her knees as soon as she sees Robert. She checks him, feeling for a pulse, I think. Then she takes her phone out of her pocket and makes a call. Ben appears suspiciously quickly wearing a baseball cap. He drags Effie away from the body, which is where the video ends.

Anna taps the touchpad again, opening another file. Then she angles the screen back to me. This camera is positioned in the same place, only on a different floor. Effie's heeled shoes come into view, with Robert by her side. He has his arm over her shoulder and he's smiling at her. She laughs at something he says and it's clear he's inebriated because he sways into her. The camera is surprisingly clear, and I get a decent view of Effie. Her eyes seem off to me, like they're glazed over. She isn't stumbling like Robert, but I sense that she isn't herself.

As they begin walking down the lower set of stairs, the door to the floor above opens. A man walks into the stairwell. He's wearing a baseball cap and gloves. I know it's him. I know the shape of him by now. He takes just one step and then he puts his hand out. I don't think Effie or Robert hear him approach. And then they disappear into the next floor. What I'm seeing is the moment he shoved them. The moment Ben May committed murder.

I let out a long breath. "Is this everything?"

She nods.

"Thank you for showing me this, Anna."

I feel shaken. What he does is evil. But is this footage enough to prove he did it? Is he visible enough? Does it look like him? I'm just not sure. I want this to be the smoking gun to take him out, but I think we need more. I need to gather more evidence. I can't risk letting him escape from justice.

CHAPTER FORTY-NINE

EFFIE

I slip into unconsciousness before claustrophobia gives me a panic attack. The dream I have is one that haunted me when I was a teenage girl. I'm at my parents' house and my mother is teaching me French. My pronunciation is terrible. Despite having a French mother, I always struggled with the accent. I'm in the living room, gazing up at the family portrait, looking at my own dead eyes. It bursts into flames. I turn to my mother and see her lighting a cigarette. She flicks it at me, and soon I'm on fire too.

When I awake, I expect to be hot, but I'm actually freezing. It's dark and smells musty. Slowly, I blink sleep from my eyes, adjusting to the gloom. My throat is raw. There's something in my mouth, cloth. It's fuzzy on my tongue and unpleasant. I can't move my arms or legs and there's a migraine throbbing between my temples.

I start to kick and flail as best I can. My screams are muffled and hurt my throat. A disembodied voice comes from nowhere.

"Be good, Effie."

It's Ben. He's watching me from the corners of his room.

Now I see the tiny cameras. I look around the dark walls, not knowing where I am. I glance down at the ties pinning me to the chair. It looks like Ben used torn-up bed sheets, not ropes. Still tight but I assume they leave less of a mark.

Tears spring into my eyes. No. *No, no, no, no, no*. This is not how it ends for me, in this dank place, tied up by my own husband. I want to throw up, but if I do, I'll choke.

I know Ben and I know he's vindictive. But I never thought he'd go this far. I never thought I'd find myself tied up, with his voice eerily floating in through the speakers set around the room. An abundance of tears fall down my cheeks.

At the sound of footsteps, I will the tears to stop falling, but panic rises in my chest. Ben approaches, a glass of water in his hands.

"If you're good, Effie, we can come to some sort of arrangement," he says. "Are you going to be good?"

He grips my face with his free hand. I manage to nod, and he smiles.

When did he get like this? Ben has always loved power. He gets off on it. But he has never been sadistic before. What brought him to this point? Or has he simply been hiding it all these years?

He's gentle as he removes the gag. Part of me wants to scream, but I need the water. I know better than to struggle in his presence. Besides, physical strength has never been an asset of mine. I'm far more likely to talk my way out of a situation, not fight my way out.

"Ben," I say, my voice pleading. "We can work this out. I made a mistake. Okay?"

"I know," he says. He brushes hair from my face as he presses the glass to my lips. "I've figured out how to make all of this better."

I take a few gulps, moistening my dry throat. He pulls the glass away.

"I'll help you with Sophie," I say. "We can blackmail her together. Like old times. Don't you miss it? Playing all those games?"

He nods. "But everything changed at the Beaumont."

"Then we change it back," I say. "It's not too late."

He kisses me on the forehead and backs away. I don't like the fact that he hasn't agreed with me. He's not saying a thing. Why is that? What does he have planned?

"Where are we?"

He looks at me with a smile. "Our new home. The cottage in the countryside you always wanted. Very quiet, very secluded. Just us."

I start to cry as he replaces the gag and turns away. I'm plunged into darkness when he walks out of the room. Panicked, I scream. I scream and scream and scream until I can't anymore. I'm muffled and exhausted. Who is going to hear me? Eventually, I start to feel woozy and realise that he's drugged me again. It must have been in the water, and I was too dehydrated to notice.

The air is so thick with decay here, rank and putrid. This is Ben's true heart and he's had it on show all this time, I just wasn't looking. But I lived in this world, didn't I? Absorbing the contents of his vile heart and letting it poison mine. It wouldn't have happened unless I wanted it to. I think I probably did want to live in that place with him, mostly because I thought I deserved it.

My cruelty never went to these lengths. This is a place Ben lives in alone, controlled solely by him. He'll be enjoying this. I'm sure it's how he envisioned winning the final game. Our dangerous arrangement is coming to an end at last.

And then a bubble of laughter works up from my throat.

Ben has no idea what I've done with the pathetic murder confession he wrote to his mother. He has no idea that David knows how to find the evidence of him murdering Robert Dinman. Well, at least I did one good thing in my life. My breathing turns shallow as I gently slip into a sleep. I hear myself, snoring softly.

My body relaxes. A sense of peace washes over me.

"Effie?"

As soon as I hear his voice I know everything is going to be okay.

My eyelids flutter open. "David?"

"It's me. Oh, Effie. I'm so sorry. Let's get you out of here."

I nod my head. "Oh God. I thought... I never thought you'd find me." My voice is high and uncertain. "I thought maybe I didn't deserve—"

He places a finger to his lips to shush me, and then he works through the ties. His green eyes crinkle at the corners and I smile.

"Can we go far away now?" I ask. When one of my hands is free, I cup his face. "Can we start over?"

"Of course we can," he says. And he kisses me, full on the lips. He tastes like honey, but perhaps that's because I'm so dehydrated and my mouth is sour.

He pulls back after our kiss and bends down to untie my feet. As I watch him work, a wash of sorrow falls on me like freezing cold water.

"I'm so sorry."

He looks up at me. "You don't need to be sorry." His hands graze my legs. "Being sorry is a weakness."

"What?"

My head lolls back. I stare up at the dark ceiling for a moment, and then back to my feet. Ben smiles at me and I recoil. I try to move but my legs and arms are still caught in their trap. I blink. Ben is gone and I'm alone.

I hear someone whisper. I strain to hear what they're saying. *No lies. No ties. No lies. No ties.*

I nod my head. Those are the rules, and I broke them when I fell in love with David. Because I did love him, I just couldn't admit it to myself. My eyes flutter open for a moment, fighting against the drug. But it's no use. As I drift back into slumber, I know I'm alone. And I know that Ben has won the game.

CHAPTER FIFTY

DAVID

Ben May no longer lives in Ivy Oaks.

I came back from the north to find the entire community talking about it. The house is empty, and he's nowhere to be seen. My heart sinks. How am I going to fulfil my promises now? To Effie, to Sophie, to Anna? I had wanted to get inside that house, somehow. And now he's gone, and no doubt he's taken every scrap of evidence with him, and he did it while I wasn't here to see. As soon as I get home, I check my house yet again for cameras, unscrewing the casing for all my appliances, taking out lightbulbs, checking the smoke alarm. It takes a few hours but once I'm done, I feel better.

Naturally, I turn to Beryl for gossip. While I'm in the kitchen preparing a sandwich, I see her taking a walk around the neighbourhood with her nurse, Holly. I have my suspicion that both of these women fuel the gossip between each other. I often see them drinking tea at the dining table, wicked grins on their faces. But maybe I'm just being sexist and they're talking politics, not gossiping about someone's botched boob job.

I hurry out of the house and jog over to them.

"Morning, Beryl," I say. "Holly. Lovely weather this morning."

Beryl smiles. "I haven't seen you around for a few days. Have you been busy?"

"I went back up north to visit my family," I say. "It looks like number one is empty. What happened?"

"Ben May left without saying a word to anyone. I didn't even see him move out. The removal company took everything out of the house without him. I suppose he'd already left. It was very odd."

"Pretty weird behaviour for someone whose wife is missing. You'd think he'd want to stay put in case she decided to come home."

"True," Beryl says. "You seem to be suspicious of him?" When she sees my expression, she lets out a laugh. "Oh, come on. You never have a good word to say about him. There was something going on between you and Effie, wasn't there?"

"No, of course not!" I protest, but Beryl purses her lips together like she doesn't believe a word I'm saying.

"Well, if you are planning to accuse him of anything, I hope you find evidence." Beryl adjusts her glasses, pushing them down her nose to regard me over the rims. "He doesn't seem like the kind of man you want to take on and lose against."

"What makes you say that?" I ask.

"Nothing behind the eyes," she says. "He's like... Like a hollow person. Someone wearing the skin of a human being. I'm old enough to know these things, you see. I've met all kinds of people in my time." She tries to smile but it comes across as a grimace, and I wonder what kind of memory she's trying to suppress. "That and the way he carried on with

Sophie Morgan. All that sneaking about, going back and forth from her house."

"Beryl, did you see Ben go to Sophie's house the night Effie disappeared?"

"No," she says. "I told the police that, but they suggested I just wasn't near the window at the time. I suppose I wasn't standing *in* the window, but I did have a decent view. I see most of the comings and goings around here. That's what happens when you're old and bored."

"Thanks, Beryl," I say. "I'll let you get back."

"She wasn't a good person either, you know. She lied. Effie that is."

"I know," I admit.

Beryl nods. "Does Deepika know she started that rumour about her children's school? Does Sophie know she was being manipulated by both of them, not just him? Because that gives them motives too."

"I guess—" I start.

"Smart," Holly says suddenly. "She's smart, you know." She taps her head. "No one listens to Mrs Scott, but they really should. She always knows everything about this place."

Beryl nods. "I've been here a long time and I've seen this place go through many changes. And what's more, I know that couple came here to cause trouble. Don't you think it was obvious? Setting up that barbecue. And let me tell you, no one moves into Ivy Oaks and is interested in anything I have to say. Not unless they're prying for information." She and Holly exchange a glance. "The Mays didn't expect Ivy Oaks to be more trouble than them, did they now?"

Holly grins. "I told you she was smart."

Beryl laughs and begins to walk away. She hesitates for a moment. "Be careful, David. I know you're doing your own investigation into Effie's disappearance. But I think you're in more dangerous waters than you realise."

Beryl is right, I do need to be careful. So I take the locked security box to a bank vault. I'm playing it safe. We all know Ben is well-practised at breaking into houses and setting traps.

In a small back room at the bank, I lay out all of the evidence I have so far. The security camera footage from the Beaumont. It would need to be verified to be admitted into evidence. Perhaps an IT expert could do that. Though Ben will be able to afford a good lawyer who may provide a rebuttal.

I have the handwritten letter, train tickets and photograph. The photograph isn't evidence, but I can at least testify these things were together like Ben kept it as a trophy. The letter would also need to be verified but who is there left to recognise Ben's handwriting? His parents are dead, his wife is missing, he has no siblings and as far as I know, he doesn't have close friends or any other family. Someone at his old job could potentially help out there but how often would Ben have written a note? Perhaps a forensic handwriting expert, but again, Ben can afford his own experts.

I have Anna's testimony. I need Sophie to retract her alibi and provide a testimony of what Ben did. But if he's smart, he will have already wiped his laptop and phone. Would he keep any of it? For leverage? In a safety deposit box like this, perhaps? Online storage under another account? A computer hidden away somewhere? I don't think I can second-guess his secrets. Sociopaths are unpredictable.

It might be time to contact the police. This might be as far as I can go.

I place everything back in the box, including the USB stick from Anna's house. Once it's safely locked away, I let out a relieved sigh. Ben May is just one man and yet even thinking about him makes my skin crawl. Sometimes I remember the sound of his voice as he told me about fucking Effie while the barbecue was going on. I picture the dead expression in his eyes.

Is he going to win this? In my darkest moments I think he might.

On the way out of the vault, I smile at the woman at the reception desk. She locks a door behind me, and I carry on into the sunshine. Summer is transitioning into autumn now, but the weather hasn't caught up, and I shield my eyes against a blinding low sun.

As I'm about to unlock the door to the car, I pull out my phone to check whether Sophie or Anna have been in touch. There is a new email, but it isn't from an account I recognise. *Bringwineoracake@freemail.com.* My heart beats hard. Effie. It has to be her.

I climb into the car and open the email. There is no message, just a heart emoji and a link to a folder. My hands are shaking as I put the car in gear. I stall it coming out of the junction onto the main road, my heart pounding against my ribs.

I set off, wanting to be home as quickly as possible to take all of this in. But the lights ahead change to red, and I slow down at a junction. Tapping my right indicator, I wait for the green light and pull out slowly. Then suddenly I see a wall of black racing towards me. It all happens so fast that I barely have time to think. The driver door slams into me as brute force pummels my entire body. When the contact occurs, an image of Lori holding red fruit in her hands flashes in front of me. We're at a strawberry field and she has punnets of her handpicked berries. She's so proud of them, and when she grins at me, there's one tooth missing right in the centre of her smile.

And then the world goes black.

BODY FOUND IN CHERWELL RIVER

The body of a thirty-year-old woman has been found in the Cherwell River. It is believed to be Euphemia May, the daughter of former supermodel Isabella Dupont. Mrs May of Ivy Oaks in Oxford has been missing for the last four weeks. Her husband and family expressed concern for their missing loved one and appealed to anyone with information to come forward.

A dog walker found the body in the water in the early hours of the morning. Thames Valley Police are currently investigating the death. They have confirmed that a body connected to the case has been found, but they have yet to give any additional information. Cause of death is yet to be determined. The family have asked for privacy during this difficult time. Further updates will follow.

CHAPTER FIFTY-ONE

SOPHIE

He's lying unconscious in the bed, tubes coming out of his nose and arms. The beeping sound of the machines feels like the thudding beat of the soundtrack to a horror movie. Every sound makes me flinch, and I can't stop staring at the door. I can't stop picturing *him* entering.

The other driver wasn't harmed. In fact, he drove away. It was a truck, and it ploughed straight into David, pinning his BMW against the traffic light pole. It then backed away, front bumper completely gone, and drove off. It was intentional. The police are still looking for the culprit. I don't believe Ben was driving, but I definitely think he was behind it. I'm sure he hired someone or blackmailed them into it. Just as I'm sure he murdered his wife.

It's like I'm walking through a dream. No, a nightmare. I'm trapped in the kind of nightmare you have as a child when you can't tell if you're asleep or awake. Ben is the person chasing you. No matter how fast you run, he's always on your heels. Sometimes, I close my eyes and I picture our bodies entwined, sheets tangled beneath us. What I gave to him that night, I gave willingly, but I gave it to a different person. I never knew the real him, but now I do. I would call him evil, but it's too reductive. Too neat. Ben is more than that.

He's also the father of my child.

What a way to come into this world.

"You look terrible."

I sit up straight. I hadn't noticed David stirring, I'd been too lost in thought. His eyes are open but narrowed, like the light is painful for him. He licks his lips, and his breath comes out ragged.

"I'll get a nurse, David. I won't be a minute."

Once I've found someone and David has been checked over and given some water, I return to my seat.

"How are you feeling?" I ask.

"Like a truck ploughed into my car. I've got a broken pelvis and a concussion apparently. Among other things."

"That's right. They sedated you for a while, but I think you woke up a bit early." I give his hand a reassuring squeeze. "Lori and your ex have been in and out. There's cards and flowers on the table. I can help you open them if you like."

"That would be great."

I fumble with the cards, tearing across envelope seams. David smiles as I read out the get well soon messages. His eyes are wet, but I'm not sure if his tears are sadness about what happened, or happiness about still being among the living. Once we're done, I hand him a tissue.

"The doctors will let them know you're awake, so they'll come visit soon, I'm sure," I say, feeling awkward David woke up to find me here and not his family. "But before I go, there's something I need to tell you."

My throat is dry as sandpiper as I prepare to tell him. While he was unconscious, I went back and forth about whether it should be me, or a family member. In the end I decided it should be me. After all, we've both been affected by the Mays. We're connected by it in a way.

"What is it?" he asks.

"Effie is dead," I say.

He flinches. Then his face pales. But he shakes his head slightly. "No, she's... She can't be, she sent me an email before the..." He trails off and stares out of the window.

"I'm so sorry, David. It's true. She has been identified."

He tries to sit up and I help him. His voice is cracked and shaky when he speaks. "Who identified her? Was it Ben?"

"Yes," I say. "And her father was there too."

It finally seems to sink in and his face crumples. I hold his hand and turn my head as he begins to cry. We sit there, not saying a word, and I offer him another tissue.

"Where's my phone?" he says suddenly. "She must still be alive. She has to be."

"I... I don't think so, David." I rummage around the room, checking the little table next to the bed. "Is this it?"

He nods, holding his hands out greedily. But once he has the phone he swears. "No battery."

"I have a charger." I grab the portable charger I keep in my bag and rest David's phone on it. He's agitated, but exhausted at the same time. I help him drink some orange squash while the phone charges.

"I was getting close," he says. "I have evidence locked away. Two security videos, a letter he wrote to his mother confessing to killing his father. A train ticket to his parents' village dated the day before Nicholas May died. I wanted him to be punished but I was also doing it so she'd finally be free. I thought she was untouchable, Sophie."

My hands begin to tremble. *Ben killed his father too?* David sees my expression and frowns.

"Sorry, you didn't know about all that, did you?"

I shake my head.

"How much charge is there?"

"Twenty per cent," I say. "Do you want it?"

He nods, holding out his hand. We then spend a couple of minutes connecting to the hospital WiFi.

"Look," he says. "She sent this to me. But how? She was already dead."

I frown, checking the date on the email. "Maybe it wasn't her."

He shakes his head. "I'm sure of it." His voice breaks and he sniffs heavily. "The email address is this stupid little joke we made together when we first met and..." He shrugs. "I just know it's her. I feel it. Maybe she's alive. What if Ben faked her death?"

It's then I realise he really loved her. I want to give him hope, but he's not making sense.

"Why would Ben do that?" I say. "I'm so sorry, but I think she probably just scheduled the email before she died."

His expression morphs into something like resignation. He lets one arm flop to the bed. "She never wanted to get caught. Maybe she wanted to throw it all away and start again. She thought she'd be gone by the time I got this." He shakes his head.

CHAPTER FIFTY-TWO

DAVID

When Sophie goes to the bathroom, I open the email again and sure enough, there's the information at the bottom revealing that Effie used a mailing list email scheduler to send me the message. My heart sinks. It was sent two weeks ago, long before her body was found.

After steadying my breathing, trying to ease the tight lump in the centre of my chest, I finally open the folder to see what she sent to me. There are video messages. Half a dozen or so. I open the first and as soon as I see her face on the screen, tears flood my eyes.

VIDEO01.MP4

Hi David. I'm sure you never expected to see my face again. Or maybe you did, I don't know. Well, here it is. And here is the shitty little room I've been staying in. Let me pan the camera for you. See, I'm alone, I'm not being held at gunpoint. It's me in the flesh talking to you.

You must be wondering why I'm sending you these videos. It's because I want you to stop this cycle. By now you must have received the envelope I sent you, the one with the letter, train tickets and photograph. I know it's not enough to put him behind bars but I'm hoping you can fill in the gaps. Did you find Anna? I hope she's working with you too. It's a lot to put on her, I know. But in a way, she owes me.

But back to the envelope. You know now that Ben murdered his father. I've known for a long time. I married him even though I always knew. But I also knew what his father did to him, and for that reason, I thought it was a one-off. I never expected him to do it again.

We both know how that turned out.

I'll get to Robert Dinman's murder later. It won't be easy to talk about for reasons you know but I'll explain everything soon. Right now, I want to tell you everything I know about Ben and every terrible thing we've done to people over the last seven years. You'll probably hate me. It's a chance I'm willing to take. And maybe you'll forgive me for dumping this burden on you. Maybe you won't. I wouldn't blame you.

By the time you get this, I'll be long gone. I actually arranged it all a while ago. I thought you might come looking for me, you see. But I'm sorry, David. I'm not a good person. I don't want to go to prison. You want me to atone, well, maybe this is a start, but I'm not ready for my punishment. Don't be too disappointed in me.

I need to tell you something and it's not easy to say. You've meant a lot to me. I've been with many men since I met Ben. Most of whom he wanted me to be with. You are the only one I've had feelings for. You're the only man I've ever loved. What I feel for you made me realise Ben and I never loved each other. We were intensely connected, but that isn't love, is it? There's no mutual respect, no equal partnership.

You made me realise I was controlled and coerced by him too. And, no, I'm not the perfect victim and I'm certainly not innocent. I won't be excusing the things I've done. But over the years Ben has manipulated me and made me in his image. I've been hurt by him many times in a hundred different ways, but I just didn't see it. And... well. You know what happened at the Beaumont Hotel but I'll get to that later.

I can't live like this anymore. When I walk down the street, I look over my shoulder. The hairs raise on the back of my neck whenever someone comes too close to me. Fear is a shadow always following me and I don't feel like I'll ever be free.

There's no way to turn back time and stop myself becoming a victim. But at least I can be the last victim. No matter what happens now, I want this to stop. I want this story to have an ending.

I feel like my life is hanging by a thread because I know who is out there, coming for me. I used to have a bright future. But now life is dark, and I want to find the sun again. I know things between us are complicated but please, if you ever had any real feelings for me, help me. Help me put an end to this sick game once and for all.

And now I'm going to play my part. Go and get a pen and paper because I'm going to give you a list of every single person Ben May victimised during our relationship. This is my testimony as his co-conspirator. When you find them, please let them know I'm sorry.

And, David? I love you. I forgive you... Let's make sure he never hurts me or anyone else, ever again.

CHAPTER FIFTY-THREE

SOPHIE

On my way back from the bathroom, I see David watching something on his phone. When I hear Effie's voice, I realise it's personal. Backing away, I take myself for a walk and find a vending machine.

With two coffees in hand, I make my way back and set one down next to David. He's totally engrossed as Effie describes in excruciating detail all the things Ben convinced her to do with the husband of someone Ben wanted to blackmail.

"There's so many of them," he mumbles. "And we need to contact them all. It's the only way to take Ben down. But I've tried to reach out to the victims before. When I did it as a journalist, they never wanted to speak. It's even more important now. If they all testify then that would be powerful. It wouldn't prove he's a murderer, but it certainly shows what he's capable of and strengthens the case." He shifts his weight in the bed, wincing in pain. "Damn. I wish I could do it, but I think I'll be in here for a couple of days."

"That's okay," I say.

"No, it's not. Time is important. The longer we leave it,

the harder he'll be to find. What if he's abroad somewhere? Criminals go missing for decades outside the country, don't they? He's got enough money to do whatever he wants."

"I've already done what you're asking me to do."

He turns to me. "What?"

"I've found the other women already."

It all started when I decided I didn't want to feel alone anymore. Lewis had a lot of issues to work through on his own. I'd cheated on him. That part we couldn't ignore. I saw the weight of it drag him down, even though he wanted us to move on. And then I found out I was pregnant, and things became even tougher.

Lewis couldn't support me while he had so much to deal with in his own head. We live together, eat together and sleep in the same bed, but it's like we're not together anymore. Part of me wonders if he'll leave once Ben is dealt with. I have a feeling he's here to protect me out of a sense of duty, but emotionally, he's checked out.

I needed to talk to someone who understood what I'd been through. But I had to do it carefully. So, I created a blog under a fake name—Francesca Sizemore—and I started talking about Ben in groups for women emotionally traumatised by grifter men. Someone pointed me to a Facebook group called the Eric Lansdown Survivors Group. As soon as I shared my story, I knew I'd found many women victimised by Ben May.

Comments dripped in one by one. They had all the same hallmarks. Revenge porn. Blackmail. Affairs. Him appearing from nowhere, bumping into him in a café, him there on a rainy day willing to help, him offering to look after their pets.

Then he'd flip and he'd become a different person. Some of these accounts went back years to when he was running a less sophisticated scam, telling women he ran a pharmaceutical company that would one day cure cancer.

There are twenty-five women in the survivors Facebook group and another six commented on my blog posts. That's thirty-one women who check their bedrooms at night to see if there are any hidden cameras, who flinch at the sound of a text message because it could be him begging for money, who on occasion have confusing feelings when remembering a kind gesture from him, or beautiful words coming out of his mouth. And we're pretty sure there are more of us out there.

While I count Effie as one of us, she did a lot of things that most of us wouldn't have done. I do think that by the time she met me, she'd had enough. I'd often wondered if the tension between them was real. Now I know that Ben murdered Effie's unborn child before I met them. The thought makes me sick to my stomach. It puts those videos of me in perspective. Does it really matter in the grand scheme of things? What matters is my baby and keeping him or her safe.

So what if the world knows I cheated on my husband? I'm a human. I make mistakes. The worst mistake I could make now is not to throw everything I've got at trying to put him behind bars. If that's the price I have to pay in order to stop Ben May then sign me up. I'm done hiding. Ben May, we're coming for you.

CHAPTER FIFTY-FOUR

BEN

I lied to my wife in her final moments. She held out hope until the end that someone would rescue her. She even thought I was David at the end. And who knows, maybe he would have played the white knight if he'd known what was happening to her. That man now proves to be a lone, tenacious fly in my ointment who insists on trying to find the evidence to bring me down. He has nothing, but he's trying very hard.

I rented the run-down cottage for a month, cash in hand, from a friend of Dominic's. We told his mate I wanted a secluded place to write and didn't mind about the basic amenities. Then I brought my wife to her new home under the cover of darkness and fed her a cocktail of painkillers to keep her compliant.

It took me a while to decide what to do with her. But deep down I always knew there was only one way this was going to end. It was her or me. She pushed it to that point. I had no choice. So, when Effie was nicely drugged up, I drove out to a secluded spot by the river. She was unconscious. I weighed her down with rocks, and gently pushed her into the water. I didn't need to worry about her being found. I wanted her to be found. Without her dead, I can't inherit her money, can I?

But now there's David, shoving a spanner in the works. Green-eyed, doughy David.

Of course, I tried leaving cameras in his house. I wanted to know what his next move would be, but the bastard always checks his own home. Every time he finds a camera, he disconnects it and bins it, no matter how sneakily I hide them. But he hasn't reported me to the police. That's how I know he doesn't have proper evidence. He has nothing.

Effie was going to leave me for this man. I'd felt the shift in her over the last few months. I suppose it's like when my dad sensed I was going to turn my back on the family, and he started up his nonsense again. He beat my mother right in front of me.

"Go on, son," he said. "Find a way to stop me."

He was daring me to hit him. I have no problem with physical violence in other situations, but with him, it was always different.

"Just go, Ben," Mum begged. "Please. Go!"

After he cracked her ribs and I did nothing about it, I realised I needed to approach it another way. My father needed to go.

I took my mother's advice and walked out of the house, leaving her in his brutish hands. Then I wrote a letter to her explaining what I was about to do.

I never sent it. After I slipped the sheet of paper into a manilla envelope, I realised that if I did send it, she'd still side with him. There's no way she'd have allowed me to do what I planned. Instead, she would have gone to the police. I pocketed the letter as I boarded the slow train that took me to

Pewsey village. From there I walked to my parents' house. It was dark by then, much easier to sneak onto the property. All I needed to do was unlock the sliding garage door and slip underneath. From there, I went into my father's car and tampered with it. I knew he'd be going for his regular Sunday drive in the morning.

As soon as I finished, I travelled back down to London and went into the office, just to be sure I had an alibi for when the accident happened. From there I waited it out. I didn't know if he'd have a little fender bender, if he'd end up a vegetable in a hospital bed, or if he'd die. I was very pleased with the result.

Mother cried for two weeks. During that time, I kept the letter in my pocket, considering actually handing it to her. I didn't, of course, because I'm not an idiot. I knew I couldn't trust her.

I wanted to hate her, but I never could. Perhaps I even loved her. Perhaps that's what love is—not being able to hate the person who is nothing but hateful to you. Which would mean I never loved Effie, because I truly did hate her by the end. I hate her lover boy too. I hate him in the same way I hated my father. In a way that forces me to act, to get this malignant presence out of my life.

It doesn't happen often—but it does happen—on occasion I allow my judgement to falter. Hiring the driver from the dark net to try and take out David was certainly a mistake. First of all, it failed to kill him, secondly, it was too soon after Effie. I'm supposed to be lying low.

There is a net tightening around me and I'm not too proud to admit when it's time to run.

A lot of British criminals run to Spain. But that feels too run-of-the-mill to me. I fancy somewhere more exotic. No, I need to go further afield. And as I already have an offshore account in Panama—with a few more grand squirreled away—it seems like the obvious choice. There are no business class tickets available, so I purchase one of the last seats in standard and hope border control isn't too busy.

No lies. No ties. The one rule Effie and I had when we played our games. I broke the first rule many times. The second rule I respected much more. The way I live, there's nothing I care about. Nothing I wouldn't leave behind in a heartbeat. My bag is packed in five minutes and I'm in a taxi on the way to the airport around fifteen minutes after that. I'll be early for the flight but that's okay.

A familiar spike of adrenaline courses through me. I've never been chased before. This is new for me. I can't say I like it as much as being the hunter, but a thrill is still a thrill.

Before I left for the airport, I had a choice. I could delete every file of every mark I've ever exploited. Or I could keep them on an external hard drive so I can still go back to them if I need to. Fear is a great motivator and a lot of what I have makes people afraid. I chose the second option and mailed it to a PO box in Panama ahead of my arrival. Everything has been wiped from my laptop and cloud. Now all I need to do is get to Panama and retrieve it.

I arrive at the airport, ready with my passport and ticket. The bored woman standing by the terminal entrance scans my ticket and checks my passport and suddenly her eyes snap into focus. She looks at me with renewed curiosity before stepping away to use her walkie-talkie.

Fuck.

Her eyes dart nervously from me to the rest of the airport. Something is wrong. Have I been put on a no fly list already? Police haven't been to interview me yet. David Holt was still in hospital yesterday. But I don't like the look in her eyes.

Standing there is attracting too much attention so I step forward and soon I'm stuck in the middle of a slow-moving queue at security. Sweat beads across my forehead as loud families unpack liquids from their carry-ons, panicking over half-empty bottles of hand sanitiser. I glance behind me, considering the option of turning around, but I'm already surrounded by people. I just have to get through to the other side and I'll be one step closer.

As I near the front of the queue, I see security guards watching me. They eyes penetrate mine. I can't tell if this is normal or whether something is wrong. I try to look bored, like a normal man waiting for his turn. But the tension is growing. Something in my gut is telling me to run. As I move forward, one of the guards points at me and I know this is a dead end.

I make a big show of acting like I've forgotten something. Then I turn around and mumble apologies to everyone around me. I start walking. Not too fast, easy does it. When border control officers lock eyes with me, I pick up the pace. But I'm so busy checking over my shoulder that I barrel straight into someone's suitcase, staggering forward, my passport flying from my hands. There are men coming towards me, there's no doubt about it. I knew it. I snatch my passport up off the floor and start sprinting through the crowds. Someone shouts behind me and I dodge through the barriers, my heart pounding, dropping both my ticket and my suitcase. If I can make it to the terminal exit. If I can push my way out of this airport. It's not possible, there are too many security guards and yet I keep going. All is lost and yet I can't stop moving.

Behind me, someone shouts, "Police!" Someone orders me to stop. I duck and dive between bewildered holiday-makers. I skip down a set of stairs, searching for another exit. Where can I go? There has to be another option. There's always another option for me. I've managed to get out of every situation I've ever been in. And then I see her. And she smiles at me. I hesitate, and someone knocks me to the ground.

This is it. I can't change this course. The game is over.

CHAPTER FIFTY-FIVE
SOPHIE

I was at the police station talking to a detective when Ben May used his passport at Heathrow Airport. It was my third visit to the station to give statements and provide evidence against Ben. Thirty-one strong women stood behind me, metaphorically, as I gave the dossier of evidence to the police. Ben's letter, the video footage of him in the stairwell of the Beaumont Hotel, Effie's videos and more. After speaking to his victims, we gathered text messages, screenshots from the videos he used to blackmail them, gifts bought by him, threatening voice notes, everything we could find.

The police listened and took it seriously. I was relieved to be heard and to be believed. But what impressed me the most was Ben being put on a wanted list. So, when he tried to use his passport at Heathrow Airport everyone sprung into action. In that moment, everyone knew that Ben May was about to escape unless quick action prevented him. Men and women in uniform rallied quickly, jumping into vans, ready to go. And because I was there, I ended up in the detective's car.

I witnessed it first-hand as Ben May was tackled to the ground. There was a bizarre moment when we came face to face and for the strangest reason, I smiled at him. That smile threw him off. It's what led to the police jumping on him. From there I watched him be stuffed into a police car, handcuffs circling his wrist. My heart pounded against my ribs. After everything he'd done, observing his downfall felt strange. I had to remind myself that I was safe now, because seeing him made me feel the opposite. He even smirked at me when they led him away.

He smirked because this isn't over. The date for the court case, where he will defend himself against multiple murder charges and blackmail charges, has been set. This is in the hands of the law now. Bail denied, Ben May will remain in prison until his day in court. He can't terrorise anyone anymore. And I can't wait to witness his day of judgement.

CHAPTER FIFTY-SIX

DAVID

Ben May is gaunt, now. He lost a lot of weight in prison. Without a decent haircut or access to hair dye, he finally looks his age. Throughout the trial he sits quietly, with his head bowed, listening to witness after witness give their testimony.

Ben May ruined my life is the repeated refrain. And it isn't just women, either. Several men come forward to talk about Ben's "financial advice" that resulted in financial ruin. Ben pocketed it all. Two or three married couples testified, including Sophie and Lewis. While Ben seduces the wife, he steals money from the husband, and then he blackmails them both to top it all off.

Ben May is a sociopath. Ben May is cruel. Ben May doesn't care about anyone but himself.

There's just one character witness to testify for Ben. A cousin. I find her words some of the most interesting of the trial. When asked what Ben was like as a child, she provides some insight into what might have made him into this monster.

"He was shy and very sensitive," she says. She has that

same plummy accent, and similar piercing eyes. Her voice is strong and clear when she speaks. "I felt sorry for him, really. His father was such a brute. No one in the family liked Mr May at all. Every summer, my mother would force me to spend time with Ben at his house. We didn't live too far away, and she'd drop me off in the morning and collect me later. While I was there, we'd walk the dogs, go on a bike ride or work on a jigsaw puzzle at the table. I often saw Mr May, Ben's father, during that time and he was never a pleasant man. He didn't really talk. I remember him calling Ben a blithering idiot when he cried after finding a dead bird."

"How old were you at this time?" asks the barrister.

"Seven," she says. "Ben is the same age, so we were both seven. When we'd go on walks away from the house, he'd sometimes start to tell me things. He hated his father but who could blame him? I saw bruises on his wrists once. But I was so young I didn't really understand what was happening." She pulls a couple of tissues from a shelf beneath the witness box and blows her nose. "I remember once, Mr May screamed at me for tracking dog poo into the house. Actually, he did more than scream, he slapped me, right across the face. Later, when my parents picked me up, I told Mummy what he did. I was crying my eyes out. Well, Mummy wasn't having that. She was always a spunky woman. She slapped him right back. He didn't know what to do, but I worry it might have made things worse for Ben after we left." She blows her nose again. "I was never allowed back, and I don't think we ever spoke to them again. My mother tends to hold a grudge." She pauses, glancing at Ben. "Look, I know he's done some awful things, and I'm not defending what he did. I don't think he would defend them either. But he had a bad start in life. I think that needs to be taken into consideration." She turns to the jury and then the judge.

It might be the first time I've felt sympathy for Ben May. But considering I walked with a cane for six months as my bones healed, it's fleeting. Ben May is not the first man to live with an abusive father and he won't be the last. He has to pay for his manipulations and crimes.

Sophie and Anna are with me every day in the courtroom, usually in the gallery, but as witnesses too. We each testify and answer the probing questions asked by the barristers. It's not an easy process. I'm exhausted when I step down from the box. Sophie's eyes fill with tears. It's been a hard road for her. After the birth of her baby daughter, Grace, she and Lewis decided to divorce. Ben's presence hung between them like a ghost, she told me. And while they're willing to co-parent, neither can live with the other any longer.

Anna has her own court date to attend soon. But the police never found out about Effie's engagement ring. Sophie and I certainly never testified to it, and Ben may have forgotten all about it in the course of the proceedings. It helped Anna secure her mother in a flat close to the hospital for the course of her chemotherapy treatments. She's doing well.

We're hopeful that Anna won't see prison time. Ben's manipulative tactics have been well documented during this trial and her lawyer is confident that a suspended sentence will be given.

The court breaks, and the jury goes away to make their decision. Sophie, Anna and I all head to a quiet coffee shop to sombrely sip lattes. Then I go home and take my daughter out for dinner. I try to hide the fact that I'm distracted by asking her a few leading questions that will entail a long answer. What is TikTok? Who is Harry Styles? I know the answers to these things of course, I just need her to talk for a while. I like hearing her voice.

Throughout all of this, there's been one question on my mind for a while—who locked Effie and Deepika in the sauna? There's no definitive answer. Effie always thought it was someone Ben had pissed off. But would they really travel down to Ivy Oaks and lock Ben's wife in a sauna? It seems odd. Sophie thinks Deepika may have been the target. It wasn't long after the rumour about Deepika buying good grades for her kids spread around Ivy Oaks. What with the other rumour that Deepika killed a dog, well, it's possible there was someone on the street who held a grudge.

I drop Lori back off at her mum's and head home to my empty house. The witness testimonies brought out quite a bit of information about Effie and the way she aided her husband's manipulations. Her flirtations with the husbands. Her seduction of Robert Dinman at the Beaumont. I wish she was here to defend herself so I could work out who I fell for. The longer time goes on, the less I'm sure. Could Effie have redeemed herself? She was the lesser of two evils, but she still did wrong.

Sleep finds me willing. I have a strong urge for hard liquor when I wake. A coffee will have to do.

The day goes by quickly. I chat to Beryl and Holly at the leisure centre, I update Aaron on the trial when I see him on my walk back home. I see the For Sale sign being taken down outside number one, Ben and Effie's old house. I wonder if there'll be someone new moving in soon. Then I go to bed and do it all again. My body feels tightly wound. But life keeps moving on.

It's the third day when the jury announce they've made their decision. I drive down to the Old Bailey one more time, barely making it in time. The gallery is full. I end up sitting at the back, spotting Sophie and Anna further forward. They decided to stay in London until the verdict is reached. I wanted to be in my own bed.

In comes the jury. My hands tighten together, wound into a knot. I lean forward as the head juror stands and the judge reads out a list of Ben's crimes. *Guilty*, the man answers. Each time he says that word, my stomach leaps into my throat. And then, the one that matters to me. The third murder. The killing of Effie May. *Guilty*.

I place my head in my hands. I could break down, right here, in front of all these people. But I pull myself together, screwing my eyes tightly shut and opening them again. My heart rattles around in my chest, but as the news sinks in, I slowly begin to relax. He's guilty. Of everything. We did it. Sophie turns around, finding my face. She smiles at me, and I smile back.

Effie's videos played in court during the trial. Her clear voice ringing through the space. I'll never forget those moments in the hospital, in pain, physically and emotionally, having just found out that Effie was dead. Then seeing her. Listening to her talk directly to me. As I heard her again, she felt more alive than ever.

Part of me never believed she was dead at all. I figured one day she'd turn up at my house in Ivy Oaks with a shop-bought cake and a bottle of wine.

It was only after the autopsy that I finally believed she was gone. After extensive forensic tests, it was clear that the body found in the river really was Effie. Ben had fed her a cocktail of prescription drugs and dumped her unconscious into the water. A cruel, cold fate that gives me nightmares.

Effie did a lot of the right things before she died, but I don't think she had any intention of turning herself in. She thought I'd receive the videos as she was safely sunning herself on a beach somewhere.

God, I loved that woman. Warts and all. She was a warrior to the end. It was her video testimony that secured the case. Her admissions about how Ben May operated and who he targeted, that was too compelling to ignore. She had been his partner in marriage and his partner in crime and she gave up everything she knew.

I wanted justice for Effie and now I have it. I watch Ben May receive three life sentences for the lives he stole. We did it, Effie. We won.

EPILOGUE

Number one doesn't stay vacant for long, but then the houses here never do. I stand at the window, watching the new residents move in. Another couple, of course. No doubt ready to settle down and start a family. They're even prettier than the ones who lived there before. I wonder if they'll be as lively as the Mays.

"He's not bad-looking," Holly says.

"Bit young for you," I say, knowing she likes her men rich and old.

Holly smiles. "Right. I'm putting the kettle on. Do you want a cup of tea?"

"Go on, then," I say.

I don't move from the window. I want to watch them for a while longer. It's always good to spend some time sussing out the new people on the street. I've been here the longest and I do it for everyone. That David fella was the one who had me the most stumped. Who knew he was an investigative journalist prying into our neighbourhood's goings-on? Thank God he ended up distracted by the Mays because if he'd gone digging too deep, he might have uncovered things he shouldn't.

I keep hoping he'll move. But he's stubborn. Perhaps me and Holly can find some ways to persuade him. She's a good sidekick, Holly. I pay her a bit extra, and she makes sure the odd dog ends up let out of the garden. She might even leave out a tin of dog food with a special surprise inside. The thing is, dogs are noisy and messy and I can't stand them. No one ever listens to me at the meetings. No one even sees me. I could complain about the annoying, yapping things until I'm blue in the face and they'd never hear me.

Shame on them.

Take that day in the sauna, for instance. No one saw me wedge that door. I wasn't going to let them die, but it was best to teach them a lesson. Deepika is insufferable. Why does she always get to host the book club? And the way she talks over me... She should learn to respect her elders.

And as for Effie May, well...

I knew exactly who she was when she moved onto the street. I recognised her, you see. It might seem strange for an old woman to track the career of a supermodel, but I've always had a vested interest in Isabella Dupont, married to the crook that is Graham Fitzalan.

My history with Ivy Oaks goes back longer than anyone here knows. You see, I was here in the eighties when the place was a psychiatric facility. It was all a big misunderstanding. I bit a woman's ear in a car park, but to be fair she did steal my parking spot. And I was under a great deal of stress at the time. It happened just after my second husband had died in a very unfortunate accident on a ski slope. Well, that kind of thing would cause anyone to lose a few marbles. The stay at a psychiatric facility was overkill, if you ask me.

It was as awful in the hospital as you can imagine. While I

had my ways of making sure I wasn't targeted by the sadistic staff, I certainly saw it happen to others.

Effie May's father helped prevent the victims and their families from receiving proper compensation. It was his underhand legal tactics that reduced the payout by thousands of pounds.

I was one of those people who lost out on the money.

As the years went by, I had a vested interest in the place. I was getting older and I never felt as though I fit in with the world. But I did inherit quite a lot of money from my third husband, who had the misfortune to fall from a cliff. Poor man. When the news popped up about turning Ivy Oaks into a residential area, I didn't just decide to buy a house, I bought shares in the company overseeing the build.

Considering I own a share in this place, and considering I survived its worst moments, I think I'm entitled to a say in the kind of people who move here. Why should I put up with obnoxious people with their loud pets and disrespectful children?

Colour me surprised when the Mays arrived and Effie May proved to be just as terrible as her father. That pizza delivery prank she pulled on me revealed her true nature. I was just a sweet old lady to her and I knew she'd done it because I saw her standing in the window at that exact moment, ready to watch me squirm in front of the delivery man. Idiot. Effie May wasn't the victim that David and Sophie made her out to be. Holly showed me more evidence online of her being terrible to other people. She played every game her con man husband played. Oh, sure, she never killed anyone like him, but a bitch is still a bitch.

The door closes at number one and Holly places a mug of hot tea on the coffee table.

"They all moved in then?" Holly says.

"Looks that way."

"How long until they move out? What's up your sleeve this time, Beryl?"

"Oh, nothing," I say. "They have to cross me first."

Holly laughs. "I wouldn't cross you, that's for sure."

I tap her shoulder. "You're just after my inheritance."

She smiles.

"Anyway," Holly says. "They look like a lovely couple. Maybe they'll settle in just fine. Maybe they'll be as nice as they look." She flashes me a wicked grin that tells me she's up for whatever I might have in mind next.

Every year I tell myself I'll stop messing with them. At some point I keep thinking my luck will run out and they'll uncover every one of my dark secrets. But they never see me. I'm invisible. And this keeps me alive. I take a deep breath, lean back in my chair, and watch the residents of Ivy Oaks living their lives. What game shall we play next?

ABOUT THE AUTHOR

Sarah A. Denzil is a British suspense writer from Derbyshire. Her books include SILENT CHILD, which has topped Kindle charts in the UK, US, and Australia. SAVING APRIL and THE BROKEN ONES are both top thirty bestsellers in the US and UK Amazon charts.

Combined, her self-published and published books, along with audiobooks and foreign translations, have sold over one million copies worldwide.

Sarah lives in Yorkshire with her husband, enjoying the scenic countryside and rather unpredictable weather. She loves to write moody, psychological books with plenty of twists and turns.

To stay updated, join the mailing list for new release announcements and special offers.

Writing as Sarah Dalton - http://www.sarahdaltonbooks.com/

ALSO BY SARAH A. DENZIL

Psychological Suspense:

Saving April

The Broken Ones

Only Daughter

The Liar's Sister

Poison Orchids

Little One

The Housemaid

My Perfect Daughter

Find Her

The Stranger in Our House

The Nice Guy

The Woman in Coach D

The Silent Child Series:

Silent Child, Book One

Stolen Girl, Book Two

Aiden's Story, a novella

Crime Fiction:

One For Sorrow (Isabel Fielding book one)

Two For Joy (Isabel Fielding book two)

Three For A Girl (Isabel Fielding book three)

The Isabel Fielding Boxed Set

Supernatural Suspense:

You Are Invited

Short suspenseful reads:

They Are Liars: A novella

Harborside Hatred (A Liars Island novella)

A Quiet Wife

In Too Deep

Printed in Great Britain
by Amazon

58522543R00189